ACQUAINTED
with the
Night

BY

ERICA ABBOTT

Bella
BOOKS

2014

Bella Books, Inc.
P.O. Box 10543
Tallahassee, FL 32302

Printed in the United States of America on acid-free paper.

First Bella Books Edition 2014

Editor: Katherine V. Forrest
Cover Designer: Judith Fellows

ISBN: 978-1-59493-404-9

Other Books by Erica Abbott

Acknowledgments

My deepest thanks goes to my wonderful family and friends for their continued love and support. I would like to especially thank my niece and nephew for some helpful late night discussions on writing and the nature of art. I am also grateful to several fellow Bella authors for their helpful advice and friendship.

Thank you to my readers for their support and the many kind words I have received about this series of books about Alex & CJ.

Everyone at Bella Books has made the evolving process of becoming an author a pleasure. My thanks especially to my publisher Linda Hill and to Karin Kallmaker, Bella editorial director, for her friendship and her advice.

To my editors Katherine V. Forrest and Cath Walker, my thanks for their thoughtful critiques, sharp eyes, and the continuing discussion concerning the proper use of the comma.

Finally, to Kathryn, I am forever grateful.

About the Author

Erica Abbott was born and raised in the Midwest, and is a graduate of the University of Denver. She has been a government lawyer and prosecutor, a college professor, sung mezzo-soprano on stage, and played first base on the diamond. She likes dogs, cats, music of all kinds, and playing bridge. She also has a love/hate relationship with golf. She lives near Denver, Colorado. This is her fourth novel.

Dedication

To my love, always and forever

PROLOGUE

The night was endless.

During the day the sunshine and doing things made it seem as if she were living a real life. She would talk to people and they would talk to her and she would work. The next day the sun would rise again and she could pretend that it was supposed to be like this all the time.

She knew she was only fooling herself, but it was all she had. So every day she would get up and go to work and smile and keep pretending.

But then night would fall and she was alone. The darkness opened over her like a black umbrella at a funeral.

She had never noticed how long night could be. During the day the hours advanced steadily, things to do, appointments to keep. At night time seemed to stop moving, no longer marching forward but swirling back and forth in a black and tortured chasm. She would sit awake looking out at the night, wondering if she would be there when the sun rose the next morning. At night she was only herself, with the pain and the grief and the aching abyss of her loneliness.

The night was endless.

CHAPTER ONE

It was drizzling an intermittent March rain as Alex Ryan ran to her truck after the school meeting. Almost all the other cars were gone from the parking lot, as she had stayed late to answer all the questions from those who had been reluctant to ask them during the meeting itself. As the Captain in charge of the Detective Squad, school safety was hardly her specialty, but she'd studied up on the initiatives enough to give a presentation as the Colfax Police Chief's representative.

She slid into the leather seat of her SUV and punched the heater on low. The interior would warm quickly, a benefit of the expensive vehicle, a gift from her partner CJ St. Clair for Alex's fortieth birthday. CJ, casual about money in a way only a woman with a trust fund could be, had actually suggested replacing it with a new one this year. Alex remembered arguing against it. "Just because you change cars every two years doesn't mean I have to," she'd told CJ.

CJ had responded, "I'll make you a deal. I'll wait until next year to buy you a new one if you promise not to try to talk me out of it then."

"CJ, sweetheart, I do not want you to keep buying me new cars."

"It's for my benefit, too," CJ asserted. "I have to ride in it half the time. And besides, I have a vested interest in keeping you as safe as possible. If you'll recall, when I met you, you were driving a ten-year-old truck that had no passenger airbag and no anti-lock brakes."

Alex couldn't argue with that. She did appreciate that this sleek black model had six airbags and traction control. She clicked her seat belt into place and pulled out of the lot. When she had safely merged onto I-225 headed south, she used her Bluetooth link to call CJ at their condo.

"Hi, darlin'," CJ answered.

"You obviously got home from the party all right."

"I left not long after you did. How did your presentation go?"

"Fine. Fortunately, no one asked me a question I couldn't answer. Chief Wylie owes me big-time for this one."

"Enough for a three-day weekend, do you think?"

"I imagine so. What did you have in mind?"

"Nothing in particular. Glenwood Springs, maybe? A little soaking in the hot springs, a little walking around in the mountains, a lot of sleeping in."

"Hmm," Alex pretended to consider. "Sounds dull. Maybe Vivien was right. We are getting to be a boring married couple."

"Do not start agreeing with her!" CJ exclaimed. "There's nothing boring about us. My other thoughts about the weekend are too lurid to communicate in a telephone call."

"Lurid is good," Alex remarked, changing lanes back to the right after passing a slow-moving pickup, the driver apparently freaked out by the wet highway. "Say more."

"You want me to talk dirty to you while you're driving at fifty-five miles an hour?" Alex heard the amusement in her voice.

"I'm considering the pros and cons," Alex said. "I guess I can wait twenty minutes. I just passed Parker Road, so I'll be home in…what the hell?"

"What?"

Alex glared at the bright lights in her rearview mirror, approaching fast in the left lane. "An idiot driver," Alex said tersely. "Going eighty, at least."

"Alex," CJ said warningly. "Do not try anything. I don't care if you're in uniform. You're in your own car and out of your jurisdiction."

"Thanks for the reminder, Lieutenant. I…"

The driver reached Alex's truck, then pulled just ahead, still in the left lane. Alex saw the brake lights, bright as rubies reflecting against the rain-slicked concrete.

"What the hell?" Alex muttered again. It was far too dark for the driver to see that she was in uniform, so the sudden braking didn't make sense…

"Alex?" CJ asked sharply in her ear.

The driver cut over in front of her abruptly, clipping Alex's front bumper. Alex tried to brake and turn the wheel away from the car at the same time, but her tires couldn't hold the pavement. In the next second her SUV sailed off the road, and Alex's world spun out of control.

CHAPTER TWO

Many times over the past three years, CJ had consciously paused to fix a memory of Alex in her mind's eye, taking an internal snapshot to freeze the image of her partner, so that she could later take the good memories out and look at them if she was lonely or troubled. Alex propped up on their couch, reading, bare feet touching CJ's calves. A sudden smile at tasting something CJ had made for her in the kitchen. Her forehead wrinkled in concentration when CJ entered her office unawares. The sight of her blue eyes first thing in the morning, bringing color to CJ's world again.

Now CJ's eyes were taking pictures she didn't want to have, memories being etched like acid on her mind. Flashing blue and red lights on the shoulder of the highway, visible from a mile away as she approached from the other side. The cluster of highway patrol, sheriff's vehicles, paramedics and a fire truck gathered untidily on the pavement or pulled onto the grass.

She turned illegally across the median and got as close as she could. When she ran out of her car, her mind took the worst picture: Alex's SUV lying at the bottom of the embankment, the roof half crushed from the vehicle rolling over, the terrible gashes in the grass, like scars.

Oh, God, a rollover. She'd been sheriff's deputy for eight years before joining the Internal Affairs Division of the Colfax Police Department, and she'd seen more fatal car rollovers than she could remember.

There were people gathered down around the vehicle, and manymore up on the shoulder. She wanted to turn and scream at all of them to get down there and help, to get Alex out of that goddamned car.

One of the men in uniform broke away and approached her. CJ wanted him to come and tell her to go away so that she could yell at him that she had to be there, that it was her life lying trapped down there in the twisted metal and broken glass.

"CJ St. Clair," the man said, and she recognized him, an old acquaintance from her days at the Roosevelt County Sheriff's office. "What are you doing here?"

"I was on the phone with her, and I heard…I called it in. She's…we're…" She couldn't form a coherent thought, much less a coherent sentence.

"Detective," he said gently, using her former rank, and she remembered his name was Bernard something, Bernie.

"She's my partner," she managed, then realizing he would misunderstand, she choked out, "We're married. Is she…"

There was no way to say the words aloud, no reality in which she would survive hearing the wrong answer to the question she couldn't ask.

Bernie said, "They're trying to get her out. She's alive, I think."

I think. She didn't know whether to fall into his arms weeping with gratitude or pound against his chest in anger for his uncertainty. She started down the hill.

He grabbed her arm. "Don't."

It gave her the excuse she wanted to scream. "Don't you tell me what to do!"

He took her other arm and hauled back her up, saying, "Detective, you have to stay here and let them work. You can't help, you'll just be in the way."

She tore her arms away from him, but knew he was right and hated him for it. "I'm sorry," she panted. "I'm sorry, Bernie, I just can't…"

"It's okay," he said. "Stay here and think good thoughts. She was wearing her seat belt, they said, and the airbags deployed. It's a big, heavy car, she could be okay."

I'm buying her a fucking tank next time, she thought desperately. *God, please, let her be alive, please.*

There was a flurry of activity at the bottom of the hill. *That has to be good. They wouldn't be working so hard, so fast, if she were already gone.* It was a fragile thought to pin the rest of her life on.

A hundred other nightmares crowded into her. She made her bargain with God: *Let her be alive. We will deal with whatever else there is, I swear, just give her back to me with her mind whole, and I promise I'll take care of the rest. Please.*

For a brief moment, she could see Alex as they lifted her onto the stretcher, her uniform dark against the white of the backboard they had her strapped onto. No one was pulling a sheet over her face, she must be breathing. Five people grabbed the stretcher and hauled it up the hill as quickly and carefully as the wet grass would allow.

CJ ran to meet them at the junction of the hill and the back of the ambulance, and this time no one tried to stop her. They had Alex in a neck brace, and the blood all over the left side of her face made CJ's heart lurch.

"Alex, darlin', I'm here," she said, trying to find someplace to touch her.

To her astonishment, Alex actually opened her eyes for a moment. Even in the harsh distortion of the flashing red lights, CJ could see her face was gray with pain.

"Sorry," Alex muttered. "Scared you, sorry."

CJ couldn't talk. One of the paramedics said, "Are you family?"

CJ nodded. Tired of euphemisms, she fumbled out, "Wife. She's my wife."

The paramedic blinked, then said, "We're taking her to Aurora Lutheran."

CJ wanted to ask how bad it was, but knew it was a useless question none of them could really answer. Instead she said, "I'm coming with you."

Alex closed her eyes again, but managed, "Please."

They let her sit by Alex's side. CJ kept a firm grip on her arm all the way to the hospital, keeping Alex with her, in this world.

* * *

CJ sat in the waiting area at the emergency room. She was attempting to send positive thoughts across the hall to Alex but all she could think about was the drama of earlier that same evening.

Before the rain, it had been a mild evening for March in Denver, and people were spilling out onto the deck and the pool area of the townhome complex where Vivien Wong lived. Music could be heard coming from within the building.

"What is that?" Alex had asked. "I've heard it before, haven't I?"

CJ listened for a moment and said, "Chaka Khan. *Through the Fire*. Sounds like Viv is going with jazz tonight."

"At least Vivien has good taste in music."

"And in best friends," CJ added lightly.

Alex laughed. "You're so modest."

CJ smiled. "Not me. I've got the most beautiful woman at the party on my arm, so I have nothing to be modest about."

She tugged at Alex's hand and led her into the room without releasing her. Alex was always careful about public displays of affection, both because she was a career police officer and because she'd fallen in love with a woman later in life, but CJ was comfortable and happy touching her. Vivien was out, and the party was sure to be filled with lesbians as well as with her business associates. Viv only gave one big party a year, and she invited just about everyone she knew.

The room was pretty full, people clumped in predictable groupings. By the food table, there was a crowd of both men and women, their casual clothing failing to conceal their ties to mortgage banking, Vivien's job. Other groups near the bar were more likely personal friends, women in everything from cocktail dresses to suits, sequins to jeans.

Alex said to CJ, "Vivien actually hired bartenders this year." She nodded at a petite brunette and a tall blond in white shirts and black ties, mixing drinks with practiced precision. The wine and liquor bottles set up on the table covered with a white tablecloth looked like the downtown Denver city skyline.

"She told me she was tired of tending bar and wanted to mingle."

"Since when did Vivien ever tend bar?" Alex asked dryly. "Last year, I think you and I did it most of the evening."

CJ laughed. "And that's why I told her to hire help this time."

Alex grinned at her. "Good thinking, sweetheart."

A moment later CJ stiffened as she glanced across the room. Alex turned around, her reaction to CJ's expression both wary and curious.

The women approached them and CJ couldn't see any graceful way to escape. "I was sure it was you," one of the women said to CJ. "It's been a while."

She hadn't changed much, CJ thought. The woman's dark hair was cut severely short, showing off diamond earrings just a bit too large to be in good taste at a casual cocktail party. She wore a pantsuit that looked like linen, and attached to her elbow was a much younger woman who was pretty in a vague way, although she was wearing too much makeup.

"It has been a long time," CJ replied. Her voice was calm, her tone carefully controlled. "Viv didn't tell me you were coming."

The woman laughed. "She didn't know I was showing up. Patty brought me, didn't you, my dear?"

Patty nodded, sliding her round blue eyes back and forth between CJ and Alex. "Um, yeah," Patty said. "I'm with Mountain Title Company. Vivien and I work together sometimes." She offered her hand. "Patty Herron."

"Alex Ryan," Alex said, her expression still cautious.

"Are you a friend of Vivien's, too?" Patty asked.

"Indirectly," Alex began. "Actually, I met her through CJ. They're old friends and—"

The other woman interrupted, still addressing CJ. "Is this the new girlfriend, honey?"

Alex narrowed her gaze. She wasn't the jealous type normally but CJ could feel Alex's temper starting to rise.

CJ said abruptly, "Alex. This is Stephanie Morrow." She added for clarification, "Steph."

CJ had only had two serious relationships before she met Alex: Laurel, her college girlfriend, and Stephanie, the real estate agent with whom she had lived for two years. CJ didn't talk much about either woman to Alex. There hadn't been any reason to: Steph was a minor chapter in her past. Alex was her present and her future.

CJ watched Alex study Stephanie. She was certainly still attractive in an edgy way, her hair molding against her head like a black skullcap. Her makeup was perfect and underneath her expensive clothes she had retained her well-maintained body. She was CJ's age, which made her seven years younger than Alex. CJ wondered if Alex was comparing herself to this flawlessly turned-out woman.

CJ found Alex's hand and tangled their fingers together in silent reassurance, silently answering Steph's question. She felt Alex's tiny tug of gratitude.

Stephanie dropped her eyes to the diamond ring and wedding band on CJ's left hand. Her manicured eyebrows rose and she murmured, "Well, well. Looks like you finally found somebody to go through that ceremony you always wanted."

CJ saw that Alex was ready to enter the conversational conflict, but she was saved from intervening by Patty's bright question.

"Oh, hey. You're CJ St. Clair, Steph's ex, right? Did anybody ever tell you that you look just like that singer? You know the one. Stephy, you know, we saw her on *Ellen*, remember? It's been a while, but you look just like her." Her look wobbled uncertainly between Stephanie and CJ, searching for help. "You know. The singer," she said again.

Steph was ignoring her, but CJ asked gently, "Are you talking about Trisha Yearwood?"

Patty clapped her hands together happily. "Yes! You're a redheaded Trisha Yearwood!"

"I have heard that once or twice," CJ said. "It's very flattering every time, though."

"You sound like her too, when you talk," Patty added, oblivious to the currents of discomfort swirling around her from the other three women. "She's from the South, isn't she? Are you?"

"I'm from Savannah, Georgia, originally," CJ explained patiently, her drawl thickening for a moment. "Trisha is from a pretty small town about two hundred miles away, I believe."

"Well, you sound just like her," Patty repeated.

Stephanie cut in with, "So what have you been doing with yourself, CJ? Aside from getting out the U-Haul. Are you still a police officer?" She shot a glance at Alex, not a friendly one.

CJ responded, "Yes, I left the sheriff's office and I'm with Colfax PD now. I'm in Internal Affairs, actually. Alex is a Captain in the Department, in charge of Investigations."

Stephanie's lips curled a little and she said, "Oh, nepotism, huh?"

Alex had just about had enough, but again CJ stepped in and said coolly, "Not at all. I'm in a different chain of command." She turned to Alex. "Would you mind getting us a drink, darlin'? I think I could use something refreshing."

"Of course," Alex said, letting CJ handle whatever was going on. "Back in a minute."

CJ watched her walk across the room then managed a few more minutes listening to Patty, who liked to chat about everyone, and fending off intrusive questions from Steph. Finally Patty said, "Steph, honey, I could use a drink too."

Steph said, "There's the bar."

Patty glared at her and huffed off in the same direction Alex had taken. CJ thought Steph would be looking for a new girlfriend pretty quickly at this rate.

"You femmes keep us busy taking care of your every need, don't you?"

CJ replied coolly, "I wouldn't say that at all. Actually, I find taking care of someone I love and being taken care of equally satisfying." She turned to go, hoping to leave the conversation behind, but Stephanie wasn't through.

"You've really got her under control, do you?"

CJ suppressed a flare of anger. She turned very deliberately and said, "I'm not going to take relationship advice from you, Steph. You don't know Alex. And you didn't really know me at all apparently, or you wouldn't have suggested a ménage à trois."

A dark red flush crept up Stephanie's neck. "You'd be surprised how well I understand you," she said acidly. "Do you still like to be fucked in the shower? You were a pain in the ass to live with, but you did like fucking."

CJ stared at her for a long moment, proud of herself for not slapping the leer from Steph's face. Then, her voice very low, CJ said, "You always were an offensive bitch, weren't you? I can't figure out why it took me so long to see that."

The angry flush reached Stephanie's cheeks. At that moment, Alex returned to hand CJ her chardonnay. CJ watched Alex read the situation and then Alex said, "Nice meeting you, Steph. I think Patty needs you. Now."

Steph gave her a glare, then she stalked away. Alex murmured, "Do I need to ruin Vivien's party by going over to slap the bitch?"

CJ looked at her in amused shock. "Why would you do that?"

"I don't know what she said to you, but I can see your canine teeth and not in your usual pretty smile."

CJ shook her head. "You always know how to make me feel better." Then she looked into Alex's stormy blue-gray eyes and murmured, "I'm sorry for bringing her into our lives, even for just a minute."

Now Alex gave her the full smile that always transformed her serious face. "Please, Red. If we have to apologize for everybody we were with before you and I met, I'd have to do seven years of penance for bringing Tony into the equation."

CJ grinned, suddenly feeling much better. "You are so right," she said with a laugh. "Dealing with your crazy ex-husband the district attorney on a weekly basis is much worse than my occasional bitchy ex-girlfriend."

Alex squeezed lime into her tonic water. "I agree." She glanced around and added, "Is Laurel here, by chance? I'm on a roll and I'd love to tell off your other cheating ex while I'm at it."

CJ laughed again. "Sorry. She's still in Georgia, last I heard. And I'm not keeping track of her. Keeping track of *you* occupies all my time."

Alex decided to take advantage of the opportunity to be affectionate in public and leaned over to kiss her, very lightly. "And that's the way I like it."

Vivien Wong joined them at that moment. She was in bright red, a tunic with a mandarin collar that emphasized her Asian features. "Okay, knock it off," she said tartly. "Jesus, I invite you two to a cocktail party so you can mingle and you just stand in the corner and neck. With each other. How boring."

CJ hugged her hostess. "I keep telling you, Viv. It's the opposite of boring, believe me."

Alex added, "And that's not really necking. I could show you the difference, if you'd like."

Vivien rolled her eyes and then hugged Alex, too. "I'd like that," she said, suggestively. Flirting with Alex was one of her occasional hobbies, but the unspoken rule was that she could only do it in full view of CJ.

"I meant with CJ, not you," Alex said with mock severity.

"Christ, you two are boring as hell!" Vivien exclaimed.

CJ laughed at her. "Not so boring," she said. "I think Alex was ready to throw a punch or two at one of your guests a minute ago."

Vivien's eyes widened. "Which one?"

CJ gestured across the room, where Steph was having what looked like a disagreement with Patty. "Stephanie," CJ said.

Vivien exclaimed, "Christ on a pancake! I had no idea Patty was bringing that cunt to my party."

CJ choked on her wine. "For heaven's sake, Viv! Just because we broke up doesn't make her a…" CJ hesitated over the word.

Vivien shook her head and turned to Alex. "For God's sake, she can't even say it, despite the fact that she presumably spends much of her leisure time in and around one. I hope to Christ she at least manages some choice language for you in bed."

CJ, suddenly angry again, demanded, "Why is everyone suddenly so interested in the details of my sex life?"

Alex's face turned hard. "Is that what Steph said to you? She really is a—"

CJ interjected, "She's not a nice person."

Vivien threw up her hands. "I give up. I'm going to go play hostess and flirt with the bartender."

"Which one?" CJ eyed the two women behind the bar.

Vivien smirked before she answered, "The blond Viking-looking one, of course. Alex, this one is all yours."

CJ watched the slow smile cross Alex's face.

"That's true," Alex murmured. "She is."

When the time came for Alex to go, she touched CJ's arm. "I'm going to go change. I'll come back and say goodbye to you before I leave."

"See you in a minute," CJ said.

Alex disposed of her glass and said goodbye to her hostess. CJ watched her walk across to Viv's townhouse, where she'd stashed her uniform earlier. After a couple of minutes CJ followed, opening and closing the door to Viv's spare bedroom quietly.

Alex turned around, surprised. "What are you doing here?" Alex asked.

"Thought I'd help you get dressed," she said in her best sultry tone.

"I've been getting dressed all by myself for about forty years," Alex remarked.

"Hmm. Then maybe I came in to help you get undressed. I'm much better at that anyway."

Alex deliberately removed her blouse and tossed it onto the bed. "I'd have to agree with that. But I have to go."

CJ crossed to her, close enough to run one long finger under Alex's bra strap, easing down to touch the soft skin at the top of her breast. "That's too bad. I love the black bra."

CJ smiled as she felt Alex's breathing speed up.

"Sweetheart, I really can't be late for this meeting."

"Oh, I know," CJ acknowledged. The finger was wandering into the valley between Alex's breasts. CJ saw her nipples tighten underneath the lace and she grinned again in approval.

"CJ, honey…"

CJ dropped her hand. The look on Alex's face was mixed relief and disappointment. "I was just making sure," she said.

"Making sure of what?" Alex demanded. "That I had to go off to a meeting in front of a couple of hundred people with my panties damp?"

CJ leaned in and murmured, "I was making sure you knew it's always you I want."

Alex said, "I think all you've proven is how much I want you."

"Good," CJ said, approvingly. "In that case, I'll wait up for you to get home."

Alex ran her nose down CJ's cheek, nuzzling her softly. "Will you? What will you be doing?"

"Hmm. Let me think. Reading, I suppose. In bed. Naked, of course."

Alex gave a little groan. "I really, really have to change clothes."

"Go ahead. I'll just watch."

"No, you won't. If I take off one more stitch with you in here, we both know what will happen."

"Umm. What was that, again?"

Alex told her in vivid terms. CJ tried to look shocked, but only managed to feel self-satisfied.

"Well, we wouldn't want that to happen, would we?" she managed after another of Alex's searing kisses.

Alex muttered, "We might."

"Now, now. You have to go to your meeting, so I'll just run along."

Alex groaned again. "So you really just dropped in here to make me crazy for you?"

"Just a reminder."

Alex pulled away a little and met her eyes. Every insecurity CJ had ever felt over two failed relationships vanished when Alex looked at her like this. "You don't have to remind me," Alex said. "I never ever forget how much I want to be with you. You're the person I waited for all my life."

CJ relaxed in her arms a little. "Not the package you expected, though?" she teased.

Alex kissed her a final time. "You're so much more than I ever thought I could have. Sometimes I can't believe how beautiful you are. Now, please get your gorgeous self out of here, or I really am not going to make that meeting."

CJ went to the door, but stopped and turned back with her hand on the knob. "Sure you trust me in the same room with Steph?" she teased again.

"Of course," Alex replied calmly. "You are carrying your backup weapon, aren't you, Lieutenant?"

CJ laughed. "Darlin', you know I never leave home without it."

"Good. Then remember to always use the force appropriate to the situation."

"You are such a cop sometimes."

"Go. I'll call you on the way home, okay?"

"Okay. Be safe, darlin'."

"Always. I have a really good reason to come home safely."

* * *

But she hadn't gotten home safely, CJ thought miserably, still sitting near the emergency room.

Nicole Ryan Castillo, walking fast, came into the waiting room. Her trench coat was thrown over jeans and a sweatshirt. CJ stood up and Nicole went immediately into her arms for a quick hug.

"What do you know?" she asked, sitting down next to CJ.

"Not much," CJ admitted. "They haven't come out yet to tell me anything. She was conscious when they put her in the ambulance, said a couple of words to me. She was in a lot of pain, though. We weren't exactly having a conversation."

Nicole gripped her hand tightly. CJ saw that she was close to panic, and it frightened her. Alex's younger sister was typically calm in a crisis, using her lawyer's logic to handle her emotions. At this moment she looked tightly wound, jaw clenched, the tiny muscles around her eyes tensed. Despite the five-year gap in age and the extra ten pounds or so that Nicole carried, CJ thought again how much she looked like Alex.

"Was she moving? Could you tell anything?" Nicole asked.

"She squeezed my hand as they took her in. They had her on a backboard, in a brace, but that's usual until they can eliminate spinal injuries. She…" CJ stumbled a little then went on, "She had some blood on her face, a cut or something, so I'm sure they're looking at her for head injuries, too."

"God damn it!" Nicole let go of CJ's hand to drop her head into her palms. CJ could see her shoulders shaking beneath the coat.

It tore at CJ's heart to see Nicole like this. She slipped her arm around her, rubbing her hand across her back, brushing away the tiny droplets of rain beaded on the waterproof material.

Nicole sat up, wiping tears away with trembling fingers. "I'm sorry," she muttered. "I should be comforting you."

"She'll be all right," CJ said, both giving and receiving the mindless comfort of ignorance.

"I just…" Nicole took a deep breath.

"It's okay, darlin'."

She took another breath and said, "I just keep thinking about Dad. I was sitting here in a room like this, with Alex, when they came out and told us he was dead."

CJ hugged her tighter. She knew the story: their father, a patrol sergeant, had been killed in a hit-and-run accident when Alex was nineteen and Nicole only fourteen. Their mother was already nine years gone from cancer, so it left just the two sisters, who were as close as two women with different lives could be.

CJ envied Alex the relationship sometimes, her own family long estranged from her because of their disapproval of her.

"We should call Paul," Nicole said suddenly, referring to Deputy Chief Paul Duncan, their godfather.

CJ said gently, "He and Betty are out of the country on a cruise, remember? That's why Alex had to cover this meeting tonight for the chief. He's got a real backlog with Paul away."

Nicole nodded unhappily. "I remember now. CJ, what happened? Alex is the best driver I know."

CJ bit her lip. "I'm not sure. She was on the phone with me, and told me someone was driving recklessly, too fast, coming up behind her. That may have had something to do with it. She didn't say she was particularly tired, I know she hadn't had anything to drink at the party we went to earlier, so it's hard for me to believe she just drove off the road. Maybe there was something on the pavement. The road was wet. Accidents happen, even to the best drivers."

Nicole shrugged out of her coat. CJ could see her trying to regain her composure, smoothing her hair and getting out a tissue to wipe the remnants of tears from her cheeks.

"I always hated that she was a police officer," she said suddenly. "I knew how dangerous it was, especially after Dad died. Alex was so determined to make a home for us, let me stay here with my friends to finish high school, but I really hated that she joined the department. It was worse when she was in uniform. The more she got promoted, the better I felt about it, knowing she wasn't on the street, you know?"

"Yes." It was all CJ said, letting Nicole talk.

"Then later I used to worry about her being, I guess, unhappy is the word," Nicole continued aimlessly. "Her relationship with Tony was never very good for her, and she just seemed to be lost. Personally, I mean. Her career was important to her, but she didn't really seem to have anything else."

"I know," CJ said.

Nicole turned to her and gave her a sad little smile. "Then you came along and changed everything. Why am I telling you all this? It's not like you don't know pretty much everything about Alex already."

CJ answered gently, "It's what we do when we're scared or stressed. We work out what we remember, what we fear, what we want, trying to make sense of what doesn't make sense. Life can be pretty random sometimes."

Nicole fixed her with an intense look that reminded her forcefully of Alex. "I know you're scared, CJ," Nicole said.

"I'm terrified," CJ said softly. "She's my whole life."

They sat together quietly for a long time.

* * *

Alex was half-propped up on the exam table, looking a little better than when CJ last saw her. The blood was gone from her face, and a small gauze pad was taped just above her left eyebrow. She wore a faded hospital gown, her right arm inside the sleeve but her left shoulder out, the ugly deep purple bruise exposed. There was a pillow propped between the arm and her body. Farther down on her bare arm her wrist was also carefully propped up, and it looked badly swollen.

But CJ really looked only at her eyes. They were a stormy dark blue-gray and CJ could see how much pain she was still in.

"Hi," Alex said.

CJ went to her, not touching anything that looked hurt. She brushed fingertips up Alex's right arm and tried to sound calm. She said, "Hey, darlin'."

There were people moving around behind her getting ready for the next procedures. CJ leaned in and kissed her very gently. Alex's mouth crooked up. She said, "Thanks, I feel better already."

"Nicole is here. She sends her love and told me to tell you thank you for wearing your seat belt."

"Tell her she's very welcome. It could have been a whole lot worse. And you tell her I'm fine."

"The doctor told me you're being a bad patient and refusing pain meds. Honey, they have to reduce the shoulder dislocation. You need to do what they tell you, and take the medicine."

"I will," Alex said. "But I have to tell you something first and I didn't want to be on drugs when I did."

"Then tell me quickly so you can get what you need."

Alex shifted slightly and winced. "The car ran me off the road."

"What?" CJ asked, in shock.

"It was light-colored, silver, gray, maybe beige. A Toyota Corolla, I think, a couple of years old or so. Partial plate is King Adam X-ray, I couldn't get the numbers."

She'd had two seconds, at the most, and she had a description and part of the license plate. CJ shook her head in wonder. Her partner really was always on duty.

"Okay, I promise I'll get it out right away. Do you think it was accidental?"

Alex looked at her hard. She said, "He clipped me on my left front bumper. Make sure they do a forensics check, there may be paint. He pulled just ahead of me at high speed, slowed to match my pace, then cut in front of me. It sure as hell didn't feel like an accident."

Was she being paranoid? CJ wondered for a moment, but doubted it. Alex didn't think that way.

"I'm on it," she said, partly because that was what Alex needed to hear to let go and let the doctors treat her injuries. "Now take the pain medicine, darlin'."

Suddenly Alex looked exhausted. She sagged back, closing her eyes. "Okay," she said with uncharacteristic acquiescence. The sound of it broke CJ's heart, but she hadn't forgotten to be grateful that Alex hadn't been hurt much worse. A young woman in scrubs stepped up and injected something into the IV line in Alex's right hand.

CJ turned back to the nearest doctor and asked, "You'll be a while, I guess?"

"Yes, we need to get a CAT scan, but it looks like only a mild concussion. We're getting a resident from plastics down here to stitch the cut on her face, to minimize the scarring, as soon as we get the shoulder taken care of, and her wrist in a cast."

CJ dropped her eyes to the injured hand. "Broken?"

"Yes, a small chip of the hamate bone, not too bad."

From the table, Alex said, "CJ?"

"Yes, darlin'?"

"My service weapon is around here somewhere. Will you secure it?"

CJ turned back to her and leaned close to her ear. "I have an idea. Why don't you let me take care of everything? Do what the doctors say, and let someone else be in control for a bit, all right? They're going to keep you overnight because you lost consciousness a couple of minutes. I'll be in your room when they take you up, and I'll stay with you tonight. You're going to be fine, so just let it go."

Alex's eyelids fluttered, the medication already taking effect. "I'm not good at that," she muttered.

"I know," CJ said, kissing her softly again. "Now behave."

"Sweetheart."

"Hmmm?"

"I am sorry. I know you were scared for me."

CJ blinked hard a couple of times, and said, "Worrying about you is just part of the deal we made. I'll see you soon."

She stepped outside the treatment room, knowing Alex would be out very soon—or at least she hoped so, praying for unconsciousness while they put her dislocated shoulder back into place and set her broken wrist.

Nicole was waiting for her on the edge of her chair. "How is she?"

CJ managed a bright smile and said, "She's okay, Nicole. We talked, she's clear-headed, and now that she let them give her something for the pain, she'll be fine."

Nicole frowned. "Why the hell didn't they give her something before?"

"She refused." CJ sighed. "She had information to give me about what happened, and she didn't want the evidence to be compromised because she was on meds when she told me. Your sister is a very stubborn woman."

"Welcome to the world of the Ryan family. Dad was just as bad."

"The important thing is that she's getting help now and she'll be fine. Do you want to wait until you can see her? It's probably going to be an hour or two before they move her upstairs."

"It's okay. David doesn't have an early lecture tomorrow, so he can get Charlie off to school in the morning. I'll see her, then go home and sleep so I can relieve you in the morning."

"They're telling me they might be able to send her home before lunch, if the CAT scans are clear."

Nicole brightened. "That's great. I'll stick around anyway. I really want to see her a minute. Why don't I get us both some coffee? I need to call David. He was really worried."

CJ smiled. "Your husband is a good guy. I'll be right here. I have a couple of calls to make."

CJ first called Lieutenant Rod Chavez, an old friend from her days as a detective with the Roosevelt County Sheriff's Department. After telling him what happened and relieving his anxiety about Alex's condition, she related the information about the vehicle that had run her off the road.

"What the hell?" he grumbled, and she could picture him tugging at his thick black mustache in irritation. "Somebody tried to kill her?"

"I have no idea, but Alex certainly thinks it was no accident."

"Well, I do believe I agree with her. That woman you're shackin' up with has good instincts, y'know."

CJ laughed for the first time in hours. "'Shacking up'? Really, you are so offensive. We are married, you know."

"Hmm, married. I'm trying to remember where I heard of such a thing."

"Put Ana on. I'll mention that to your wife and we'll see how that bad back of yours survives you sleeping on the couch."

"Hell, how d'you think I got the bad back in the first place? If you'll excuse me, I think I'll just make a call or two and see what we've got."

"Call me back on my cell, will you? I'm staying here. They're keeping her overnight."

"Will do. Tell Alex to rest, okay?"

She called Vivien next, and got a cranky greeting. "What the fuck, CJ?"

"Oh, sorry, darlin'. Did I interrupt something?"

"Yes and no. You failed to interrupt rounds one and two, but have managed to screw with round three."

"Viv. Too much information. Way too much."

"Hey, you called and you asked. I trust this is some kind of emergency."

CJ explained, and spent several minutes reassuring her about Alex's condition.

"Do you want me to come to the hospital?" Vivien demanded.

"Not directly. I came here in the ambulance with Alex, so what I need for you to do is go and pick up my car. It's on I-225 southbound, just south of the Parker Road exit. You'll need to drive it here, which means you'll have to take a cab to get to it."

"Wait a sec." There was a muffled conversation that CJ assumed was Vivien getting rid of that night's date. After a minute, Vivien got back on and said, "Don't worry. Marja will drive me there, and I'll bring your car to the hospital. She'll follow me and bring me back. I've still got your spare set of keys around here somewhere."

"Marja?"

Vivien cleared her throat. "Blond bartender," she added.

"Oh. Of course. Thanks for doing this and thank, um, Marja for me, too."

"No problem. We'll see you inside an hour."

CJ studied her phone with an air of disbelief. How on earth did Vivien do it? She must have dated at least fifty women in the seven years or so CJ had known her, if "dated" was the right word.

Nicole returned with coffee, remembering to bring two tiny containers of half and half for CJ. In a few minutes CJ's cell rang again, the caller ID showing Rod Chavez's home number.

"I am a very suspicious man," he began.

"What is it?"

"Patrol unit found the car a few minutes ago. It was abandoned, in a Home Depot parking lot on East Mississippi."

"Wait. That's north of the accident. Alex was traveling south."

"Yeah. Interestin', isn't it? He, she or they must have turned around. If we hadn't had a description and the partial from Alex, we probably wouldn't have found it for a day or two. Anyway, the car was reported stolen from a parking lot at Aurora Mall around eight or so this evening. And, no surprise, there's some damage to the right front bumper. We're gettin' it towed so we can look for prints and match the damage."

"Let me get this straight. They took it from Aurora Mall, and then they dump it a few hours later less than a mile away? And in the meantime, they drive it fewer than ten miles, run Alex off the road and then drive it back to virtually where they stole it in the first place?"

"Yep, and if you think that sounds screwy, I'm on board the train with you. Something smells bad, *pelirroja*."

CJ closed her phone and sipped at her coffee thoughtfully. Something did indeed smell bad, and it wasn't the hospital coffee.

CHAPTER THREE

Alex struggled to manage her purse and briefcase while she opened the door to their condominium without moving her shoulder too much. Her wrist, in a soft cast after almost two months, was healing without much discomfort, but her shoulder continued to give her pain even between physical therapy sessions.

She got the door open and gratefully dumped everything she was carrying onto the table in the foyer. She stepped over CJ's shoes left discarded in the front hall, as usual. She called out, "Kitchen or bedroom?"

"Kitchen," CJ responded. Her voice sounded brittle to Alex's ears.

Alex found CJ standing next to the kitchen island, savagely chopping celery on the wooden cutting board.

"Um, hi," Alex said tentatively. "You have a bad day?"

CJ continued slashing at the vegetables. The knife was making dull thuds against the wooden board.

"Sweetheart?" Alex ventured.

CJ threw the chopped celery into the frying pan behind her on the stovetop, and started hacking away at a carrot.

"My day was just peachy. And how was *your* day?" CJ asked, through a tense jaw.

"Okay," Alex said. "Limited duty isn't really much of a strain for me, since it's pretty much all I do anyway. I had some statistic reports to write. You want to tell me what's wrong?"

"You didn't have any special issues today?" CJ asked tersely.

Alex put her hand over CJ's hands to stop the relentless chopping. "Apparently you know that I did. Are we going to talk about this?"

CJ slapped the knife down and Alex caught her glare. "Steph called me. Can you imagine how pleasant that conversation was? I would have been happy never to see the woman again after our little encounter in March, and now she calls me to tell me you're harassing her."

"I'm not harassing her," Alex said, trying to keep her voice mild. "She had an FTA, so I sent out a patrol unit to her office."

"You sent a patrol unit out because she failed to appear for a *speeding* ticket?" CJ exclaimed. "That sounds a lot like harassment to me."

"I was just getting her attention," Alex countered.

"Oh stop it, Alex! You're not fooling me and you're not being honest with yourself. Despite the fact that you have not one shred of evidence that she had anything to do with the accident, you keep after her."

"That's not exactly accurate," Alex said coolly. "It's a bit much of a coincidence that we have an unpleasant encounter with the woman and a few hours later someone tries to kill me."

"Alex, for God's sake," CJ said, exasperated. "Motive is not evidence. She has an alibi. She says she was with Patty all evening. Patty confirms that. Besides which, the woman does not have the skills to boost a Toyota, much less handle the demolition driving it would take to run you off the highway."

"You don't know that."

"Yes, I do! Alex, I lived with her for two years. She could not have pulled that off. And Patty just isn't smart enough to lie successfully. She didn't do it, Alex. Give it up."

Alex said stubbornly, "One phone call and she could easily have hired someone to do it for her."

CJ leaned across the island with her hands braced on the granite top. "You think she has a car thief on call, just in case she needs one? Listen to yourself, Alex. She had a couple of hours. She couldn't go through the Yellow Pages or go online and do a search for 'murderer for hire.' You're not making sense."

Alex crossed her arms and wished she hadn't as the pain shot through her shoulder. "It's still too big a coincidence."

"Coincidences do happen. Alex, have you had a pain pill today?"

The twinge from her shoulder must have shown on her face, Alex decided. "No. I don't need one."

CJ said, "I disagree. Stop being such a martyr and take one. I'll finish dinner."

Alex narrowed her eyes. "Does this mean we're through with this fight?"

"Up to you," CJ said, but her voice had softened in tone. "I said what I wanted to say. At least Steph called me instead of Paul, but I don't think she'll stop at calling your boss next time." Her voice gentled further. "And if Paul has to log an official complaint, the Internal Affairs Inspector will be assigned to investigate."

Alex recognized CJ's attempts to end the argument with a gentle joke. "Well, that's okay then," she said with a little smile. "I've got a lot of influence with the head of IA."

"Do you?"

Alex leaned into her for a kiss. "I'm pretty sure."

CJ stroked Alex's cheek gently with her fingertips. "Will you please think about what I said? Going after Steph without any proof is a bad idea."

Alex frowned. "You seem a little too worried about Stephanie's feelings for my taste."

"You know what? I don't give a flying hushpuppy about Stephanie Morrow or what she thinks or how she feels. But I care very much about you, your mental health and your career. So do me a favor, will you? Until or unless we get some evidence, just let it go, all right?"

Alex stared into CJ's bright green eyes. "You know that's not exactly the way I work."

Very quietly CJ said, "I do know that. And you know sometimes we just can't solve every case."

Alex turned away. "I'm well aware of that. Whoever ran my father down twenty-four years ago is still out there somewhere."

She felt CJ come around behind her. The next moment she felt CJ's arms circle around her waist. Alex leaned back into the warmth of CJ's body and felt herself relax.

Into her ear, CJ murmured, "I'm sorry, darlin'. I should have realized why this was so difficult for you. I just want you to recover from what happened, whatever it takes. I love you, you do know that?"

"I know, sweetheart. And I promise I won't talk to Stephanie again unless we get something else to go on, all right?"

"All right. Good. I know how hard this is for you, and I admire your ability to…what's the word?"

"Grow? Change? Evolve?"

CJ laughed. "One of those, anyway."

* * *

Alex had a new mystery novel. She was reading studiously, propped up at her end of the couch. CJ closed her book and let it slip to the floor by the couch with a small thump. She stretched luxuriously and said, "God Bless the Fourth of July. I just love these three-day weekends."

Alex looked at her over the top of her own book. "Do you? I get antsy away from work too long."

"Well, there's a surprise. I swear, if it weren't for my cooking, you'd never come home from work at all."

Alex set her book, open, on the back of the sofa. "Yeah, I only come home for your meatloaf."

CJ managed a pout. "Oh, darn. I thought it was the irresistible allure of my sexual charms. And by the way, I've been thinking about spicing up my meatloaf recipe. Maybe chile peppers?"

Alex said, "I don't think you should touch the ancient family meatloaf recipe."

"Your opinion is duly noted. So what time is the Ryan family picnic on Monday? Noon?"

"Yes," Alex answered.

"Nicole reserved one of the shelters, right?"

"My sister, the woman who puts brushing her teeth in her daily planner? Yes, dear, she reserved the picnic shelter."

"Have I mentioned recently how happy I am that you finally got that cast off your wrist?"

"Why, yes, you did mention it. And you also remarked on how pleased you were that the physical therapy on my shoulder was successfully completed."

"I did, didn't I?" CJ said, trying to look innocent while pressing her bare foot along Alex's calf.

"I just wish we'd found whoever ran me off the damn road," Alex said unhappily.

"Could you maybe not go into that again?" CJ stretched once more, and brushed one foot up the inner seam of Alex's shorts. It sent a pleasant little thrill of pleasure directly up Alex's leg.

"Why don't you want to discuss the case?" she teased.

"Because I'm trying to seduce you."

"Right here on the couch?"

CJ gave her a look of pure heat. Alex sat up a little and murmured, "Come here."

CJ got onto her hands and knees and slowly crawled down the long sofa toward Alex, the expression on her face far from innocent. Alex felt her heart beat faster. When CJ got to her, Alex said, "Sorry it's been a while."

CJ looked into her eyes. She murmured, "Don't apologize, Irish. Just make it up to me."

Her tone was lighthearted, but Alex suddenly wanted nothing more than to do just that. She began caressing CJ through her T-shirt. CJ leaned into the touch, then reached down to take the shirt off.

"Nope," Alex said, and leaned forward to nuzzle her breasts through the fabric.

CJ made a little hissing noise as Alex used her teeth, biting lightly at her lover's nipples, still protected by both shirt and bra. Alex put her hands up under the shirt, stroking CJ's belly and continuing to work her mouth until she had CJ moaning loudly.

Alex pulled at the waistband of CJ's shorts, pulling shorts and underwear down and off without moving her mouth away from CJ's breasts. CJ went to her knees over Alex, her arms propping her over Alex's body.

Alex stroked up from CJ's knees, across her naked thighs and down. CJ moaned again and began to push her hips into Alex.

"So impatient," Alex whispered.

"Honey, please."

Alex continued her touching until CJ was grinding against her in need. Then Alex found her wetness and caressed her, lightly at first, then with more and more determination.

CJ dropped her head on Alex's shoulder, breathing hard into her neck. "God, Alex, touch me."

Alex stroked her firmly, knowing exactly where and how to move for CJ until she felt the pulsing climax against her hand.

CJ pressed her damp forehead to Alex's, and Alex shifted up to kiss her for the first time, CJ breathing into her mouth.

It filled her with joy to know just what CJ needed and to give it to her. After a moment, CJ lifted her head and Alex saw the flush across her throat, the darkly-dilated irises crowding out the deep green of her eyes.

"You're not finished," Alex said, a statement rather than a question.

"More," was all CJ said.

"My favorite word," Alex murmured.

She shifted both of them until CJ was on her back on the couch. Alex kissed her deeply and slid her fingers into CJ, feeling rather than hearing CJ cry out into her mouth. Alex moved with her, CJ rising and falling with her hand, taking and somehow giving to Alex at the same time.

CJ came again, with Alex's hand buried deep within her. She finally grasped Alex's wrist to stop her, muttering, "Okay, okay."

Alex stopped moving but stayed where she was, relishing the tight grip of CJ's muscles, holding Alex within her body. When CJ finally stirred, Alex withdrew slowly and reluctantly.

"God," CJ sighed. "Can you even feel your fingers anymore?"

Alex wiggled them. "All present and accounted for." She leaned down and kissed the deep pink flush on CJ's chest. "Better, sweetheart?"

"Holy Mother, yes. Darlin', you make me feel so—"

"Satisfied?" Alex said lightly. "Fulfilled? Transported?"

CJ looked at her seriously. "Loved, honey. You make me feel loved."

Alex lay happily with her for a few minutes.

"Shoulder okay?" CJ asked, after a while.

"Everything is great, stop worrying."

"I wasn't worrying, I was just doing a preliminary check."

"Preliminary to what?"

"This."

With gentle movements, CJ slipped out from under Alex and turned her onto her back. She got to her knees on the floor beside Alex and, tugging at her shorts, said, "I think we should lose these, hmm?"

Alex helped her, and moments later CJ was kissing her thighs. Alex lifted one bare leg to the back of the couch, and put her other foot on the floor, opening herself to CJ's mouth.

CJ murmured, "Ready for me already, darlin'?"

"Oh, yes," Alex said, her voice rough with need.

Smiling, CJ lowered her head happily. Alex closed her eyes against the familiar sensation of CJ's mouth against her, heat spreading out like a flash fire through her body. She was so close already, making love to CJ all the foreplay she usually needed for her own arousal.

CJ was thorough as always, but Alex urged her to finish with her hands on the back of CJ's head. The strength of her climax took her by surprise, flooding her with both pleasure and relief before she sagged back in exhaustion.

When Alex could move again, she felt CJ shift against her leg. CJ was sprawled, her long legs under the coffee table, her head resting on Alex's thigh. Alex reached down and ran her fingers through CJ's red hair. CJ moved up, and Alex wiped moisture from CJ's face. "You're a mess," she chided.

"God, you taste good."

"I taste like sex. Yours, in fact."

Alex sighed happily. "I'm calling our insurance agent on Tuesday. We've got to take out an insurance rider on your tongue."

CJ laughed. "And people say you don't have a sense of humor."

In mock indignation, Alex demanded, "People? What people?"

"Ah, let me think. My friends, your friends, our co-workers, your family..."

"Stop already." Alex sighed heavily, then said quietly, "Did I mention how much I love you?"

"You did. And darlin', I love you too. Even without a sense of humor."

CHAPTER FOUR

Even eight months later, Alex could remember almost every detail of that day with CJ, making love on the couch, the last weekend she was happy.

Alex had seen a psychologist twice in her life before. The Colfax Police Department required a fitness for duty interview for every officer involved in a shooting incident before they were cleared to return to work. There had been the first time almost fifteen years ago, an exchange of shots with a suspect after a traffic stop when she was still a patrol officer. No one had been hurt and she hadn't had a lot of residual anxiety about it.

The second time had been much worse: a suspect shot dead and CJ badly injured. That one had been pretty dreadful for a while, but not because of what she had done—rather, it had been the prospect of losing CJ that had fueled her nightmares for weeks. The intervening three years had let the recollections lose some of their potency, but like the scar on CJ's chest, the memory remained, however faded.

Even so, each of those occasions had been brief encounters, a single visit and evaluation, and not by Alex's choice. This time felt different in many ways, and Alex twisted uncomfortably in her seat in the waiting room, wondering again if she'd made the right decision to come here. Her pain felt too vast to be contained or explained by another person, even one trained to help.

There was a buzz at the assistant's desk, and without further communication, the young woman seated there said, "Dr. Wheeler is ready, Ms. Ryan. You can go on in."

The inner office, unlike the impersonal standard office décor of the waiting room, seemed to reflect a specific personality. The chairs were white leather, as was the couch, and the small side tables were glass-topped metal. There was, to Alex's surprise, no desk, but there was a chair with a small laptop on the table beside it. The walls held several paintings, abstracts with swirling colors and vague shapes. Alex wondered if they were some sort of informal Rorschach test.

Besides the door from the outer office, there was another door on the opposite side, and Alex wondered if it was a separate exit, since she hadn't seen anyone emerge from this room through the waiting room. There was a glass, open shelf bookcase on one wall holding a few small chessboards, their pieces neatly lined up in the ranks. There were no other knickknacks, no books or magazines, not even an ashtray.

After a few seconds, the unidentified door opened and a woman came in, closing it behind her.

"I'm sorry," she said. "I made the mistake of taking a phone call. I'm Elaine Wheeler."

Alex offered her hand. "Alex Ryan."

"It's good to meet you. Please, sit wherever you'd like."

As expected, Wheeler took the chair by the laptop, and Alex sat across from her in one of the chairs, the leather soft and welcoming. Wheeler tapped a couple of keys, then turned away from the keyboard and met Alex's gaze.

She was a little younger than Alex, she guessed, late thirties. Her blond hair was already going silvery gray, but her face was almost unlined below strongly marked eyebrows. Wheeler wasn't in a suit but was wearing a pair of slacks and a turquoise blouse that set off her fair coloring. The clothes fit her well, although she looked to Alex's eye to be fifteen pounds away from slender. She wore a modern-looking pair of glasses, the eyes behind them a light blue. She had a relaxed expression, pleasant enough but inquisitive.

Alex felt another frisson of apprehension. Was she going to be able to open herself enough to this stranger to get what she needed? Was getting help even possible?

Wheeler said, "I'd like to start by telling you how I work. Then I'd like for you to talk about yourself, telling me as much as you can about what has brought you to me. All right?"

Alex tried to relax a little, glad to hear that the psychologist was going to talk first. "Yes," she said.

"As you know, from our talk on the phone, I am a clinical psychologist licensed by the state, which means that I can practice psychotherapy but, unlike a psychiatrist, I cannot prescribe medications for your condition. If, in my opinion, medication is indicated, I will work with your physician as necessary. All right?"

"I understand." She hesitated a moment, and Wheeler smiled gently.

"You'll have to be able to tell me what your questions are as we go along, if we're going to be able to work together."

"I'd like to avoid any use of drugs," Alex admitted.

"They may not be necessary, but I would like to ask why you're opposed."

Alex took a deep breath. "I'm a police officer. If I'm on a prescribed medication for anything psychological, I'd need to report it and I'd like to avoid that. If we can."

"I see. Do you think your issues are connected to your job?"

"No. I'm very certain of that."

Wheeler nodded and continued, "All right. I focus on what is technically called cognitive behavioral therapy and interpersonal psychotherapy, which really just means I work with patients to help them solve their problems by talking with them about what they're doing and why they're doing it, hoping to change perceptions and behaviors that are causing them problems in their everyday life. It's a therapy that works well for many disorders. I'd like to know more about you, and what you see as your issues, so we can see if I'm likely to be able to help you. If I don't think I can help, I'll try to refer you to someone who may be better able to do so."

"Fair enough," Alex said. "I have to tell you I'm not sure anyone can help, really."

Wheeler gave the gentle smile again. "Perhaps not, but I do hope so. Tell me about yourself. May I call you Alex?"

"Of course."

"You can call me Elaine if that's comfortable for you. Or Dr. Wheeler if you'd prefer."

"I'm not sure where to start," Alex said.

"Anywhere you'd like. Perhaps you could tell me how you're feeling right now?"

Alex looked away, seeing the neatly lined up chess pieces and wondering whether her life would ever make sense to her again. Some days were agonizing, the pain like a constant bitter taste in her mouth. Other days she was numb, stumbling through her work and her interactions with other people feeling like a ghost, not really present. There was anger, and grief, and loneliness that tore at her in the night.

"I'm hurting," Alex finally said, simply. "I can't sleep well. Every night seems to go on endlessly. I'm restless, sometimes until dawn. I'm not interested in eating, I have no energy for work, and I've always been able to work effectively, no matter what else was going on in my life. Now I can hardly seem to function." She gave Wheeler a sharp look and added, "I know I'm depressed."

"How long have you felt this way?" Wheeler asked in a soft tone.

"Since last July twelfth," Alex said wearily.

Wheeler said thoughtfully, "Such a precise date indicates that there was a specific event that happened at that time, I assume?"

"Yes," Alex said. "I—"

The emotions hit her like an electrical charge, twisting her inside. She dropped her head into her hands, feeling hot tears begin to run down her cheeks, salty when they reached her lips.

She thought she would be used to the pain by now, that the sorrow that had become her daily companion would have inured her to the question of what had happened, but the grief ripped through her again as if newly formed.

Dr. Wheeler rose, got a box of tissues, handed it to her. "Take your time," she said softly.

Alex wiped her eyes, crumpling the tissue in her hand. "Sorry," she managed.

"Don't apologize. We're accustomed to apologizing for displays of emotion in public, but if you can't cry in your therapist's office, where can you cry?"

Alex looked up at the unexpected flash of quiet humor. "It probably won't be the last time," she admitted.

Wheeler cocked her head a little at Alex. "I'm guessing you're not normally an emotional woman."

"That's true. How would you know that?"

"I've worked with people in the helping professions before. If you were emotionally volatile, you probably wouldn't still be a police officer. Or at least not a good one. Are you?"

Alex appreciated the change of subject to permit her to regain her composure. "I'm a captain, in charge of the detectives at the Colfax PD. I've been a police officer for almost twenty-four years."

"That sounds like a lot of responsibility. Do you like your job?"

Alex couldn't figure out the background questions from the ones that were really important, so she decided to just answer everything as well as she could. "I always have," she said. "Lately, nothing seems enjoyable to me."

Quietly, Wheeler asked, "You're obviously in a lot of distress. Have you considered suicide?"

Alex knew the importance of this question. An honest "yes" would probably get her medicated at best, suspended from the job at worst. Her Catholic upbringing meant that she hadn't considered it very seriously, though there had been a few moments over the last months when the thought of pulling the trigger had been tempting. It wasn't that she wanted to be dead as much as she was desperate for the pain to stop.

"No," Alex said. "But I'm just so tired of hurting all the time."

Wheeler leaned back and rested her arms on the arms of her chair. "I understand. Tell me why you joined the police force."

Alex went briefly through a summary of her life: the loss of her parents, raising Nicole, her brief and unhappy marriage to Tony, the death of Tony's niece, her niece, when she was only nine, her promotions. She had done enough research before selecting Elaine Wheeler to know that the next part of her story wouldn't cause an issue.

"I met another officer at work," Alex explained. "A woman. She asked me out and we became involved. We married out of state, and have been living together for the last three years."

As she expected, Wheeler nodded calmly. "Tell me about her," Wheeler asked.

Alex shifted uncomfortably. "This is difficult for me," she said. "We have—had—a good marriage. I love her and I know she loves me. Or she did."

Wheeler said, "Why is this difficult?"

"She's the reason I'm here."

"Are you interested in therapy to help you salvage this relationship?" Wheeler asked.

"I don't think that's going to be possible," Alex said sadly.

"Why is that?"

The tears threatened again, but Alex bit them back fiercely, using all of her strength to try to maintain her composure.

"Alex?" Wheeler's voice was gentle again. "Why isn't that possible?"

"Because I have no idea where she is," Alex said at length. "She left me. She left me, and I don't know why."

CHAPTER FIVE

"God damn it, Fullerton!" Alex was yelling at the detective in her office. "You're not some rookie. What the hell were you thinking?"

Her voice was carrying into the outer bullpen where her detectives sat to work when they weren't in the field. She saw a couple of them look up into her office in surprise. Alex certainly had a temper, but screaming was out of the ordinary for her.

Across the bullpen, Sergeant Frank Morelli nudged his partner Detective Chris Andersen, the youngest detective in the room and the only other woman. Morelli was Alex's senior detective, her informal right-hand man. Chris Andersen had been her most difficult challenge as an employee. Chris had seemed determined to start an affair with Alex, but their issues had been settled. Alex thought Chris had the most potential to be a good investigator among all her staff, but she still had a lot to learn.

Chris met Alex's eyes through the office window and then glanced meaningfully at Detective Roger Fullerton, the object of Alex's tirade. Chris knew better than to smile, but she did slowly nod as if to say, whatever you're doing to him, he deserves it.

Alex turned her glare back to Roger and said, "Well? I'm waiting, Detective."

Roger, his voice surly, muttered, "Waiting for what?"

"Your explanation," Alex snapped back at him. Fullerton's partner, Kelly Porter wiggled uncomfortably in Alex's other visitor's chair. Porter was a bland, baby-faced man who looked younger than his thirty-six years, and he'd been suffering as Fullerton's partner for almost five of them.

Porter tried to defuse Alex with, "Captain, the guy was being really non-cooperative."

Alex swept her gaze to him and he swallowed. "I'll deal with you in a minute, Detective. At this moment, I'm still waiting to hear your partner's explanation about why I have not one, not two, but *three* citizen complaints on my desk about you and your actions yesterday."

"Jesus, Captain," Fullerton griped. "The scum we arrest are presumed innocent. How come I don't get the same break as the bad guys?"

Alex felt her temper ratchet upward from anger to fury. "Unlike you," she snarled fiercely, "I have an answer for the question. Because we're the damn *good* guys, Roger. The cops get held to the highest possible standard for our conduct so people can tell the difference between us and the so-called 'scum.' We play by the rules, not just some of the time, but all the time, you understand me? That's what *makes* us the good guys. We do not scream at citizens, or threaten them, or push them to get what we want. Particularly seventy-four-year-old citizens. That was an *assault* you committed, are you aware of that?"

"I was doing my job, *ma'am*." He was all but snarling at her. "He was fucking with us. You been gone so long you forgot what it's like on the street, actually doing the job. You have no fucking idea."

She could see Porter go pale at this level of insubordination. Suddenly the fury that had been boiling her veins turned to ice.

She was done with Fullerton. He'd been nothing but trouble from the day he'd swaggered into the bullpen, tormenting Porter, Chris, and anyone else he didn't like. Most of the other detectives avoided him, and a few, like Frank and Chris, actively disliked him.

"That's it," Alex said, surprised at how cool she sounded. "Badge and gun, right now. I'm putting you on administrative leave and recommending that you be suspended pending both an Internal Affairs investigation and an investigation to determine if possible criminal charges should be brought."

He jumped from his chair and Porter actually scrambled up beside him, looking ready to either flee or grab him.

"You stupid bitch!" Fullerton screamed. "You have no fucking idea how to do the job, you know that? Or is it that you just like fucking around with guys? Oh, wait, that's right, you don't actually fuck guys anymore, do you?"

Porter went an even deadlier shade of white. Through the glass, Alex saw both Frank and Chris get to their feet and start toward her office.

Alex felt herself actually tremble with the effort to stay in control. She said, "The difference between a police officer and a bully with a badge is self-control. However frustrated you were at Mr. Sato, you had no right to touch him. Take me, for example. Right now, I'm exercising my self-control not to break your jaw so I don't have to listen to you anymore."

Fullerton lunged at her, actually taking a clumsy swing over her desktop. She backed away easily, and by the time she got to her feet, Porter, Frank and Chris had Fullerton in a three-way vise. Porter looked as if he were in shock, Frank was furious, and Chris looked actually pleased at being able to pull Fullerton's arm behind his back.

Fullerton was still screaming at Alex, but she couldn't hear his words anymore. When he stopped for breath, she said to her officers, "Let him go."

The detectives stepped back warily. She looked at him and said, "Badge and gun, Fullerton. IA will be in touch."

He threw his badge down and reached for his service weapon. Chris Andersen stepped up next to him and said quietly, "Be really careful, Fullerton."

He glared at her, then swiveled his head back to Alex. "This isn't over. I'm calling the PBA and getting a lawyer."

"Be my guest," Alex said coolly. "Call the Police Benevolent Association or the mayor or whoever you want. Just get out."

When he was gone, she sat back down in her chair again, feeling drained. When she glanced up, the three detectives were still in her office, watching her.

"Kelly," she said. "You weren't named in the complaints. Internal Affairs will want to talk to you, but you're not the subject of the investigation yet. What I need you to do in the meantime is go back through what you and Roger had on your desks so we can figure out how to get you some help. All right?"

He still looked as if he were in shock.

"Kelly? You okay?" Frank asked.

"Yeah. Yeah, I'm fine," Porter rubbed a hand over his face. "I'll get right on it, Captain."

Frank walked him to the door, and turned back to look at Alex. "I'll go give him a hand," he said. "If you need me, you know where to find me, Captain."

Frank Morelli was being her friend, she knew that. She nodded and said only, "Thank you, Sergeant."

When the men had gone, Chris Andersen lingered in the doorway.

"Yes, Detective?" Alex asked.

Chris cleared her throat. "Everyone heard it," she said. "And there's not a cop out there who won't be very happy to testify about what happened. Fullerton is an asshole, and we'd be glad to be rid of him."

Alex just nodded, trying to figure out yet again how she could feel so empty, so hopeless. Was the rest of her life going to be like this, a black hole of anger and sorrow?

"Captain?"

"Thanks for your help, Chris."

"I..." Chris seemed to hesitate, and Alex looked at her. "What is it?"

"If this is none of my business, just say so. But you...I mean, we've been kinda worried...oh, hell, I really suck at this shit."

"Chris, if you have something to say, just say it."

Chris ran her hands through her short, blond hair in embarrassment. "Frank and I were talking. You haven't been yourself since...you know. Is there anything we can do? I mean, you could just maybe come over for dinner, or something? Beth is a great cook, and I just..." Both her voice and her look softened. "You were a good friend to us, Beth and me, when we needed it. You and...um, Inspector St. Clair both. It's, uh, hard to see you so, ah, unhappy."

Her words twisted inside Alex. She couldn't even sort out what she was feeling. Everyone had just been trying to ignore what had happened to her, trying to act normal, especially Chris, perhaps because of their past stormy issues. The Chris Andersen she knew was tough and self-sufficient, largely uninterested in other people's problems. Perhaps being with Beth Rivera, her girlfriend, had begun to change Chris. An invitation to dinner was deeply surprising to Alex, and touched her unexpectedly.

"Tell Beth thanks," Alex said. "I need a little more time, I think, but I will come to dinner sometime, if the invitation is still open."

Chris nodded gravely, but Alex could see that she was pleased. "Anytime. I mean that, Captain."

"Thanks, Detective."

She called Sergeant McCarthy, CJ's former assistant in Internal Affairs, to give him the information about Fullerton.

"Hey, Captain, I'm glad you called," McCarthy said when she was finished. "I got a call yesterday from the DA. They wanted to know about an Internal Affairs investigation on, um..."

Alex heard him scrabbling through the paperwork on his desk. "On Detective Kinsey?" she supplied.

"Yeah. Kinsey. Apparently they're getting ready to go to trial on some case where he's the witness and the DA is worried that we'll have to tell the defense about the IA investigation. You know, exculpatory evidence."

Alex snorted into the phone. "The DA does not need to do a Brady disclosure on Detective Kinsey because he screwed up his timesheets."

McCarthy said, "Okay, but the DA said it might reflect on his truthfulness as a witness, so he wanted me to send the IA file over to them."

Alex sighed. After the scene with Fullerton, she did not need the unpleasantness of a conversation with her ex-husband, the current District Attorney. "I'll call him myself and explain exactly why he does not need the IA file, Sergeant."

McCarthy sounded fulsomely grateful. "Thanks, Captain. Thanks a lot."

It took her a couple of minutes to gather the strength to even dial his number. Everything seemed difficult for her lately. In the beginning, after CJ had left, she had spent weeks doing everything to find her. When every effort proved futile, her failure took her energy with it. Now even getting through the day was almost too difficult to manage.

As she waited for her ex to pick up his line, Alex could only think that the conversation she was about to have would never have happened if CJ had still been on the job. CJ would have known the answer and probably would have taken some pleasure in calling Tony to tell him how wrong he was. Tony had never liked CJ and hated that Alex was married to her. CJ had tried to treat him with equanimity, but eventually had surrendered to her deep resentment of his interference in Alex's life.

"Alex." Tony's deep baritone sounded warm. "To what do I owe the pleasure?"

God, she hated that he always sounded as if he were still interested in her. "Not pleasure, Tony, business. I'm calling about Detective Kinsey."

"Kinsey. Kinsey. Which case is that?"

Alex sighed. It took her three minutes to remind him about the topic and another ten to explain why his office did not need the IA file. Finally he said, "Look, I get it. You don't want your guy to look bad. But I don't need an accusation from the defendant's lawyer that we didn't disclose the evidence, so humor me on this."

"You want me to send you the IA file and hang my detective out to dry because you're afraid to look bad to the public defender's office?" Alex snapped at him. "When did you stop acting like a DA and start acting like a politician?"

"The District Attorney is an elected official," he said, his tone defensive. "Alex, you've been around enough to know how things work. You can't do any good unless you're in a position to do good, and sometimes you have to do something expedient to get there."

"Save it for your next Rotary Club speech, Tony. I am never going to agree with you that the ends justify the means. I've never been afraid to admit when we had a bad apple in the department, but Kinsey isn't a liar. He made a mistake, but you don't have to tell the PD about it because it's not going to have an impact on his credibility. Okay?"

"Yes, okay." She could tell he was unhappy about it.

She was ready to hang up but Tony said in a mollifying tone, "So how are you doing, Alex? We haven't talked for a while."

"I'm fine," she lied.

"No, really. I mean, it's been a long time and I figured since you haven't heard anything from her—"

"What?" Alex cut in. "You thought you were safe to assume that I was over it by now?"

"Come on, don't be like that." His voice turned condescending. "I'm worried about you, honey. She treated you like shit, taking off like that."

"Stop it," Alex said, weary of the conversation and of him. "I've told you this before. My current marriage is none of your business. I'm not interested in your worry about me, I'm not interested in your opinion of CJ and I'm definitely not interested in anything personal you have to say to me. Goodbye, Tony."

She managed to hang up without slamming the phone down, then tried to shut everything off, to concentrate on the latest index crime section of the Uniform Crime Reports. Her pain was beginning to feel like a permanent change in her, as if her eyes had somehow changed color. How long would it be before she stopped reaching for the phone in the middle of the day to call CJ? How long would it be before she stopped reaching for her in the night?

She looked up to see Deputy Chief Paul Duncan in her doorway. Sighing, she put the UCR aside and said, "Paul, come in. Are you here about Roger?"

He wedged his bulky body down carefully into her visitor's chair, a frown wrinkling his already lined forehead. His bad hip must be bothering him again, Alex thought. Glancing down at his hands, she wondered if he hadn't developed some arthritis in the thick, gnarled fingers.

Paul smoothed down the navy blue tie on his uniform. "Sergeant McCarthy called me. Said you put Fullerton on leave pending an IA."

She nodded, and briefly described the complaints and the encounter in her office, watching his frown deepen with every word.

"You think I shouldn't have put him on admin leave?" she finished, reacting to his expression.

"Well, hell, Alex, of course you should. Aside from the pretty serious citizen complaints, he can't talk to a superior that way, much less take a swing at one. I know you haven't been happy with him for a while."

She sat back in her chair. His bald head didn't prevent her from noticing how much gray was in his mustache. Paul was her father's friend, her own godfather, her mentor during her career. She loved and respected him, but she sometimes wondered if the respect ran both ways. She knew he'd never fully approved of her relationship with CJ.

"It's true I've never been satisfied with Fullerton's work," Alex answered. "Apart from everything else, he's just not a very good cop. He blames other people for his own mistakes and he's a complainer."

"Well, he's gone too far this time," Paul said firmly. "When the investigation is completed, you should be rid of him for good."

"I hope you're right." She watched him rub a hand over his gleaming black skull, shaved completely clean, and added, "What else is on your mind, Chief?"

Her use of his title caused him to flinch a little and then she realized whatever it was he wanted was personal.

"Alex," he said. "I got a call from Chief Wylie. He wants to recruit for the vacancy."

She knew what he meant, but she didn't want to acknowledge it. "I'm not sure how that concerns me, Paul."

He frowned again and said, "We kept the Internal Affairs position open as long as we possibly could."

"I didn't ask you to do that. She resigned, that's what her letter said, didn't it?"

"Yes, but no one resigns and leaves the same day unless... unless there are other circumstances."

And that was the truth of it, she thought. The real reason she was going to therapy, the real reason that everyone was looking at her with pity, the real reason she couldn't sleep at night. Because there were other circumstances. She just had no idea what they were.

What did I do wrong? she asked herself, as she had every day since CJ left. *What did I do that was so terrible that she had to leave me, leave her job and home and friends to get away from me?*

"This has nothing to do with me," Alex said bitterly. "The chief wants to hire a new Internal Affairs Inspector. Fine. Clearly his former one isn't coming back."

Paul gave her a look she could hardly bear. "I'm sorry, Alex," he rumbled. "I know you're upset."

Upset? That was hardly the word.

He added, "I feel responsible. I should have talked you out of this at the time, I just thought—"

Her anger flared again. "Thought what, Paul? That you could talk me out of loving a woman? That you could convince me it was a passing phase? You know better."

He looked angry, too. "I thought you would know how transient those relationships could be. I was afraid you'd get hurt."

She wanted to explode. "Transient? What the hell are you saying, Paul? That two women couldn't form a 'real' relationship? Jesus, I was with CJ for three years, longer than I was married to Tony, and believe me, I was a hell of a lot happier. I *loved* her, Paul. I wasn't with her so I could get laid, for Christ's sake!"

He winced at her words. "Alex, you know I'm not saying that. I'm just saying—"

"You know what? At this moment, I don't really care *what* you're trying to say, *Chief*. Just save it."

They sat a moment, staring at each other, Alex still angry, Paul wheezing a little as he tried to calm down.

"All right," he said, at length. "I thought you might want to go down and get whatever she left in her office. Personal effects."

Personal effects sounded as if CJ were dead, Alex thought. She sometimes wondered, in the depths of her despair, if it would have been easier if CJ *had* died. At least it would have been over, she'd know why CJ left, and that she was never coming back. Hope that she might someday see her again had never quite gone away, torturing her every day.

"All right," she said, shuffling through the paperwork on her desk. She knew she should have done the cleanup of CJ's office months ago. She'd been dreading this, to finally admit that CJ wasn't coming home. "I'll manage it later. This week sometime, is that soon enough?"

Paul stood unhappily. "Yes, fine. Alex, I…"

For a moment she thought he might apologize, but he said only, "How's Nicole doing?"

"Not great. She's getting through it." She looked up at him and added, "We have a lot in common these days."

He flinched again, then said, "Tell her Betty and I want you both to come to the house next week for dinner sometime. It'll be like when you were teenagers again, when your Dad had to work late, and we fed you, remember?"

No, Alex thought, it was never going to be like that again, but all she said was, "I'm seeing Nicole tonight. I'll tell her, Paul."

She knew she was taking her anger out him a little unfairly. After the scene with Fullerton and then the conversation with Tony, she just didn't have any patience left for him. She added, "My love to Betty."

He nodded and left her alone.

CHAPTER SIX

Alex sat with her sister in the backyard as the temperature cooled. The day had been an unexpected harbinger of spring for March, warm and sunny, but it was still going down to the forties tonight. Nicole had lit the firepit on the deck now that Charlie was safely in bed.

She'd also taken out the scotch, and she was on her second, and last, drink of the evening. Alex, who still had to drive home, had stopped at one, and was drinking coffee.

They didn't say anything for a long time, staring into the flames, flickering orange tongues under the starry night. Nicole lived in Lone Pine, far enough away from the lights of Denver that they could see a few bright pinpoints of light in the endless black above them.

Dinner had been filled with safe topics, mostly driven by Charlie and the challenges of being a fourth grader. He was a great talker for his age, and kept mother and aunt entertained through his macaroni and cheese and chocolate pudding.

He'd finally stopped asking for his Aunt CJ a couple of months ago, but Alex saw him looking at the passenger side door every time she drove up, still hoping to see her emerge and give him a hug. *I know how he feels.*

Alex said, "I saw Paul today. He and Betty want us over for dinner next week."

Nicole took a drink. "Just like old times, I guess."

"Something like that."

"I think Charlie has a sleepover a week from Friday, if I remember the date right. We could go then."

Alex said, "Well, I'm free."

Nicole gave her a sharp look that Alex could feel even in the dark. "Alex."

"Don't start, okay?"

They sat for a while longer, then suddenly Nicole said, "You are not going to believe what happened to me today."

"What?"

"Somebody asked me out. On a date."

Alex almost dropped her mug. "You're kidding."

"Well, don't sound quite so shocked. I'm not *that* old."

"I didn't mean that. I just meant—didn't he know? It's only been eight months."

Nicole said harshly, "I *know* how long it's been, Alex. It's not like there's a time limit. They don't make you wear widow's weeds for a year anymore."

Alex reached for her hand. "Nic, that's not what I meant. You know that."

Nicole clinked the ice in her glass. "I know," she said quietly.

"So who was it?"

"What? Oh, another attorney. I've known him a while. He's been divorced for a few years, and has a son a couple of years older than Charlie. We would swap child-raising stories sometimes. He's a nice guy. I've never heard him trash his ex-wife, for example. Seems like a good father, at least."

Something in her voice caught Alex's attention. "Did you say yes? To going out, I mean?"

Nicole took another drink. "Sort of. He's got his son a week from Saturday. We're taking the boys to the Avalanche game in the afternoon. We're meeting them there, and probably going for pizza or something after. Not much of a date, chaperoned by a couple of elementary schoolers. But sometimes—I don't know, Alex, I guess I just get lonely for a little adult male conversation that isn't about depositions and subpoenas."

"It's okay, Nic."

She sighed. "Is it? A year ago, I thought I knew what my life would be. Now, David's gone and I have to start thinking differently. I mean, Charlie lost his father."

"You don't have to find him another one, Nic."

"I know. I know you're right, I just keep thinking. I don't want to be alone the rest of my life. I miss David every single day, but I don't owe his memory the rest of my life, do I?"

How was she supposed to answer that? "Of course not," Alex answered.

Nicole put her glass down on the table with a sharp clank. "You think I'm a terrible person."

"Don't be ridiculous," Alex said forcefully. "You're my sister and you've been through something awful. I want you to be happy, that's all."

"For a long time after David died," Nicole said, "I didn't want to be happy. At first, I couldn't be, and then, when it got a little easier, I felt guilty."

"Survivors usually feel guilty."

"I know. I'm thankful for the grief support group you recommended. They've really been great. I think—for the first time, I think I can see that I might be able to be happy again. Not today, or tomorrow, but someday."

"Maybe Saturday," Alex said gently.

Nicole laughed a little. "Not quite that soon," she admitted. "But someday. Jesus, Alex. I really miss sleeping with someone else. Not just sex, although that, too. Just being held by somebody when the lights go out."

"Yes," Alex said, her voice almost a whisper. "I know."

Nicole turned to her. "God, I'm an insensitive jerk. Alex, I'm sorry."

"You don't have to apologize, Nic. It's not quite the same."

"Isn't it? I mean, I know David's never coming back, but lonely is lonely, however it happens."

Alex drank coffee and felt the warmth and the bitter taste of it on her tongue. "Paul said something today about how he should have tried to warn me that relationships 'like that' wouldn't last."

Nicole said angrily, "I hope you told him off."

"I did, and I wasn't very gentle about it, either," Alex admitted. "God, Nic, how could he even think that? It was as if he thought we were just playing at marriage, or something. Although," she added bitterly, "maybe one of us was."

"You don't believe that," Nicole said strongly.

Alex looked up at the stars. "I don't know what the hell I believe anymore. How could she leave me, Nic? What did I do? What didn't I do? I don't have a fucking clue."

After a long pause, Nicole said softly, "Alex, maybe you should see somebody. A professional, I mean. You're grieving, too."

"I'm ahead of you. I saw a therapist last week. My second appointment is tomorrow."

Nicole gripped her wrist. "I'm really glad. And I'm proud of you. I know how hard it is for you to admit you need help."

"I need something," Alex admitted. "I can't live like this. It's killing me inch by inch, Nic. Living without her is destroying me."

Nicole said sharply, "You can't let it. I know how hard it is. I really do."

Alex gave her a sad smile. "Well, you seem to be getting over it a lot better than I am."

Nicole released her fingers and sat back. "I had Charlie to consider. I had to pull myself together, for him."

"Yes," Alex said. "I guess I'm just not motivated enough to get over her."

"Listen to me. I need you, Alex. Charlie needs you. Promise me you'll try."

Alex said nothing, and Nicole said, "You're scaring me. Stop."

Alex finally answered, "I promise, Nic. I just don't know how much longer I can take feeling like this."

CHAPTER SEVEN

"We talked last week about how you were feeling," Elaine Wheeler said to Alex. "Today I'd like for you to tell me more about what you expect to get from therapy."

Alex smoothed her hand over the white leather on the arm of the chair and said, "I'm not completely sure. I know I want to stop hurting so much, I suppose."

"Why do you think it hasn't gotten better, over time?"

"I don't know. Maybe because my life feels as if it's somehow pending. Like I'm waiting for something."

"What do you think you're waiting for?"

She tried to sort through an answer that made sense.

Wheeler said, "This will work more effectively if you try to respond as honestly as you can, without worrying about how you think it will sound."

Alex almost smiled. It was like questioning a suspect. You were always trying for the most spontaneous, least rehearsed reaction.

"I'm waiting for her to come back to me," she said simply.

"Do you believe that will happen?" Wheeler asked.

"Do I believe it? No," Alex responded. "Do I still have some hope that she might come back to me? Yes."

"Why is that?"

"I suppose because it's human nature to hope, even against all odds, for what we want. CJ didn't just vanish, go missing. She went into work, worked half a day, wrote a letter of resignation, withdrew some money from her account, and apparently went home to our condo and packed a few clothes. Then she drove away and no one has heard from her since."

"Did she leave you a note?"

"Yes. It was not helpful," Alex said shortly.

Wheeler looked at her curiously. "I'm not sure what you mean by 'not helpful.'"

"It didn't tell me anything I needed to know. She didn't explain why she was leaving, or what I did wrong to make her leave. She said exactly two things, and neither one of them made much sense, in that context."

Wheeler tapped a finger against her chin. "I'm interested in your perception that you feel as if you did something to make her leave. Why do you feel that way?"

Alex felt frustrated. "Well, it seems obvious to me. If she were upset about her job, or somebody else in her life, a friend, she could have changed that without vanishing. It had to be something about me, or our relationship."

"Couldn't she have changed that without disappearing?"

"She could have," Alex admitted. "But it was probably easier for her to just walk away from me than to stay and face telling me—whatever it was. She did that once before, walked out on a lover."

"Tell me about that."

Alex sighed. "When CJ was nineteen, she met a woman at college. She fell in love with her, and CJ told her family she was gay. They basically disowned her, never spoke with her again. She stayed with this woman, believing they were in love and going to build a life together. They lived together for four years, then CJ walked in to find Laurel with another woman in bed. CJ threw her out, and then she ran away, left Georgia and moved here. She hasn't been back since, not even when her father died a couple of years ago, because she knows her family doesn't want to see her."

Wheeler said gently, "And you believe this is the same thing as before?"

Did she? Alex thought about it a minute. "I guess I do. I don't know. I didn't cheat on her, but I must have done something. All I know is when something went wrong with her first relationship, CJ left. So I must have done something wrong. What else can I think?"

"Was there another occasion where CJ acted in this way?" Wheeler asked.

"She had another serious relationship with a woman, after she moved here," Alex said. "But after they broke up, she didn't take off. In fact, I met the woman, her ex, last year. In fact, almost exactly a year ago."

"Did CJ seem disturbed by that meeting? Do you think it precipitated her leaving?"

Again, Alex thought a moment, then shook her head. "No. I met Stephanie in March, and CJ didn't take off until July. She mostly seemed worried about my reaction to meeting her. And we did fight about my belief that Steph was responsible for the accident, although I've never been able to prove it." Alex looked away. "Maybe that disagreement was more serious than I thought."

"What accident?" Wheeler asked, frowning.

Alex briefly explained what had happened last March. When she was finished, Wheeler asked, "CJ left the relationship with Steph but she didn't leave town, then."

"No. That's true."

"But you think she ran away from you."

"Look," Alex said in exasperation, "I see what your point is. Maybe a pattern I thought I saw isn't there at all. I think she really left Georgia, not so much because of what happened with Laurel, but because her family cut off their relationship with her. That hurt her a lot, I know."

She thought she saw a brief flicker of something in Wheeler's eyes. "But you still believe that CJ left because of you?"

"Yes," Alex answered. "You don't know how hard I tried to find her.

"Talked to her friends, even tried to talk to her family, not that they would speak to me. I called every police department and sheriff's office in the state, I think, trying to locate her. She must have wanted to disappear really badly. Disappear so even I couldn't find her." With a slowly dawning realization, Alex added, "And I think I can give you a real answer to your question."

"Which question was that?"

"You started out today by asking what I was looking to get from therapy."

"Yes. And what do you think that is?"

Alex took a deep breath and released it. "I want to know—no, I *need* to know why she left me. If I can resolve that, somehow, even if it's only in my own mind, maybe I can move on. I'll always love her, but maybe someday I'll be able to see a life without her, a future, if I can just understand the past."

Wheeler looked at her speculatively. "Knowing what other people's motives are isn't always possible," she said. "But I do believe that you can come to understand what has happened in your life, from your own perspective. If you can come to understand your own motives, why you made the decisions you made, you can change your behaviors." She smiled at Alex and added, "It's a goal we can work toward."

* * *

It was dark by the time Alex got home to the condo. She turned on the lights in the foyer as she took off her jacket and threw her keys on the table. As she hung up her coat, she looked down, as she had every evening since last July, hoping to find a pair of CJ's discarded shoes on the floor of the entryway.

CJ always stepped out of her shoes as soon as she walked in the door, a habit that had driven Alex a little crazy. Why didn't she walk a few more feet and take them off in their closet? Alex had to avoid tripping over them every time she came home.

But there were no shoes on the floor after CJ had come home that last time. Alex looked every night, waiting for CJ to come home and make everything right again.

The session with Dr. Wheeler, helpful though it was, had exhausted her. She couldn't decide which was more difficult: talking about CJ to her therapist, or not talking about CJ to everyone else.

She walked down the hall to the master bedroom. Her service weapon, a Glock semiautomatic, went locked into a small safe built into the closet. She tossed her blouse into the hamper, carefully hung up her slacks and then unstrapped her backup gun from her ankle. The Smith and Wesson revolver was a short-barreled hammerless thirty-eight caliber. She put the smaller gun, still holstered, in the drawer of the bedside table on her side. Loaded, it weighed just about a pound, and she was always happy to get it off her leg.

Alex slept only on her side of the bed. Both the phone and the alarm clock were on her side. CJ's side held only a lamp, and a volume of Robert Frost poetry, the book she'd been halfway through rereading when she left. Alex sometimes wondered if the cleaning service was curious about why they kept having to shift the same book to dust twice a month.

She hadn't gotten rid of anything, given away CJ's extensive shoe collection or moved her clothes out of the closet. Sometimes, when she was really hurting, she could go into the closet and put her face in one of CJ's jackets and catch the faintest breath of her scent clinging to the clothes. It had taken her weeks before she had been able to wash the sheets on their bed.

Alex pulled on sweatpants and a T-shirt, then went back out into the kitchen to search for something to eat. There wasn't much, but she found a container of leftover pasta salad that would do. She was never very hungry anymore, but she ate whenever she remembered to do so.

She finished the food, rinsed out the container and put everything in the dishwasher. She didn't have to run it very often anymore, not like when CJ was cooking. Alex often complained to her partner that she could use half the pans in the kitchen to make a simple omelet. Alex wished that she had to clean up after CJ now.

She lay on the couch and picked up a book, but nothing caught her attention. She closed her eyes, exhausted but not sleepy.

When the phone rang, she jerked up, the book falling to the floor with a thud. The caller ID surprised her.

"Hi, Vivien," she said. "Have you heard something?"

She'd only talked to Vivien about once a month since that first frantic week, when everyone CJ knew was exchanging what seemed like constant phone calls, text messages and emails. Now every conversation Alex had with Vivien, or for that matter with Rod Chavez or anyone else, began with the same words, and Vivien gave the same answer as always.

"Nothing." Vivien sighed. "How are you doing?"

"About the same," Alex answered honestly. "How are you?"

She tried to remember that she wasn't the only person CJ had left behind, that she didn't have exclusive rights to missing her. Vivien had suffered, in a different way, almost as much as Alex had herself.

This time Vivien hesitated over the question. After a moment, she said, "I have kind of a weird request. Could we go out sometime, like dinner or maybe lunch this weekend? I'd really like to talk to you."

"Of course," Alex said automatically. She and Vivien had never been as close as CJ might have liked—best friend and wife were too different for that. But Alex liked Vivien, in moderate doses, and she knew how much CJ loved Viv. She felt as if she'd gotten custody of Vivien somehow.

"Good," Vivien sounded relieved, as if she'd been afraid Alex might refuse the invitation. "I need a friendly ear. Well, some advice, actually."

"Is this about CJ?" Alex had to ask.

"Not at all. Though I have to tell you that if she were here, she'd be the one I'd be asking."

Alex wasn't sure how to take this news. "So, what, I'm pinch-hitting for her?"

"Sort of. Not exactly, I just…oh, fuck, Alex. I just don't know who else to talk to. About this. And you're the only other person I know who would really understand."

Really confused now, Alex asked, "Are you having trouble with the law, Vivien?"

"No! Nothing like that. I just want to talk to you. In person, okay?"

They settled on lunch at the Great Northern Tavern on Saturday, and Alex hung up, still wondering what Vivien wanted to talk about.

CHAPTER EIGHT

Late on Friday afternoon, Alex was doing a quick read through the latest *Police Chief* magazine when Frank Morelli knocked on her open door.

"Got a minute?" he asked.

"Of course. I was just thinking about you, in fact."

"You were reading the magazine and thinking about me?" he kidded her.

Alex smiled a little. "I was, actually. I was thinking about asking Wylie if I could take you to the IACP conference in October."

"Really?" Frank looked pleased and surprised. "And why would I be going to the International Association of Chiefs of Police conference?"

"Because they have a lot of training sessions. For example, you could take a session on first line supervision."

"Something you're trying to tell me, boss?"

Alex sat back and looked at him. Frank had an open, friendly air about him that made him good with victims and helped calm tense situations. He was only a little younger than Alex, with almost twenty years' solid experience behind him.

"Let's just say I'm thinking about succession planning," Alex said. "I hope you'll be making lieutenant someday very soon, and maybe captain after that. Training is always a good thing."

Suddenly he looked apprehensive. "Jesus, Alex, are you going somewhere? You're not going to quit or anything, are you?"

"No, of course not," she answered quickly. "Why would you think that?"

"You…" he stopped and suddenly sat down heavily in her visitor's chair. "I just thought that maybe you were so unhappy you were gonna quit." He stopped and looked at her with sad brown eyes.

"I am unhappy," she said quietly. "Quitting wouldn't help that. God, if I couldn't come to work I'd be completely round the bend by now."

"Oh, man. You had me scared there for a minute."

"Frank, what did you want?"

He cleared his throat, clearly a little embarrassed. "I was just checking up on you. You were pretty upset with Fullerton the other day. Not that the jerk-off didn't deserve it, but you're not much for screaming. I just wondered how you were doing."

He was being nice, and Alex tried not to resent being asked, once again, how she was feeling. How did everyone *think* she was feeling? What words could she use that would tell the story? Empty? Aching? Angry? All of those emotions, and others she could hardly name.

"About as well as I can be, I guess," Alex answered him.

He continued to look at her steadily. "I wish it hadn't happened," he said softly. "Everything that happened last summer, but mostly I'm really sorry she left. I really am."

"I know, Frank. Thanks for caring," she said gently.

He got up and said on his way out, "Jennifer told me to ask you over to dinner sometime. If you can stand to have dinner with a fourteen-year-old smart-ass at the table, we'd love to have you."

Jesus, Alex thought, what was it with the sudden avalanche of invitations to feed her? Chris, Paul, Vivien, and now Frank. Did she look like she'd lost weight or something?

"Thanks, Frank," she said, without pursuing it. "And thank Jennifer for me. We'll set it up sometime." She glanced at the clock and saw how late it was. "And could you mind the fort for a few minutes? I have to go downstairs and do something. I'll be back."

"Sure thing."

* * *

Sergeant McCarthy looked up from his desk as she went into his tiny office on the first floor.

"Captain," he said in greeting, looking uncomfortable. "The chief told me you'd be by."

"How are you, Chad?" Alex asked kindly.

"Okay," he answered, rubbing the tiny bald spot on his crown. "Busy, you know."

"I know," Alex said. She fought an irrational urge to apologize, as if his having to manage the flood of work was somehow her fault. "I'll need a box or something, I guess."

"Yeah, I got an empty copier box in there for you. If you need another one, let me know, but I don't think there's that much personal stuff. Just the bottom couple a drawers in the desk. All the files and stuff are locked up."

"Of course. Thanks for getting things ready."

"Sure thing." He chewed on his lip a moment, then blurted, "I'm really sorry, y'know. About the Inspector. I really liked her."

Me, too, Alex thought. Everyone is sorry. "Thanks, Chad," was all she could say.

She went into CJ's small office. Crammed into the room were desk, office chair, one visitor's chair and a trio of filing cabinets that took up most of the space. Alex went over and got the empty box, then sat in CJ's chair.

She looked for a moment out CJ's window. In the park on the other side of the parking lot the aspens weren't budding yet, their pale trunks still stark against the slowly ripening grass. Soon they would be bright with green leaves that shimmered in the faintest summer breeze, before turning deep gold in the fall, a uniquely Colorado sight that had always lifted her heart.

But not last autumn. Most of the last year had been so filled with pain that all the beauty had been crowded out, as if everything were blurred with tears. Would she ever be able to see the beauty around her again?

She opened the drawers. In the bottom one was a small makeup case that held mascara, blusher and a compact, along with a mirror. There was also a hairbrush and a toothbrush, carefully capped, with a small tube of toothpaste. At the bottom of the case was a lone earring, the post broken. Alex dumped it all out onto the desk, staring at the earring for a moment.

One earring, broken, lost from its mate. Useless.

She pushed everything into the trashcan with a brutal sweep, even the case. If you wanted it, she thought angrily, you should have taken it with you. You shouldn't have just left it behind.

She opened the next drawer. It held a couple of file folders, and she put them on the desk to see if they were work files.

The first folder was labeled Personal. Alex rifled through it, and found copies of CJ's paperwork, insurance forms, leave requests and such. She put the file in the box to take it home and shred the contents.

The second file was labeled Notes. She had just begun to open it when her cell phone rang. The number came up as Nicole's cell phone.

"Hi," Alex said. "What's up?"

"Thank goodness I got you," Nicole said briskly. "Listen, I'm stuck here at the office on some problem with a Motion to Compel. Is there any way you can pick Charlie up from after school care and take him home? I'll be there as soon as I can."

"It's not a problem, Nic," Alex said, dumping the other file folder into the box. "Do you want me to feed him?"

"Oh, God, would you? That'd be great. They'll send somebody out for sandwiches, and I can eat here if I don't have to worry about him. Just don't try to cook anything in my kitchen."

"Very funny. We'll stop on the way home."

"Okay. Not too much junk. Try to negotiate a reasonably nutritious meal, please."

"I'll do my best," Alex agreed.

She took CJ's umbrella, and the spare jacket she had kept hanging on the back of the door, along with her gold pen and nameplate, putting them all in the box. She could finish going through the second file later—if there was something that belonged at the office, she could always bring it back.

* * *

Charlie frowned, his dark eyebrows drawing together. For a not-quite-ten-year-old, he looked gravely serious.

"Can I have a cheeseburger?" he asked.

"It's 'may I have a cheeseburger,' and yes, you may. But you have to choose: soft drink or french fries. Not both."

She met his eyes in the rearview mirror from where he was securely strapped in backseat.

"But if I get french fries," he asked cagily, "I have to have something to drink."

"Yep," Alex agreed. "And it will be milk."

The frown deepened. "I could have a milkshake," he suggested.

"Nope. Milkshakes are desserts, not drinks, and we agreed on a popsicle later, right?"

"Yeah," he sighed. "Okay. Cheeseburger and french fries."

"Okay," Alex said. "And we're drinking all of our milk."

"Are you getting milk, too?" he asked warily.

"I am, in fact," Alex said. "Deal?"

"Deal."

They went inside, and when he'd eaten everything, she released him to go to the attached play area, watching him climb on everything that could be climbed. He'd done the best of all of them, she thought, bouncing back from losing his father better than either she or Nicole could have hoped for. The bad dreams had been rare, and they had gone away completely, but then he hadn't really seen much of what happened. Thank God—and CJ, she thought—for that.

She knew he missed CJ too. He didn't always differentiate between his two aunts, not caring that Alex was the one related to him. He'd worshipped CJ, and she seemed to love him, always thinking about what he needed and cooking special things for him—his favorite chocolate chip cookies, pasta without too much garlic in the sauce.

How could you do this? Alex asked CJ the mental question for the hundredth time. *If you were angry with me, even if you didn't love me anymore, how could you leave everybody else you loved, people who cared about you? Vivien, Rod and Ana Chavez, even Chad McCarthy, for God's sake. How could you leave a ten-year-old boy who adored you without even saying goodbye to him? Because you didn't love me anymore?*

Somewhere deep within herself, Alex knew that she simply couldn't believe that CJ had stopped loving her. It wasn't as if they'd been distant from each other. Maybe the fight about Steph had been more serious than she thought. Maybe Alex really had driven her away somehow.

She could remember the last time they'd made love with vivid clarity. It had been a Sunday, the day after David's funeral, and Alex had been so distraught about Nicole that CJ had come to her, the comforting caresses becoming more than that. Alex remembered lying awake in CJ's arms for an hour afterward, feeling her skin, smelling her scent, drawing strength and peace from being her arms. She could feel CJ's love and caring for her in every breath.

And two days later she leaves me? Was I the only one feeling our love? Was she deceiving me somehow?

She couldn't believe it. No matter what it seemed to be, she simply could not believe it.

CHAPTER NINE

Alex watched as Vivien picked at her salad. It had beautifully cooked maple-cured salmon on top of it, a lovely medium rare pink, but Vivien looked only slightly more interested in her food than Alex was.

They had exchanged pleasantries, the usual lack of information about CJ and her whereabouts, and a brief discussion about their jobs. As usual, Vivien complained about the mortgage banking business, and Alex complained about how much paperwork an administrative position included.

Whatever had prompted Vivien to suggest lunch hadn't been revealed yet, and Alex was determined to let Vivien bring it up when she was ready. She'd eaten a number of meals with Vivien over the last three years, but she couldn't remember ever meeting with her without CJ. No, there had been the planning lunch for CJ's surprise thirty-fifth birthday party, but they'd had plenty to talk about then.

Vivien finally looked up and said, "I really appreciate this."

"I haven't done anything yet," Alex said mildly.

"You agreed to meet me," Vivien said. "That's something."

Alex sat back in the booth, shaped to look like a train car seat to carry out the railway theme of the restaurant. "Vivien. If you need anything, I'll try to help."

Vivien gave her a sharp look. She had her shiny black hair pulled back today, and was wearing what was for her casual Saturday clothes: designer jeans (although Alex had no idea which designer), and a deep purple sweater that looked like cashmere. Alex was sure the matching purple pumps with the two-inch heels were designer, too, since Vivien and CJ had shared a passion for beautiful—and expensive—footwear.

"You don't have to be nice to me," Vivien said suddenly. "I mean, just because of CJ."

The remark surprised Alex. She answered, "It's not like I'm making a big sacrifice, Vivien. I like you. And even if I didn't, CJ loved you, and that's a good enough reason for me to help you if I can."

She watched as Vivien looked away and blinked hard.

"Fuck," Vivien muttered. "I really miss her, Alex."

"I know."

She shot her dark gaze back to Alex's face and said, "I used to be jealous, you know. I'm way past that now, but I was for a while."

"I understand," Alex said gently. "I just assume every woman I met had a little crush on her."

Vivien gave her the sharp look again and said, "Jesus, I wasn't jealous of *you*. CJ and I worked out the 'we'd be terrible as lovers' issues years ago. No, I was jealous of her. Well, both of you really."

Alex frowned into her soup. Was Vivien, after all this time, making a real pass at her?

Vivien sighed and said, "I just—I was a little jealous that she finally found somebody to love her the way she deserved to be loved, you know? But I was really happy for her, too. She was so happy with you, Alex. So…I don't know, it was like somebody finally turned on the big light inside of her and let it shine out." She mangled a piece of salmon with her fork and said, "Christ on a surfboard, I sound like an idiot. What the fuck happened, Alex? Why the hell did she take off and leave both of us?"

Alex knew the questions were rhetorical. There had been an unpleasant conversation between them that first week after CJ left, with Vivien screaming at Alex, demanding to know what she'd done to drive CJ away. She'd apologized later, more than once. Alex had forgiven her without a qualm. She'd had her own share of irrational anger, some of it lingering still. A part of her was so angry with CJ that she wondered how long it would take for that forgiveness to come.

"I have no idea why she left," Alex answered. "God, I wish I did know."

They ate in silence for a minute, until Vivien said, "Look, I need your advice. Like I told you on the phone, I'd ask CJ if she were here, but you're the only other person I know who might even begin to understand."

Alex pushed her soup bowl away and said, "Okay. I'm listening."

Vivien took a deep breath, and then asked, "Do you remember the blond bartender, the one I hired for the party at my house the night you had your accident last March?"

Alex searched her memory for a moment, then said, "I do, actually. She drove you over to pick up CJ's car, didn't she?"

Vivien brightened. "Yes, that's right. That's the night we met. Her name is Marja Erickson."

"You're still seeing her?" Alex tried to keep the shock out of her voice, but Vivien laughed.

"Yeah, I know. You're thinking about calling the Guinness people to find out if my dating the same woman for a whole year is a new record. Well, let me tell you—it sure as hell is."

"I'm not sure what to say," Alex said. "Congratulations?"

Vivien held up one hand. "Too soon, I think. Anyway, that's what I need to ask you about."

"Okay," Alex said, puzzled.

"How—" Vivien took a deep breath and began again. "How do you know if you're in love? I mean, really love, not all that other stuff, like lust and friendship and all the crap people think is love."

"Vivien," Alex said, trying to get over her shock. "You're in love with this woman?"

"Oh, fuck. How the hell would I know? That's what I'm asking you."

"I have no way on earth of knowing whether you're in love with her or not. I don't know you well enough to tell and I don't know her at all. How could I possibly help you with this?"

Vivien put her fork down and sighed. "Just tell me what it was like for you. How did you know CJ was the right woman? Or are you doubting that now?"

Alex looked away across the restaurant. There were a lot of couples, a few looking happy, others just bored. There was a group of women at one table, celebrating a birthday or a shower or something. Two men sat at another table, and something about them told Alex they were more to each other than just friends.

Was she doubting that CJ was the right woman, that she had ever been the right person for her? She certainly helped Alex come to peace with her attraction to women, a long struggle fueled by a Catholic upbringing and a bad early marriage. Because of CJ, Alex knew, with complete certainty, that if she could ever fall in love with someone again, it would be with a woman.

"I'm not doubting how I felt about CJ," she answered the question. "Maybe I'm doubting whether I was right for her. I'm angry, I'm hurt, I'm really confused, but I haven't stopped loving her. I knew then, and I know now, that she was the right person for me."

"But how did you know?" Vivien pressed her. "I know CJ, and it had to be more than great sex."

Alex felt herself flush a little, but answered, "I don't know about anybody else, but I think we had great sex because we were in love, not the other way around."

"I get that, but what was it? Help me out here, Alex. Sometimes I look at Marj and I think I'm already there, other times I just want to jump in my car and run away."

Alex flinched involuntarily, and Vivien exclaimed, "Oh, fuck! I'm sorry."

"It's okay. Look, I don't know what to tell you. I could tell you all those things from romance novels, that looking at her made my heart beat faster, that I thought about her all the time, that I would have driven a thousand miles just to hear her laugh. I could give you a list of things I loved about her, but it wasn't really any of that that made me sure I loved her. It was—"

"What?"

"It was how she made me feel about myself," Alex answered slowly. "It wasn't just how I felt about her, but how I felt about me, about us. She made me stronger, more caring. She both accepted me for who I was, completely, and at the same time made me want to be a better person. The day early on when I thought I'd disappointed her, that I'd lost her forever, I was frantic. That's when I knew, for certain, that I loved her. When I looked into her eyes and saw the rest of my life, I knew."

It was Vivien's turn to look across the restaurant thoughtfully. Alex said softly, "Why don't you tell me about her?"

"We don't have anything in common," Vivien began with a sigh. "She grew up on some ranch somewhere down in southeastern Colorado, which is a long way from San Francisco. She's tending bar to work her way through graduate school. Get this, she wants to be a social worker, can you believe that? She's out to her friends, but not to her family, and she's only twenty-eight. Fuck the casbah, what am I thinking?"

Alex said, "You're giving me a biography, not telling me about her. What's she like?"

"Oh," Vivien said, and Alex watched her typically cynical expression soften. "She's—I guess you'd say she's the strong, silent type. Kind of butch, the best kind, really, really thoughtful. She doesn't talk a lot, but she loves to read. When I've had a bad day, she'll just sit there and read and let me calm down until I'm ready to talk, then she'll listen to whatever bullshit I've got to say. If she gets home before I do, she'll make dinner. I mean, she's not an awesome cook like CJ, but she makes stuff I like."

"Wait," Alex interrupted. "You're *living* with her?"

Vivien, who could discuss cunnilingus in a crowded public elevator without a qualm, actually blushed.

"Well. Yes. It was stupid for her to pay rent on her apartment when her money is tight, and she was at my house every night anyway. And before you say anything, she's not after me for my money. She pays me every month, expenses, and goes grocery shopping. She takes the light rail to school, that kind of thing."

Alex was still trying to process Vivien living with the same woman for almost a year. "And you haven't driven her crazy yet?" she asked lightly.

"Damn it, Alex." Vivien sighed. "She's fucking incredible in bed. But some nights, you know, I just want to…and she's there for that, too. I'm starting to look forward to just hanging around the house on Sunday mornings so we can have brunch and light a fire. Christ, I sound so domesticated!"

Alex had to laugh. "Vivien, there's nothing wrong with that."

"Come on, Alex. Can you seriously see me sleeping with just one woman for the rest of my life?"

"That's not the point. Can you?"

Vivien nodded at the waiter who came to clear their plates away. When he was gone, she said, "I don't know. But the alternative is not being with her. She's, um, into monogamy, can you believe that? So I can be with just her, or be without her."

"Can you?" Alex asked again. "Can you be without her?"

Vivien was silent a long time, staring down at the table.

"I think," Alex said gently, "you've answered your own question. Vivien, you already know the answers. Just accept whatever it is. It'll be okay."

"Will it?" her voice was just above a whisper.

"I know it's scary as hell. But look at it this way. You can't go back. We never can. You can only go forward. And you can go forward with her, or without her. Give yourself a chance, if that's what you want. Okay?"

"Okay," she said at last. "You know, you're not so bad at this. CJ would be proud of you."

"I think she might just be proud of you. Once she got over the shock, of course."

* * *

Alex remembered the conversation with Vivien at her next session when Wheeler asked, "Tell me about your relationship with CJ. How long were you together?"

"Three years," Alex answered. "What kind of things do you want to know? I love her. She loved me, too."

"You are still sure of that," Wheeler said, not quite a question.

"I know she did. I don't know what to think now."

"Did you fight?"

"Everybody fights," Alex said dismissively. "Of course we did."

"About what kinds of things?"

Alex considered. "I would get mad at her for being late all the time. We had a yelling match in the car one time on the way to my godfather's house for dinner, and when we got there, dinner wasn't even in the oven yet. She's not very tidy, and I would get aggravated with her for leaving stuff all over the condo. She has half-read books everywhere, and leaves her shoes in the front hall for me to trip over. I think she's too careless with her money, but that's probably because I rarely had very much and she has way more than she can spend. Her grandfather left her a lot of money in a trust, and she doesn't pay much attention to how much things cost. I can get compulsive about things, so occasionally she had to sort of call me on obsessing about stuff that wasn't really important. She's a night owl, and I'm a morning person, so we had to work that out a little. Things like that."

After a moment of thought, Alex continued, "We did have a pretty serious disagreement a couple of months before she left." She described the fight about Steph, and Alex's suspicion that Steph had been behind the attempt on her life. "It came up a couple of times after that because I had trouble letting go of her as a suspect. In fact," she hesitated before continuing, "we had another brief fight about it the night before she left. I was never able to let go of thinking Steph was involved."

"You had a fight about this the night before she disappeared," Wheeler repeated. "But you don't think this disagreement was the reason she left?"

Alex sighed. "I didn't think so, but now I wonder. I can be difficult once I get onto something, stubborn. I'm sure it frustrated her. She was pretty pissed off at me."

"What about the money issue? Did you resolve that?"

"That was easy once we talked about it. We pretty much fixed it by opening a joint account for the household stuff, and I pay the bills out of it. Her trust fund is separate, and I try not to pay any attention to what she does with the rest of her money. She will buy me a way too expensive present once in a while, but I've learned to just let that go. It's not really a big deal anymore."

"Did you have communication issues? Trust issues?"

Alex smiled a little. "Communication was not too big a problem. Sometimes she had to prod me a little to get me to open up, but I'm a lot better than I was. Getting CJ to communicate is not an issue, believe me. She's very much a 'what you see is what you get' kind of woman. I'm not that way, but she knows me very well by now. Or she did, anyway." She shifted a little uncomfortably, and added, "As for trust—the worst fight we ever had was when she thought I was cheating on her. She was wrong. I've never cheated on her, and I never would."

"How did you resolve that?"

Alex met her look. "I told her the truth, and she believed me. That was the end of it. She's never referred to it since. CJ doesn't hold grudges." *Or at least I don't think she did, but maybe I was wrong.*

Wheeler asked calmly, "And how was your physical relationship?"

Alex shifted again, and finally answered, "I don't remember ever having a single cross word with her about sex. We talked, and there were a few things to work out, like there always is in a new relationship. I'd never slept with a woman before CJ, and it took me a while to get through just being overwhelmed by how…" she struggled for the right words, "how emotionally satisfying it was. I was overcome for a while, all those new feelings. Emotions, I mean, not physical feelings. Sometimes I was still overwhelmed, even after living with her for almost three years. It was always good between us. I was still very attracted to her, and she apparently felt the same way about me—she initiated sex a lot. Is this what you wanted to know?"

Wheeler tapped her fingertip on the arm of her chair. "When most couples have issues, they normally center around communication or trust, money or sex. I'm not a marriage counselor, but it doesn't sound as if you had any major issues around any of those."

"No," Alex said, with what she hoped sounded like complete conviction. "I don't think we did."

Wheeler looked thoughtful for a moment, then said, "Let me ask you another question. Last week, you said you thought what you needed from therapy was to answer the question of why CJ left you, so that you could move on. Do you still feel that way?"

"Yes," Alex said firmly. "Very much so."

"I think I should ask you why you are convinced that CJ left you."

Alex looked at her in confusion. "What do you mean? She was living with me, and she disappeared."

"Let me rephrase. Why are you convinced that she left *you*?"

"I don't understand. She left everyone in her life, her friends, her job and co-workers, my nephew, whom she adored."

"She left her life."

"Well, yes. What are you saying?"

"I'm just asking you to consider whether you were the reason she left. Are there any other possibilities?"

Alex just stared at her. She'd never, for one moment, considered that her pain was some kind of collateral damage in CJ's departure.

"But why?" she demanded. "What other reason could she possibly have had?"

"I don't know," Wheeler responded gently. "Do you?"

Alex sat back, combing thoroughly through her mind for other possibilities. "I suppose if she were sick, dying or something, and wanted to spare me, spare all of us from that. But she wasn't sick. I have access to her medical records through the department's health insurance website because we have each other's passwords. She had a physical two months before, everything was fine, mammogram, pap smear, everything. She had no symptoms of any kind. She was fine."

"All right. What else?"

Alex felt her anger flare suddenly. "Why are you asking me this?" she snapped. "Are you suggesting that she left me for someone else?"

"I'm not suggesting anything except that you should look for other possibilities. Do you think she was having an affair?"

"Jesus God, no. Even if she were the kind of woman who would, and she wasn't, she just didn't have time. We often drove to work in the same car, went home together, we had lunch together about half the time. She worked one floor below me, I saw her every single day. We were in bed together almost every night. The only time she could have been seeing someone else would have been about ten minutes a week."

"All right. She didn't leave with someone else. Why did she leave?"

"I told you, I don't *know!* Yes, we had a fight, but everybody fights! I don't know why she left. That's what I need to figure out."

Wheeler looked at her steadily for a moment, then said, "What I'm suggesting to you is that you do know. You have told me several times that you loved CJ, and that you believed CJ loved you as well. Do you really believe that still?"

"Yes," Alex said, her voice hoarse. "Yes."

"Could your belief that she left you be rooted in the number of people in your life who left you prematurely? You told me your mother died when you were ten, your father was killed when you were nineteen, and you lost your niece to cancer when she was a child. Even your ex-husband."

"I left him," Alex mumbled, her mind still reeling. "And my parents, my niece, didn't leave me. They died."

"Those are still losses. You've lost a lot of people. Could you be seeing CJ as just one more person no longer in your life, one more person you lost?"

"I didn't *lose* her," Alex muttered again. "She *left* me."

"She's still lost to you," Wheeler answered.

Grief broke loose inside her, like a giant piece of an iceberg tearing free. Alex began to weep, angrily this time. Wheeler let her get up and pace for a while as the tears streamed down her face, with Alex furiously hurling them from her cheeks as she stalked around the office. When they subsided, Wheeler wordlessly handed her the tissue box again.

"God," Alex said, "I've never been so confused in my life. What are you saying? Just tell me, for God's sake."

Wheeler leaned forward until Alex was able to meet her ice-blue gaze. "Alex. I don't know what your personal spiritual beliefs are, but I think it's very possible that you know what happened, in your soul, on some deep level. If you knew CJ as well as you seem to have done, you know why she would leave. You may not be sure of all of the circumstances, but in some way, I think you know why she left. If you can't tell me, at least tell yourself."

Alex continued to stare at her. Wheeler said, "You're thinking too hard. Think less, feel more. Sit back, close your eyes a moment. I'm going to ask you again, and you're going to answer me, all right?"

Slowly Alex sat back in the leather chair, trying consciously to let her body relax, trying to empty her mind. After what seemed to be a long time, she heard Wheeler's voice asking quietly, "Why did CJ leave, Alex?"

The words left her before she could catch them.

"Because she loved me," Alex answered.

That answer made no sense at all. Alex could only wonder if it was the right one.

CHAPTER TEN

Alex was sitting in her living room on Saturday night with the Denver Nuggets basketball game on the television, the sound muted. She had a book in her hand, but she was not paying much attention to either the game or the reading. Her phone rang, surprising her.

"Hi," Nicole said. "I didn't wake you up, did I?"

"It's only nine forty-five. Not even I go to sleep that early."

"You have been," Nicole countered.

"Going to bed, yes," Alex admitted. "Not sleeping. Are you calling to recap the date?"

"I am, actually. How high school is that?"

"Pretty close. Want to tell me what you wore?"

"Oh, stop it."

"Is Charlie asleep?"

"Crashed out like a toddler. It's been a carbohydrate-filled afternoon, between popcorn and soda at the game and pizza after that."

"You sound wiped out yourself."

"A little bit. It was mostly the strain of being on a date, something I haven't done, by my calculation, for a good sixteen years."

"How much did it feel like a date, given that you had a ten- and twelve-year-old with you?"

"Not very," Nicole admitted. "But that was mostly because of Bill. It felt a lot more like a family outing, if you know what I mean."

"Not entirely. Did you have a chance to talk?"

"More than you'd think. Fortunately, the boys got along very well. Bill's son Drew was nice to Charlie, and I think my son has a serious case of hero worship. A sixth grader seems very grown up to him."

"It's funny," Alex said, "how much difference a year or two makes at that age. Any age difference less than a decade now feels like nothing."

Neither of them mentioned that CJ had been seven years younger than Alex. Nicole said, "Bill was very laid-back about it all. But the best part was that we got to talk about things other than work and our kids. Really, you have no idea how wonderful it was to discuss a book other than *Peter Pan*."

Alex's heart ached for her sister. Alex had tried so hard her whole life to protect Nicole, and she'd been unable to shield her from the worst heartache of all.

"Sounds promising," she said.

"Early days. But he is very nice, and we do have some things in common."

"So," Alex whispered, "did you get a kiss goodnight?"

"You are bad. Yes, a very chaste one on the cheek. But we did agree to go out again, without Charlie and Drew this time."

"Even more promising."

Nicole was quiet a moment, then asked, "Alex, do you think it's too soon?"

"Honestly, Nic, the only question that matters is whether *you* think it's too soon. Does it feel wrong?"

Her sister's sigh came clearly over the phone line. "No. I kept spending the whole afternoon wondering when I would be stricken with guilt over David, but I just felt sad. I just *hate* it that he won't be here to see Charlie grow up. It's so goddamned unfair."

"Yes," Alex could only agree. "It's goddamned unfair."

"Anyway, it was a nice afternoon, and Charlie enjoyed it. So we'll see how it goes."

Moving on, Alex thought. Vivien, Charlie, Nicole, other people were taking up their lives again, slowly recovering. Was she recovering?

As she brushed her teeth she looked at herself in the mirror, something she had avoided the last few months. She looked thin, not in a healthy, lean way, but in a "not eating well" sort of way. She'd actually been getting up earlier to go running on the weekday mornings, and taking longer runs on Saturday and Sunday.

Usually CJ had gone running with her on weekends, and as a result the runs were actually shorter, more relaxed. Often CJ would lure her back into bed. It had been one of their favorite times to talk, touch, make love.

Alex snapped off the bathroom lights so she didn't have to look at her face anymore, the skin stretched high over her sharp cheekbones, her eyes dark and smudged. *I look like a refugee. I hardly look as though I'm recovering.*

She undressed and crawled naked between the sheets. CJ liked sleeping nude, and Alex had grown accustomed to the pleasure of it. She turned off the bedside light and lay still, staring into the darkness.

Some nights the memories were of good times, the best moments of her relationship to CJ playing out before her mind's eye. In some ways, those were the worst, because Alex always remembered the sadness coming underneath the joy. Other nights she replayed other, more terrible moments.

This night, she remembered every moment of the afternoon of last July Fourth.

"How many people are we feeding?" Alex had complained as she hauled the cooler across the grass to the picnic pavilion.

"Oh, come on now," CJ had responded, her arms full of paper plates, napkins, utensils and cups. "My favorite nephew is a growing boy."

"He's nine years old."

"And this is the time to make sure he grows up nice, strong and tall."

"Honey, have you checked out his gene pool lately? If he finishes taller than five seven, it'll be a miracle."

CJ drew herself up to her full height. "I'm hoping to contribute by osmosis."

Alex laughed at her and murmured, "Always the optimist, my treetop lover."

CJ laughed too as they were met by Charlie, running jubilantly across the grass. "Aunt Alex!" he yelled. "Aunt CJ! Mom says you have watermelon!"

Alex grinned at CJ and said, "We sure do. Want to take a peek?"

"Yeah!"

Alex showed him the big slices wrapped in clear plastic wrap and tucked into the cooler. He helped her drag the wheeled cooler the rest of the way to the table.

"Hey, guys," Nicole greeted them, kissing Alex and then CJ. "Glad you got here. The chef was getting ready to throw the burgers on."

David, standing by the grill, rolled his eyes. "Dear, I keep telling you that you can't put the food on as soon as you light the coals." He made eye contact with CJ and added, "It's a genetic defect in the Ryans. High intelligence coupled with a complete lack of cooking acumen."

CJ went over to hug him and said, "Well, thank goodness they have us, then."

"Yep. I'm pretty sure they married us for our kitchen skills."

Mindful of Charlie a few feet away helping to unload plastic containers of food, CJ merely lifted her eyebrows and murmured, "Well, in *your* case maybe."

David gave a hearty laugh. Nicole said suspiciously, "What are you two cooking up over there?"

"I'm not cooking anything, dear," David said mildly. "The coals aren't ready yet. We need about five more minutes."

CJ looked at Nicole and said, "Would it be okay if Charlie and I went over to the play area for a bit? We promise to be back for lunch."

Charlie jumped off the picnic table bench and said, "Yeah!"

"You want to come, Aunt Alex?" CJ asked.

"I think I'll stay here and supervise," Alex said. "Maybe later we can walk down to the pond and look at the ducks before fireworks."

"Fireworks!" Charlie yelled happily and took off at a run toward the slide and swings.

Nicole said, "Do you remember when we used to run everywhere?"

CJ, trotting after Charlie, said over her shoulder, "Talk to your sister. She still does that."

Alex and Nicole finished setting up the table, then Nicole fixed lemonade, asking David every sixty seconds if it was time to put the meat on. Finally David asked Alex, "Are you like this with CJ?"

"Like what?" Alex asked innocently.

"Annoyingly compulsive."

Nicole said with asperity, "I'd like to point out that it's people like us who get things done in the world."

David wandered back over to give her a kiss. "And people like CJ and me that make sure people like you have fun," he responded mildly.

Nicole reached up and brushed a leaf from his apron, which featured Uncle Sam and read "With Liberty and Hamburgers for all." With a note of humor in her voice, she asked, "Is it time to put the burgers on yet, sweetheart?"

Eyes twinkling, David said, "Why, I believe it is." He strolled back to the barbeque grill and picked up the plate.

Alex looked over to see CJ pushing Charlie on a swing in the warm afternoon, the sunlight bouncing from her red hair like a flame. Then a loud noise penetrated Alex's consciousness, and she looked around for the source.

There was a sedan driving recklessly across the grass of the park, scattering pedestrians and picnickers. The car was heading toward them. A drunk driver?

From the driver's side open window, she saw a sudden flash. Alex had time for one scream.

"CJ! Gun!"

As adrenaline flooded her, the scene unfolded for a moment in slow motion. CJ grabbed Charlie from the swing and rolled them both beneath the metal slide, curling herself around Charlie entirely.

Alex heard the first gunshot as she grabbed for Nicole, shoving her under the concrete picnic table, and trying to wedge herself under as well. Nicole was screaming for Charlie, for David, and Alex gripped her tightly as bullets seemed to pour around them like hail. Alex felt something hit her back, a spray of dirt or a chip of concrete, but it didn't hurt enough to be a bullet. She tried to count the gunshots but there were too many. *More than one gun*, she thought.

Time had slowed so much it seemed like forever before the firing stopped, although it was probably less than a minute. She heard the engine roar away, and she rolled out, trying to spot a license plate, but it had been carefully mud-splattered to be unreadable.

Alex scrambled to her feet, looking desperately for CJ. She was still curled motionless beneath the slide, Charlie wrapped in her arms.

"CJ!" Alex yelled frantically. "Are you hurt?"

No, God, please, I can't take that again.

She watched CJ unfold herself and get to her feet, saw her lift Charlie into her arms and speak briefly to him, her hands touching him slightly.

"Okay! We're okay!" CJ called, beginning to move back toward them.

The next moment, Alex became aware of Nicole screaming behind her, and she turned.

David was on the ground, the white apron bloodied and torn. Nicole was bending over him, hysterical and trying to get him to talk to her.

Alex whirled back to CJ and said, "Take Charlie away."

CJ's green eyes went wide, then she grasped Charlie firmly with one arm against her shoulder and turned away again, groping with her free hand for her cell phone.

Alex went to Nicole and said, "Honey, please, let me look at him."

"No, no," Nicole was moaning loudly.

"Nic, please. Let me help."

"David, talk to me! Honey, please..."

Alex said, "Here, move here." Nicole shifted, reaching for David's hand.

Jesus, her brother-in-law was mess. She tried to see where he was hit, but it looked like he'd been used for target practice—chest, abdomen, arm. So much blood.

Far away, she could hear sirens beginning their journey, and she mentally blessed CJ for calling and knowing what to say. She knew CJ had what little description they had on the car already on broadcast. With any luck, a patrol unit would spot it in a minute or two.

Alex was afraid to feel for a pulse, but she did anyway, putting two fingers against his neck, feeling for his carotid artery. She thought she felt a flutter, but the harder she pressed, the less there was to feel. She moved to the other side, but there was nothing.

Nicole was sobbing against her, still holding David's lifeless hand.

The rest of the memories always came in pieces: the useless ambulance ride, after which David was solemnly pronounced dead on arrival. Nicole's incoherent grief, Charlie crying. Alex took them home, while CJ went back to help with the investigation. Alex called Frank Morelli and Chris Andersen, her best team, to take the case, and they left their holiday celebrations to get there within the hour.

But despite two dozen witnesses in the park, lots of physical evidence from tire tracks to bullets, they'd never found a single suspect. Twenty-six bullets had been fired at them, and no one else in the park had been hurt, so it seemed as if they had been targeted. But why? David had been a college history professor. At Alex's insistence, Frank and Chris had dug into every aspect of his life, of Nicole's caseload at her law firm, and they had come up with nothing: no motive, no suspects.

Nicole had survived by writing it off as some drug-fueled violent spree, tragic and random. Part of Alex had wanted to do that, too, but the absence of any suspects made her suspicious. Men too drunk or too high to know what they were doing didn't cover their tracks—or their license plates—quite so successfully. Yet she hadn't been able to come up with a single good reason why anyone would want to kill any of them.

Alex hadn't been able to stop thinking about being run off the highway last March. It seemed impossible that David's shooting was connected to the attempt on her life, yet it seemed equally unlikely that they were unrelated, chance events. Two violent occurrences in four months couldn't be coincidental, yet she hadn't been able to see any link between the two.

They had buried David that Saturday. And the next Tuesday, CJ had disappeared.

Alex kept thinking there had to be another connection, something, that somehow made David's murder relevant to CJ leaving.

She left because she loves me.

There wasn't anymore logic to it now than there had been when she'd said it out loud in Dr. Wheeler's office.

Alex turned over in the bed, curled on her side, facing the empty side of the bed to her left, CJ's side. She had tried sleeping in the middle, trying to take up the whole mattress, but it hadn't worked. She hadn't told Dr. Wheeler what was in the note CJ had left for her, but she had it memorized, and it had never made much sense to her, not from the moment she'd first read it, stunned and shocked, in the foyer of the condo.

I have to go. Please don't look for me. On the love I know you have for me, I beg you not to look. And for the love of God, take very good care of yourself.

Alex had refused CJ's request and had looked everywhere for her, in vain. What had CJ been thinking?

She was tired of questions with no answers, so tired of being alone. She should go out tomorrow, to Regina or some other lesbian bar, and pick somebody up for a night of mindless sex. She wished that she were Vivien, who could manage that with aplomb.

Then Alex wanted to laugh. No, Vivien was home with the woman who had finally tamed her, settling down awkwardly into the different challenges of a long-term relationship. Even Nicole had been out on a date. She was the only one alone.

No, she thought again. That's not quite true. Wherever she is, CJ is alone, too.

Or perhaps not.

That thought tortured her for another hour before she finally fell asleep.

* * *

Sunday morning she put the laundry in, then began reorganizing the kitchen cabinets. It was what she did when she was stressed or upset. That and running, and after really looking at herself yesterday, she decided she needed to give herself a day off from exercise.

By evening she was jittery, restless, unable to sit and relax. She hadn't spoken to anyone all day and, despite her desperate thoughts from last night, she had no desire to go out and see anyone, much less a stranger.

She had no desire of any kind, she thought sadly. The sexual rebirth she'd experienced the first time she'd slept with CJ had led to a pleasant, constant simmer of arousal, sometimes bubbling quietly in the background, sometimes boiling over into a passion that CJ could always quench. From the day CJ left, it was as if the heat inside her been shut off. CJ had apparently taken Alex's sexual desire away with her when she left, and some days Alex wondered if she'd ever want to sleep with anyone again.

All right. At least I'm going to take one or two of those dinner invitations I keep getting. Maybe Chris or her partner Beth know some nice single woman to introduce me to. If I don't find a way out of this soon, I really am going to be alone for the rest of my life.

She hadn't yet straightened up the second bedroom that they used as an office. Alex had her desktop computer set up in there on one desk, and CJ often used her laptop on the table near the other chair. The laptop had gone with CJ in her car, and Alex's emails to her had, not surprisingly, gone unanswered. Alex hadn't sent any messages for months.

She straightened up her desk, which didn't really need it, and paid a couple of bills online. As she logged off, she saw the box of files she'd taken from CJ's office on Friday, and decided to finish up with them.

She ran the paperwork with CJ's personal information on it, the leave slips and copies of insurance information, through the shredder. She'd forgotten the second file folder marked Notes, and she picked it up.

A glassine, transparent evidence envelope slipped out and fell onto the floor. Alex frowned at it. CJ wouldn't have evidence in her office, certainly not in a personal file. Whatever it was would have been logged into the evidence room.

Picking up the envelope, she saw that there were two items inside. There was a standard business-sized paper envelope with only "Lieutenant C. St. Clair" typed on it, no return address. Alex's frown deepened—it wasn't the type of interoffice envelope they used in the department, yet this one hadn't been sent in the mail, either. There was no stamp, no address other than the name. Hand-delivered?

She turned the glassine envelope over. There was a single piece of letter-sized paper that had originally been folded in thirds to fit into the paper envelope, she assumed. She read the typewritten lines on the sheet.

I meant what I said before. Leave her right now. This minute. Don't go back to her, don't explain, don't see her. If you don't leave, I will kill her. I am watching you and I will kill her. I won't miss a third time.

Alex stared at the words for a full minute, rereading them again and again.

She had always seen the past as a stained glass window, with the scene and colors fixed and unchanging. But the past was really a kaleidoscope—a single turn changed the image. The colors were different, and the picture of the past had been transformed, changed to something else entirely.

One moment and everything had shifted, not the facts, but what they all meant. CJ was still gone, but she hadn't left Alex to get away from her. She'd left to save her life.

She really had left because of love.

Alex let the envelope slip from her fingers onto the floor again, but wasn't aware of it. Her mind was racing.

I won't miss a third time.

The shooting in the park—the bullets had been meant for her. And the first time, that had to be the car that ran her off the road in March. CJ had every reason to think that whoever was threatening Alex was deadly earnest. The first attempt had left Alex battered, the second had left David dead.

A spear of pain shot through her. Her suspicions had been right: the two incidents had been connected, connected to her. David's death was her fault. Nicole was a widow because of her. She tried to shake off the guilt that suddenly washed over her.

It wasn't her fault. It was the fault of whoever was trying to kill her.

Alex looked down at the evidence envelope. CJ had preserved it, just in case there were fingerprints or other forensic evidence to be gained from it. She must have thought Alex would find it more quickly than she did. Perhaps that was why she'd left a letter of resignation, hoping to prompt a fast and thorough search of her office. Alex's first search the day after CJ left had clearly been too been cursory. Alex had been looking for something obvious, a receipt for plane tickets, something, not this hidden note in a file folder.

Some detective I am! Useless!

What did the writer want? For Alex to be dead? Then why warn CJ, why not just finish the job? There had been no attempts in the last eight months.

Jesus, no wonder CJ told me to be careful. She must have been worried out of her mind.

The thought of CJ, probably frantic with anxiety, hurrying away to protect her, hit her in a rush. *She loved me, she loved me,* Alex repeated to herself in wonderment. *She loved me enough to leave everything and everyone behind, for me.*

But unless there was something on the paper or envelope, there were no clues, Alex thought in frustration.

No, that wasn't right. Memory came back to her in jagged pieces. In the few days between David's murder and CJ's disappearance, CJ had been almost beside herself to find out what had happened, urging Alex and her detectives to locate the car and the men who had driven it, far beyond just a desire for justice.

Alex read the note in her hand again. *I meant what I said before.* There had been at least one another note, or an anonymous phone call, before this final threat. CJ must have been frantic.

God, CJ, why didn't you just tell me?

What did the writer want? Alex thought she knew the answer, and energy flooded through her body.

Aloud she said, "Whoever you are, I'm coming for you. I'm going to find you, you son of a bitch."

CHAPTER ELEVEN

Alex had finished with her usual Monday morning case review with the entire staff of detectives. As they were gathering up notepads and coffee cups, and divvying up the last of the doughnuts, Alex said, "Kelly, Frank, Chris. Please sit down again."

The others shot a curious look at the trio before filing out. Alex saw Chris give Frank a questioning look, and saw his answering *I have no idea* shrug in return. Kelly Porter as usual just looked nervous.

"All right," Alex began. "I have good news."

Chris said, "First a staff meeting without having to put up with Fullerton whining, and now more good news. This Monday keeps getting better and better."

Frank Morelli eyed Alex and said, "You look like the news is really good, Cap. You must have gotten a good night's sleep last night."

"The first one in a long time," Alex admitted. "You first, Kelly. I've a new partner assigned for you, a patrol officer who passed the detective exam and was next up on the promotions list."

"You want me to break in a rookie?" Porter asked in amazement.

"I have every confidence in you, Detective Porter," Alex responded. "You've been here long enough to know your way around, and I know you'll do a good job."

"But, um, what if Fullerton comes back? He's not fired, is he?"

"He's not fired, but he's suspended pending the result of the IA. I'll deal with whatever happens when it happens. He might be back, he might be fired, he might get demoted. I received permission from Deputy Chief Duncan to fill the position because we need the help now. Don't worry about Roger. Whatever happens, he won't be coming back to work with you."

Porter looked as if she'd just given him a birthday present. "Really, Captain?"

Alex smiled at him. "Really. Your new partner reports Wednesday, and after I speak with her, I'll send her over to you and you can start filling her in on your open cases."

"Okay. A woman?"

"Detective Adamcyzk. Yes, she is a woman. And you're fine with that, correct?" she asked firmly.

Porter gave her the most genuine grin she'd ever seen from him. "Yes, ma'am."

"Okay. Get back to work."

When he'd gone, Alex went over and closed the door behind him. Then she came back and sat down across from Frank and Chris, and passed each of them a file folder.

"Another reason we got an immediate replacement for Fullerton," she began, "is because you two are getting a cold case back, and I'm making it priority one for you two."

"Cold case?" Frank asked. "Which one?"

"The murder of David Castillo," Alex replied grimly.

Chris Andersen exclaimed, "No shit! Please tell me you've got a lead."

"I do," Alex said. "But it's going to take a minute to explain."

She told them to open their folders and said, "What we have now are two things we didn't have before: a clear motive, and at least a preliminary list of suspects."

Frank, staring down at the photocopy of the note CJ had received said, "What the hell, Captain? Somebody was trying to kill you?"

"Looks like it. The original note is down at the lab where I delivered it this morning. I told them you two were getting the case back, so they should give you whatever they can get, but I'm not holding my breath. Follow up with them if you haven't heard in a couple of days."

Chris made a note, then said, "Okay. What about the list of suspects?"

Alex said, "That one took me a while. Look, you can run a list of everybody I ever arrested, but it makes no sense that they would send this note to CJ."

Frank said, "I give up. What the hell about this does make sense?"

Taking a deep breath, Alex said, "Someone who wants CJ."

"Run that by me again?" he asked.

"It's the only thing that makes sense," she said. "First they try to kill me, to get me out of the way. When that doesn't work, they threaten her, to get her away from me. It's her they want. I'm just in the way."

Frank sat back, deeply perplexed. Chris said slowly, "Somebody jealous of you. A stranger who's turned into a stalker, you think? Or somebody she knows, or knew?"

"I hope to hell it's the second one, because somebody from the first category is going to be hard to find at this point, given that CJ has disappeared. And if it's some anonymous stalker, it could be a man or a woman. At least if it's somebody from CJ's romantic past, we know it's a woman."

"Wait," Frank said. "What about her family? She's got money, I know. Maybe somebody's after that."

Alex looked at him, surprised that she hadn't considered that. "I don't think there's anything about her money that could be a motive. It's in a trust, left to her by her grandfather, administered by a lawyer who's an old family friend. And her mother and her brother haven't had any contact with her for years, at least that I know of. It's hard for me to see how getting me killed would be of benefit to her family, but I'll check them out."

Chris met her eyes and said suddenly, "She didn't just disappear, did she? Not the way everybody thought. Fuck, Captain, she left to save you, didn't she?"

"Looks like it," Alex said calmly, her voice not betraying her emotion.

"Oh, my God," Frank said. "Captain—Alex, this is—I mean, it's awful, but it's great, too, isn't it? She didn't just take off. She had a reason. Holy shit."

"Yes," Alex agreed. "She had a reason. I wish to God she'd just told me, but she didn't. So now we have to find out whoever it was that sent this note, find out who killed my brother-in-law, so she can come home. So if you look at the next page, I've listed the people I think are the best possibilities."

Both detectives turned the page. Alex said, "I've given you whatever contact information I have, and I want you to just listen a minute to what I know about each of them so you can tell me what you think."

Chris readied her pen again as Alex began.

"Stephanie Morrow. She and CJ lived together for a couple of years, a year or so before we met. She's a local real estate agent, I've got her information there."

"Why'd they break up?" Chris asked.

Alex cleared her throat, then answered, "A variety of reasons, I think. The precipitating incident was Stephanie's request to have another woman go to bed with them. CJ refused, and Stephanie moved out."

Frank made a little choking sound, and Chris gave him a brief elbow in the ribs.

"Better stop doing the visual on that one, partner," she smirked.

"The interesting thing," Alex continued, "is that I met Stephanie for the first time the night somebody ran me off the road. I find the timing—let's say I found it highly coincidental.

She was with a woman named Patty Herron the evening I met her. I got her phone numbers this morning from a friend of CJ's, the one who hosted the party. I don't imagine Patty is involved, but you never know. She might at least be helpful with possible alibi information."

"Got it," Chris said. "Laurel Halliday?"

"CJ's first girlfriend. She was an economics instructor. They were together for several years, until CJ caught her cheating. CJ hasn't seen her in twelve years, so I'm thinking she's a long shot, but anything is possible. I don't have contact information for her, so you'll have to do some digging."

"Do you have a photo? That might help," Frank suggested.

"Good idea. I don't know, but I'll check some of CJ's stuff at the condo and see if she's got a college scrapbook or yearbook somewhere."

Chris was staring at the next name on the list. "Are you serious, Captain? District Attorney Tony Bradford?"

Alex nodded solemnly. "Another long shot, but they have a difficult history together. My ex-husband hates that I'm remarried, and he specifically hates that I'm married to a woman because he thinks it's bad for his political career for his ex-wife to be gay. He thought CJ was trying to sabotage his campaign during the last election."

Chris said in disgust, "Yeah, I remember that real well."

Frank said, "Christ, you seriously want us to investigate the District Attorney?"

"I do. It's hard for me to believe that he would actually try to kill me, but I've heard a rumor or two that he wants to run for a senate seat in a couple of years, and he is not a man of—let's say, he's not a man of high moral standards. It's possible this whole thing was a double-bluff to get CJ out of the way."

Frank looked at Chris and said, "Well, this is shaping up to be a whole lot of fun."

"Anybody else?" Chris asked.

Alex hesitated, then said, "There's one other possibility, but I'm going to check that one out myself. If I turn up anything, I'll let you know. Meantime, everyone else is fair game. Clear?"

"Oh, yeah," Chris said, as they gathered their files and notes together. "This is going to be a whole lot of fun."

* * *

Alex sat in her car outside the townhouse, remembering why she had always hated surveillance assignments. Sitting patiently was not one of her signature skills. It was getting close to dusk when she saw a tall woman carrying a backpack slung over one shoulder walking up the sidewalk to the front door.

On the way to the townhouse, Alex had already established the location of the nearest RTD bus stop, and this pedestrian was coming from the right direction. When she approached the unit and took out a key, Alex saw fair hair shining in the porch light that had come on automatically a few moments ago.

Alex gave her five minutes, then went up and knocked on the door.

"Yes?" She was tall and very blond. Her coloring reminded Alex of Chris Andersen.

Alex showed her badge and ID. "My name is Alex Ryan, Colfax Police Department. Are you Marja Erickson?"

She looked a little worried, but said, "Yes. What is it?"

"I'd like to ask you a couple of questions. May I come in?"

She'd used her badge to make access to the house easier, easier than telling Marja she was a friend of Vivien's. When they were in the living room, Marja turned to her suddenly and said, "Oh, my God. Is Vivien all right? She's not—"

Alex kicked herself mentally for scaring the woman and said quickly, "She's fine. This won't take long. I just need to ask you a couple of questions, as I said."

"Oh. Okay. Would you like some coffee or something?"

"No, nothing. Thank you."

They sat down in Vivien's carefully furnished living room that could have been a cover photo for an Ethan Allen catalog. Alex looked Marja over, curious about Vivien's new girlfriend.

She was as tall as CJ, but with a completely different body. CJ was all lush curves and feminine to her fingertips. Marja had shoulders to rival an NBA player and Alex imagined she could easily bench press the couch. Her hair was in a casual braid, and she looked like the grad student she was, dressed in jeans, sneakers and a gray University of Denver sweatshirt. Her complexion had a healthy glow, and even with no makeup she had strong, compelling features.

A woman more different from the carefully groomed and fussy Vivien was hard to imagine. Maybe that was the attraction.

"I need to verify some information," Alex said, "and I think you can help me. I'm trying to establish where Vivien Wong was on a couple of dates. Last year, actually."

Alex didn't believe that Vivien had anything to do with the attacks on her, or the note to CJ, but she was going to feel a lot better in a few minutes if she could actually prove it.

Marja said quietly, "I'll help if I can."

"I'm hoping the first one is easy. I understand you first met Vivien the evening you were hired to serve as a bartender at a party she was giving."

"Yes." Well, Vivien told her Marja wasn't a big talker.

"Do you remember the date?"

"March sixteenth. Last year."

"Good. I don't need any details, but I do need to know if Vivien was here all evening. All night."

Marja stared at her, and said, "Can I ask what this is about?"

"It's really just routine. I'm verifying her whereabouts for that night."

Marja looked unconvinced by Alex's explanation, but she answered, "Yes."

"Yes, what?"

"Yes, she was here all night. With me."

"She didn't leave?"

"No. I left about seven the next morning, and she was here all night."

"You're sure she didn't leave for any period? Perhaps when you were sleeping?" Alex tried to be tactful.

Marja's color rose a little, but she said, "She got up to go to the kitchen and get us some water about four o'clock. We weren't really sleeping much. She was here."

Alex tried another angle. "Did she make a phone call at any time? Especially before, say, ten thirty that night?"

"No."

"You're sure?"

"Really sure."

She could have set something up ahead of time, Alex knew, but it was hard to imagine that she wouldn't have had to make at least one verifying phone call, either before or after. "One last question, Ms. Erickson. Do you happen to remember where you were last July Fourth?"

Marja stared at her a moment, then shrugged and said, "Yes. We went to Georgetown, up in the mountains, you know. They have a five-K run, and I did that, then we saw the fire hose races, and watched the fireworks over the lake. We stayed in a bed-and-breakfast the night before, then drove back down after the fireworks, since Viv had to work the next day." She frowned, then added, "I remember she got a phone call from a friend of hers, something about a shooting…"

The door from the garage opened, and Vivien called out, "Hey, baby, are you home yet?"

Alex got to her feet as Marja went to greet Vivien.

"Honey," Marja said. "There's a police officer here."

"Alex!" Vivien exclaimed when she came into the room. "What's going on? Have you heard something?"

"Not directly," Alex said. "But I do have something to tell you. Can we all sit down?"

"What the hell is going on?" Vivien asked again. She put her briefcase on the sofa table and unbuttoned the short jacket of her charcoal-gray suit.

Marja looked at Alex, then said to Vivien, "She was asking questions about you, hon. Do you know her?"

Vivien gave Alex a sharp look.

Alex said, "I needed to confirm your whereabouts, Vivien. For the night I had the accident, and for the day David was killed."

"What on earth for?"

Alex sighed. "It's kind of a long story. But one I think you need to hear."

"I'm listening," Vivien said cautiously.

"Okay. But first, I want to apologize. You weren't really a suspect, but I needed to make sure you weren't trying to fool me."

"About what?"

"About how you really feel about CJ," Alex admitted.

Marja said, "Maybe I should go start dinner, or something."

Vivien gripped her hand tightly, ignoring Alex for the moment. "There is absolutely nothing on this topic you can't hear," she said, her voice harsh. "Isn't that right, Alex?"

Alex read Vivien's look, not the one directed at her, but the one she'd directed at Marja. If Vivien was lying about what she felt for her lover, Alex would turn in her badge.

"I actually think that's right," Alex said.

Marja looked from Vivien to Alex and back again. "Viv, who is she?" Marj finally asked.

"A friend, or so I thought," Vivien said acerbically. "This is the woman married to CJ St. Clair, my best friend. Or perhaps my former best friend. Which is it, Alex?"

Alex sighed. "CJ didn't want to leave, Vivien. Not you, and certainly not me. Let me explain."

When she was finished, Vivien was crying and Alex had brushed away a few tears herself. Marja didn't say a word, but halfway through the story she slipped one long arm around Vivien's delicate shoulders and held on.

"Christ on a kite, why the fuck didn't she just tell us?" Vivien finally said.

"She didn't want to risk it, I guess," Alex said. "I don't really understand it myself."

"All this time…" Vivien began, then choked up again.

Marja squeezed her tightly, and then said, "You should have known she'd never leave voluntarily. She loved you guys, right? So I think I should go make dinner now, and we can talk about all the positive memories you have about her, so when I meet her I can tell her how much good stuff you told me."

She went into the kitchen, and Alex watched Vivien's eyes following her.

"She's amazing, isn't she?" Vivien asked.

"I like her," Alex said.

"Me, too. She makes me feel like a fucking teenager."

"I'm sorry for the questions, Vivien. I needed to be sure you weren't harboring some secret obsession with CJ."

Vivien wiped her eyes. "I love CJ to pieces," she answered. "But not like that. The only person I've ever felt that way about is her," she said, looking toward the kitchen.

Alex, satisfied, said, "I know."

CHAPTER TWELVE

On Wednesday morning, Alex got to her office at eight a.m. exactly to find someone already waiting outside for her. The woman was somewhere in her early thirties, dark hair and pale complexion, with deep-set, dark eyes. Something about her features looked vaguely Slavic. The next moment, Alex remembered: her new detective was reporting today. With everything else, she'd forgotten.

"Detective Adamcyzk," Alex greeted her. "I'm Captain Alex Ryan. You're early."

"Didn't want to be late on the first day," she said easily.

"Come on in."

They sat in Alex's office, and Alex said, "I've read your jacket, of course. What would you like to tell me in addition to that?"

The open-ended question seemed to fluster her a little, but she straightened in her chair and brushed her palms against her khaki slacks. "I liked patrol just fine," she answered. "But I really wanted a gold shield, to be a detective. I'm hoping to get to work as soon as I can."

"Good," Alex said, "because there's always plenty to do. But I just wanted to get to know you a little better. Your first name is…" She glanced down at the label on Adamcyzk's file again. "Jolenta? Am I saying that correctly?"

"Yes. You got Adamcyzk right, too, which is pretty rare. Jolenta is my grandmother's name, she immigrated from Kraków after the war. I go by Jo."

"Kraków? Isn't that where Pope John Paul II was from?"

"You're right," Jo said, trying to conceal her surprise. "He wasn't born there, but he was the Archbishop there for a while. You a Catholic?"

"Sort of," Alex answered honestly, and that got a smile from Jo Adamcyzk.

"Me, too," she said. "A sort of Catholic."

"You have family here?" Alex asked.

Jo shook her head. "They're back in the Chicago area, mostly. I moved out here after high school."

Alex looked at her appraisingly. "Why Denver?"

After a moment, Jo answered carefully, "Change of scene. God knows the weather is a lot better. Scenery, too."

There was more to that story, Alex thought. Some problem with her family, maybe, like CJ. Alex said, "You'll want to meet Sergeant Frank Morelli, my senior detective. He's from the Chicago area, too."

"Okay. Will he be my partner?"

"No, I'm assigning you to Kelly Porter. He's been here five years, long enough to know what's going on, but new enough that he'll remember what it was like to be the new guy. He should treat you right, but if you have any problems, I have an open door. Work hard and use good sense, and I won't mess with you. We have a staff meeting every Monday morning at eight to go over caseloads, and as the new gold shield you'll be bringing the doughnuts for a while. Do you have any questions?"

"No, ma'am."

"Good. Let's go out and I'll introduce you around a little."

The first people she ran into were Chris Andersen and Frank Morelli, who were in a huddle at their desks in deep discussion.

Alex introduced Jo Adamcyzk to them both, and said to Frank, "Got another cop from Chicago for you."

"Yeah?" Frank said happily. "What neighborhood?"

"Roseland."

"Geez, that's a way out there. Tough neighborhood."

"What about you?"

"Harlem Avenue."

"Uh-oh." Jo smiled. "Northsider."

"Hell, yeah. Oh, man, I bet you're a Sox fan."

"Of course. And you root for the Cubbies, I'm sure."

"Well, of course."

"Poor guy." Jo turned to Alex. "My team won a World Series a few years back. His hasn't even been close for a hundred years."

"At least I'm rooting for Chicago's favorite team," Frank retorted.

"Bite me," Jo said, in a friendly tone.

Chris looked at Alex and said, "Do you have any idea what the hell they're talking about?"

"Not much," Alex conceded. "Let me introduce you to your new partner, Detective Adamcyzk. You and Frank can trade insults later."

On her way back to her office after getting Jo settled in with Kelly, she said to Frank and Chris, "You have stuff to tell me yet?"

The two partners exchanged a look, and Frank said, "Yeah, I think so. Is now okay? We got interviews later."

"Absolutely. Come on in."

As they sat down, Chris said to Alex, "Looks like another one for the team."

"Excuse me?"

Chris smirked and said, "I think our new girl there is a family member, Captain."

Frank said, "Okay, my turn to be confused."

Chris turned to him and said, "Get with it, Frankie. Adamcyzk is gay."

He looked at her in surprise. "Really, Hans? Has she got a tattoo on her forehead that I missed?"

"Don't call me Hans," Chris retorted. "Your problem is that you're not tuned into the cosmic vibrations of lesbianese."

"Well, you got that right. Hanging out with you all day probably made me immune."

Chris rolled her eyes and said to Alex, "I'm right, aren't I, Captain?"

Alex responded dryly, "I have no idea. That wasn't in her file."

"Funny, Captain."

Alex said, "Could we get down to it, please? I can tell you that neither CJ's mother or brother left town on the relevant dates, and there's no angle on CJ's trust fund that seems relevant. What do you two know that you didn't know Monday morning?"

Frank started with, "As we all suspected, the lab was no help. Common paper and envelope, written on an ink-jet printer, no prints except for Lieutenant St. Clair's. No fibers, no DNA on the envelope either, so he or she didn't lick it closed. Zip."

Alex sighed. "Too bad, but, as you say, not surprising. What else?"

Chris said, "I've been trying to track down Halliday. She was on the faculty at, uh, Oglethorpe University, a private school in Atlanta. Or she was until a little over a year ago."

"What happened?"

"She apparently just walked out the door. Quit and left, in the middle of the semester, no less. University won't say anything else and we haven't tracked her down yet. Still working on it."

Alex considered the problem thoughtfully for a moment.

"We talked to both Patty Herron and Stephanie Morrow yesterday," Frank said. "And we've got an appointment with District Attorney Bradford in an hour and a half."

Alex suppressed a sigh. She knew she'd be getting an unpleasant phone call from Tony later. "What did you get from Morrow and Herron?"

The two detectives exchanged a glance. "Told you it would be fun," Chris muttered.

"Herron was very talkative, but not real helpful," Frank said. "She did remember the night of the cocktail party last March pretty clearly. Said she and Morrow had a hell of a fight on the way home that evening."

Alex asked, "Did she say what it was about?"

Frank suddenly looked a little uncomfortable, and he shifted his body a little toward Chris, as if to say "you take this one."

Chris said coolly, "They had a fight about Lieutenant St. Clair. Herron's version is that she made the mistake of saying something about how nice she thought St. Clair was, and then Morrow started going off on what a bitch St. Clair had been when they were together, what a snob she was, stuff like that. Apparently it pissed Herron off, and they continued the fight until the early morning hours."

"I see," Alex said calmly. CJ was the least pretentious woman she knew, but she did have money and had had a rigidly proper Southern upbringing, so she could see how Stephanie could twist that into snobbery. "The important point being that they were together all night?"

"Yeah," Frank jumped in now that Chris had done the heavy lifting. "She said Morrow didn't call anybody all evening."

It was the same story Alex had from Patty Herron last March. "What about July Fourth?" Alex asked. "What was Stephanie Morrow up to then?"

"Herron didn't have any idea," Frank said. "They had broken up and she told us she hasn't spoken to Morrow in months."

Alex sat back, reflecting. All the frustrating problems she'd had with Stephanie Morrow as a suspect in her automobile accident last March were still there. Presumably Stephanie had no idea she would meet Alex that night, although she probably anticipated seeing CJ again at Vivien's party, so how could she have set up the attempt on her life in advance? There was no evidence, other than a motive, linking Stephanie to the crime.

"What about the interview with Morrow?" Alex asked.

"What a clusterfuck that was," Frank said, half amused, half annoyed. "She did *not* want to talk to us. We went twelve rounds on 'Do you have a warrant?', 'I'm gonna call my lawyer' and 'She's harassing me again.' Jesus."

"I see," Alex said appraisingly. "What was your assessment of her?"

"She was pissed off," Frank answered succinctly.

Alex frowned at him, and Chris stepped in with, "She was mad, but I think that was all, Captain. She didn't seem afraid, or defensive, just nasty. Of course, she could be hiding something else but I don't think so. She assumed you had sent us over there to harass her about the car accident again. When I told her we were investigating a murder, she seemed to calm down a little."

"And once you got there, what did she have to say?"

"Nothing that would help us," Chris answered.

Alex noticed the way she'd unconsciously taken over the report from Frank. Was it because she'd taken the lead in the interviews? Alex somehow doubted it. Chris was settling down nicely from a slightly reckless officer into a very sound detective. She'd always been a hard worker, but Alex was seeing signs of maturity and good judgment, too. She wondered if this was Beth Rivera's stabilizing influence on her lover.

God knows CJ changed me for the better.

"To summarize," Chris continued, "she didn't know anything. She didn't run you off the road, she didn't murder Castillo, she hasn't seen or spoken to St. Clair since the cocktail party. As she put it in no uncertain terms, I hope I never see the bitch again. End quote. If she's harboring a secret obsessive passion for St. Clair, she's hiding it real well."

"And you think she's telling the truth?" Alex pressed her.

"I do," Chris responded, meeting her eyes. "But we thought we'd drop in on her again around the end of the week, just to see if she remembered anything. Mostly to remind her we're still around."

"Good plan. Anything else?"

Frank said, "Like we said, we're seeing Bradford later. We'll let you know how that goes."

He shot a warning look at Chris, who subtly shook him off. What were they disagreeing about? Alex wondered.

Chris lifted her chin an inch and said, "Captain, we wondered if we should consider another possibility. Another motive."

Frank made an unhappy noise, and Alex could see that he didn't want Chris discussing this with her, for some reason.

Gently, Alex said, "Frank, it's all right. What's your theory, Andersen?"

"Maybe this whole thing is just what it looks like. Somebody who's interested in hurting you, end of story. Both attempts seem to have been directed at you. And short of killing you, what's the one thing somebody could do to harm you? Hurt your family, or…"

She left the rest unsaid. Alex finished it for her.

"Take CJ away from me," Alex said quietly.

"Maybe that's what this is. Not someone after St. Clair. Maybe somebody who hates you enough to mess with your life in every way they can."

Frank shifted uncomfortably again. Alex said, "I have to grant you that it's possible. But if it's not CJ's family, then it's got to be a pretty limited pool of suspects. I haven't been working a caseload for a lot of years now. We can count the arrests I've made in the last six years on one hand."

Stubbornly, Chris said, "Then it should be easy to locate all those perps, shouldn't it, Captain?"

Alex said tersely, "It's your case, Detectives. If you think you should pursue this line of inquiry, do it. I have a strong instinct that tells me this is about CJ, not me directly, but I could be wrong. In the end, all that matters is finding out who the bad guy is. So go do that."

Chris looked fiercely determined as she said, "We're on it, Captain."

* * *

Alex closed her office door after lunch and went online to find the telephone number she needed. It took a couple of minutes to get through to Roger Edgarton, senior partner in one of Savannah's oldest and most prestigious law firms. She finally had to invoke CJ's name to do it, remembering at the last minute to call her Belle, from Christabelle, the name she'd grown up using.

While she waited for Edgarton to come on the line, she remembered the first time she'd talked to him. He had called her the day after CJ had been hurt, the only conversation of any length she'd ever had with him. She had talked to him briefly a couple of times since, when he'd called the condo for some reason, but she didn't know him at all except through CJ's stories. He'd been a friend of her grandfather's, the grandfather who had left her a sizeable trust fund which had financially cushioned the blow of her family's rejection of her. It made Alex sad every time she thought about it. CJ's mother and brother refused to have any part of her life because CJ was gay. Even her father, who would have accepted her, cut off contact with his daughter because of his wife. What a foolish waste.

A man's deep voice boomed in her ear. "This is Roger Edgarton."

"Mr. Edgarton, this is Alex Ryan. I'm Belle's partner, as you may remember."

"I do, indeed." She caught a note of something she couldn't define in his voice.

"I'm calling for your help. I'm not sure if you can help us, but if you can, I would be very grateful."

The note of hesitation was stronger. "I'm not sure if I will be able to assist you or not," he said. How could he say that when she hadn't even asked her favor yet? Alex wondered.

She explained what she wanted. When she was finished, there was a moment's silence on the line. "I may be able to help with that," he said carefully. "I'll make some calls."

Alex said, "I thank you for this, Mr. Edgarton. If CJ were here, she would thank you as well."

He rumbled, "I am sure that you are acting in her best interests. My client and I have discussed you, Miss Ryan, as you may be aware. I confess that I did a background check on you when you and Belle first became involved."

Alex hadn't known, but wasn't surprised. "I'm sure you were acting in her best interests as well," she said calmly. "I know CJ has a lot of money."

"Yes. Well. She seemed very happy with you, Miss Ryan. I'm very fond of Belle, as if she were one of my own daughters, and I was very pleased that she was happy in her life. Having to leave you made her very—"

He stopped abruptly, and Alex found herself gripping the telephone so tightly her fingers went white. Why hadn't she thought about this before? "You know where she is," she said, making the words a statement rather than a question.

He cleared his throat, a sound like a low growl. "Any information I might or might not have would be covered by attorney-client privilege," he said. "Especially since I have been clearly instructed not to reveal that information to you except under very specific conditions."

"What?" Alex asked, thunderstruck. "Are you saying you *could* tell me where she is?"

"I have been instructed not to discuss this with you unless you can verify your identity to me, in person, and provide me with satisfactory evidence that the threat to you has been removed. Short of meeting these conditions, I am not authorized to discuss this matter with you further. Except for this: I was instructed to provide you with a few pieces of information if you should contact me."

It was as if someone were providing her with a breath of fresh air after she'd been held under the water for a long time. She gripped the phone impossibly tighter and said, "What is this information?"

"She asked me to repeat to you her request for you to refrain from seeking her out," he said. "But I can tell you that she is well, or she was when we last had contact. And she did ask me to tell you that she is sorry, and…" He cleared his throat, and finally added, "She asked me to tell you that she loves you."

Alex gulped more air into her lungs, as if she'd been a hairsbreadth from drowning. CJ was all right.

She still loves me. "Thank you," she choked out.

"I'm pleased that you contacted me," Edgarton said. "I thought this was information that you needed to hear. I will contact you soon about your other request for information."

"Yes," Alex managed. "And I hope, Mr. Edgarton, to meet you in person very soon."

CHAPTER THIRTEEN

Alex stared at Elaine Wheeler and said, "I don't understand. Are you saying that nothing has changed?"

"Not at all," Wheeler said. "Certainly your understanding of CJ's motive for leaving casts many of the facts in a different light. What I am suggesting to you is that not everything has necessarily changed."

Alex shook her head.

"Let me ask you this," Wheeler persisted gently. "How do you feel now?"

"Everything is different," Alex said forcefully. "I've had three decent nights' sleep in a row. I have energy to work, I'm even eating better. It's like turning a corner."

"Those are all good things," Wheeler conceded. "But let me rephrase the question: how do you feel about CJ now?"

Alex stared at her again. "I feel the same way about her as I did before," she said.

"How was that?"

"I love her," Alex said angrily. "I loved her before, and I still love her."

"Yes. And how else do you feel?"

"How else…" Alex stopped, trying to calm herself, trying to understand the emotions roiling inside of her.

Wheeler waited patiently.

"I'm still sad," Alex finally admitted. "She's still gone, I'm still alone. When I'm working, it's better, but when I go home at night, she's not there. I just miss her. I miss her singing in the kitchen, I miss talking about our day together, I miss holding her.

"And—"

"Yes?" Wheeler said encouragingly.

"I'm angry," Alex admitted. "I'm mad she didn't come to me, mad she couldn't trust me with this. I understand why she left, I do, but part of me wants to scream at her for not being able to trust me to handle the situation. She just ran away. I mean, she thought she was doing the right thing, I know that, but I'm still angry at her. And damn it, I feel guilty about being mad at her. None of this was her fault and she did what she thought she had to do to protect me. I just wish she hadn't left."

When she ran out of words, Wheeler looked at her. "So, despite discovering the reason CJ went away, you're lonely, angry and feeling guilty, is that about right?"

Alex sat back and gave her a wry smile. "Yes, but other than that, I'm fine."

Wheeler returned the smile. "What do you want now?"

"What do I want? I want her back. I want to solve this, and I want the life we were making together back again. That's what I want."

"But you know," Wheeler said, "all these feelings you're having won't just magically go away. If CJ were to walk into the room right now, you'd still have a lot to get through. And so, I imagine, would she."

"Yes," Alex said, half in agreement and half a question.

Wheeler continued, "You've been feeling very sad for a long time now. And fearful and perhaps even hopeless. And angry."

Angry? Yes, she admitted, without even knowing where to direct her anger. At CJ? Herself? God or fate or karma? Suddenly she asked, "Do you think CJ is angry, too? At me?"

"I don't know. I don't know her. But it's certainly possible. Regardless of the circumstances, she's uprooted her entire life and she's suffering from many losses, too."

Alex thought about that for a minute. She knew CJ better than anyone, and Wheeler was right. Wherever she was, CJ was lonely too, missing her, and no doubt feeling guilty about leaving. She was undoubtedly angry at whoever had caused all of this. And maybe she was angry with Alex, for not solving the case sooner, and letting her come home. Alex was a good detective, but she could see now that grief had made her careless, and depression had robbed her of the energy to act.

She'd thought all she had to do was find the bad guy, solve the case, and that would fix everything. They could return to normal and be together again. She saw now that the road back was long and twisted, blockaded with recriminations and grief over what had happened: the attempt on her life, David's death, and their painful separation.

"You look sad," Wheeler said softly.

"I am sad," Alex conceded. "I'm not sure we can ever go back to where we were before. And it makes me angry to think that whoever is doing this to us could damage our relationship from the outside. I thought no one would ever be able to do that. I guess I was wrong."

Wheeler said, "So, grieving, guilty, lonely, angry, and wrong as well?"

Alex looked up quickly to see that Wheeler was actually joking. "Well, yeah," Alex said, trying to shift the sadness that had settled around her shoulders. "Think I might need therapy?"

Wheeler said, "Yes. But I don't want you to feel hopeless. You can work through grief and anger and sadness. If you can't go back to the relationship you had before, look at it this way: relationships are never static. Your relationship would have changed in some ways in any event. Instead of seeing this as a tragic circumstance, you can use it. Together, you may even be able to make your relationship even more solid than you thought it was before. Sometimes going through difficult times makes people, and couples, better and stronger. If you—and CJ—are willing to work at resolving the emotions you're going through now, you may come out the other side even better together."

Alex gave her a crooked smile. "I can't imagine," she said, dryly. "Better than we were before? Seems impossible to me."

* * *

Alex was sorting through a box of CJ's belongings. The box had been stuffed in the back of the closet in the spare bedroom, and Alex had never looked through it before. She pulled it out into the middle of the room and sat on the floor to go through it.

She found what she was looking for, a couple of photo albums. She pulled the first one out and opened it up.

These were family photos, beginning with a chubby baby CJ in a studio portrait. There was another studio shot, a year or so later, of CJ with her older brother. He looked sturdy and solemn in his suit with short pants, narrow bow tie underneath his double chin, his blond hair carefully combed. The toddler CJ was laughing into the camera, and it made Alex happy to see her. *Thirty plus years later, that grin hadn't changed much*, she thought.

She paged through the photos. There was a family shot of the four St. Clairs. Her father, the physician, looked aristocratic but friendly in his seersucker suit, the very picture of the trusted family doctor. Lydia St. Clair was tall and aesthetic looking, carefully dressed, her dark red hair looking as though it had been dyed. Clay was casual in T-shirt and shorts, still a chunky, towheaded boy. CJ was also dressed for summer in shorts and a sleeveless blouse, her bright red hair in a single braid down her back, her smile revealing a missing front tooth.

Alex smiled back at six-year-old CJ, who looked like a happy little girl. Each parent had a hand on her shoulder, and Alex could almost tell from everyone's expressions what was going on. CJ was a daddy's girl. Clay was no one's favorite, and he had a slightly surly expression that said he knew that already, even at age nine.

CJ's mother somehow managed to convey that she didn't approve of her daughter's scraped knee or her muddy shoes.

"Oh, sweetheart," Alex muttered aloud to CJ's photograph, "it's going to get worse before it gets better."

She paged through the rest of that book, watching CJ and her brother grow up, seeing her parents age. Her father's hair got white, her mother's more and more aggressively red. Clay got broader. There was one picture of him in a high school football uniform, another of him in a University of Georgia football uniform, the surly expression still firmly in place. There was a nice photo of CJ and her date to some dance, maybe the senior prom. CJ looked stunning to Alex, voluptuous in an emerald gown with spaghetti straps that showed off her shoulders and décolletage. The young man with her looked stiffly uncomfortable in his summer tuxedo, handing the wrist corsage to CJ in the shot. As usual, CJ looked happy.

There were a few more snapshots, CJ in her dorm room as a college freshman, a shot of her standing outside her sorority. Then there was an abrupt end to that book, the last couple of pages blank. Alex set it aside and tackled the second album.

The next volume was only about half-filled, but there were no more family photos. There were some of CJ with people Alex didn't know, classmates, sorority sisters. Then the pictures began to feature another woman, and Alex knew she was looking at Laurel Halliday.

Laurel was an attractive woman, a few years older than CJ. In every shot, she looked cool and composed. In the pictures of the two of them together, Alex saw the adoration on CJ's face as clearly as the sun shining, but Laurel's expression never varied—she inevitably looked proud of herself.

Proud of having landed CJ? Alex wondered. She pulled out a good close-up of Laurel by herself to give to Frank and Chris.

A page or two later, the content changed. There were, not to Alex's surprise, a few photos of CJ with Vivien, one at what looked like a friend's shower, the women all wearing bows from packages in their hair. The unadulterated joy of the pictures with Laurel was gone, but CJ still looked as if she were having a good time.

She turned yet another page, and saw CJ with Stephanie. They had actually made a nice-looking pair, Stephanie's dark looks and angular body contrasting nicely with CJ's red hair and curves. But Alex could see, beneath CJ's smile, slight signs of strain around her eyes, clues that told her that something between them hadn't been right from the beginning.

Something about Stephanie felt off to her. She couldn't imagine CJ staying with Stephanie if she had been physically abusive, but there were other ways to be abusive in a relationship that were less obvious.

She finished going through the book. The next-to-the last page had a picture of CJ with Rod and Ana Chavez, and another of CJ in a Roosevelt County Sheriff's uniform getting the medal for the shooting incident when she was on loan to the Feds.

The last page had only one photograph, centered on the middle of the page. It was a picture Nicole had taken of the two of them in her backyard when they'd only been dating a few months. CJ was sitting on a lawn recliner on the back deck, Alex sitting in front of her, between her legs, with CJ's arms wrapped around her.

Alex was looking away from the camera into the yard, at Charlie, probably. But CJ was looking at Alex, and Alex saw the difference between this expression and the ones she'd seen directed at Laurel and at Stephanie. CJ's face was open, relaxed, joyful, just like the little six-year-old girl she'd been years before.

It was the last photo in the book, as if CJ had finally ended the journey. Alex knew it was just the fact that everyone had switched to digital cameras, and that CJ had dozens of photographs of them on her laptop, but looking at the picture touched her softly, somewhere deep.

We'll get it back, Alex promised CJ, promised herself. *I promise we'll get us back, somehow.*

The telephone rang, and Alex had to hoist herself up, reminding herself that she might be just a bit too old to sit on the floor for an hour. She grimaced when she saw the caller ID, but punched the phone on.

"Hello, Tony," she said.

"Alex," he said, sounding weary. "What the hell are you doing?"

"At this precise moment, I'm talking on the phone," Alex replied.

"You know what I mean," he said, his voice turning truculent. "I had two of your detectives in my office asking me a million questions about you, CJ, our relationship and where the hell I was half of last year. What the fuck is going on?"

"I'm guessing they actually explained to you at the time what was going on. Did you find their explanation inadequate?"

"Don't play stupid games with me, Alex," he snapped. "How dare you put me on some suspect list?"

"Just exploring all the possibilities," she said calmly. "Somebody murdered David, tried twice to kill me and threatened CJ. You've at least got a motive."

"What are you saying, for crissakes?"

"That you actively dislike CJ, you hate that I married her and you would do anything to end our relationship."

"Married!" he snorted. "As if two women—"

"Don't," Alex said very sharply. "You have no idea what you're talking about, so keep your ignorant, bigoted opinions to yourself. Are we done now? Because I have many, many other better things to do than to talk to you."

She heard him breathing heavily for a moment. Finally he said, "Look, I had nothing to do with any of this. I can't say I'm surprised CJ took off, but I didn't do anything to cause it. And believe it or not, I have no interest one way or another whether you're with CJ or not. I'm...I've been seeing someone. It's getting serious."

"A woman?" Alex couldn't help herself.

"Fuck you, Alex! Of *course* it's a *woman*. We've been dating for a while and—well, I'm thinking of asking her to marry me."

Alex sorted through a jumble of emotions: surprise, relief, skepticism. "I hope it works out for you, then," she said.

"Do you, really?"

Yes. Because then maybe you'll leave us the hell alone. "I do, actually, Tony. I hope you'll be very happy."

"And you'll call off your dogs?" he pressed.

"Are you making an harassment complaint?" she retorted.

"Well, no—"

"I didn't think so," Alex said crisply. "In that case, let's just let my detectives investigate their case, all right? If you have a legitimate complaint, you know where to find me."

She punched the phone off.

CHAPTER FOURTEEN

Alex was in her office, ostensibly reading arrest reports, but in reality going over the murder case. By midmorning, the bullpen was sparsely populated, most of her detectives out on calls or interviews. She watched Kelly Porter say something to Jo Adamcyzk, who nodded. They both headed toward the elevators. Frank was at his desk, with Chris leaning over his arm, both of them looking at something on his computer monitor. Gonzales was at his usual place by the coffeepot, surveying the morning's leftover blueberry breakfast crumb cake, homemade by Jennifer Morelli, who sent Frank in with baking once a week. Alex had eaten a small piece herself and it was up to Jennifer's usual high standard.

She pulled out her photocopy of the crime scene report on David's murder. Twenty-six bullets were fired in less than a minute. About half had been nine millimeter, the others thirty-eight caliber. Was there one shooter, switching guns? It seemed unlikely. The car hadn't stopped moving long enough for one man to empty two clips and drive at the same time.

So, two shooters then. And they'd gotten away so quickly that no patrol unit spotted them. That meant they'd hidden the car somewhere close to the park and escaped in another vehicle, or on foot. And later, somehow, they had returned to get rid of the car they'd used in the shooting, probably chopping it up for parts.

All in all, a well-planned operation, but clumsily executed. It seemed to her as if there were two sets of hands on the crime. Good strategy, poor tactics. The killers should have driven straight to the pavilion, stopped the car and taken a moment to aim. Neither she nor CJ had been armed that day. It would have been the world's easiest assassination.

Instead, they had started shooting too early. No one could have mistaken David for her—they had simply fired wildly at everyone in the picnic shelter.

Whoever had planned this, Alex realized, hadn't been in the car that day. She seriously doubted that Laurel, Stephanie or even Tony had the knowledge and ability to steal and hot-wire the car that had run her off the road in March. And she simply couldn't see any of them stealing a car and taking a dozen potshots at her family.

"They hired somebody," Alex said aloud. Why hadn't she thought of this before? She seriously doubted Laurel or Stephanie had the connections to find a local hit man, but Tony, on the other hand…he had an entire office full of file folders with the location of a variety of criminals, from whom he could pick and choose.

Oh, that was absurd. Tony is a slimy toad, she thought, but he's hardly going to go through his case files to find a handy contract killer.

Her thoughts were interrupted by her telephone. "Ryan," she answered.

"Captain, thank God," a panicky male voice said.

"Who is this?" Alex demanded.

"McCarthy, down in Internal Affairs," he said breathlessly. "Jesus, Captain, get the hell out of there!"

"Slow down. What's happening?"

"I just interviewed Fullerton. He got up in the middle of the interview and said he was going to have this out with you personally. He's on his way up there!"

Alex stood up and said, "Listen to me, Sergeant. Call Deputy Chief Duncan, and if you can't get him, call Chief Wylie. Tell whoever you get what you just told me. Did Fullerton take the elevator or the stairs?"

"I don't...oh, wait, the elevator."

That gave her an extra thirty seconds. "Was he armed?"

"I don't know. I mean, you got him to turn his service weapon in when he was suspended, but he might have a backup gun—"

She didn't waste time on another word. She ran into the bullpen and barked, "Gonzales, go downstairs and notify the watch commander we have a situation. Fullerton is on his way up here. He may or may not have a gun. Take the stairs. Go!"

The startled detective sprinted toward the stairs.

Frank and Chris were already on their feet. "Elevator?" Chris said.

"Yes. Frank, go around the corner by the restrooms where he won't see you. Chris, you wait in the door to the stairwell. I'm going to meet him at the elevator and see if I can calm him down."

"Is that a good idea?" Chris asked grimly, already moving toward the hall.

"Maybe so, maybe not," Alex conceded. "Get in position."

She pulled her backup revolver from her ankle holster and stuck it in the back waistband of her pants. It was against regulations, but she wanted it very handy and invisible in case Fullerton was intent on violence.

Alex could see Frank just around the corner to her left. Chris had the stairwell door slightly cracked open to her right. Her heart was pounding, but it made her feel better to know she had two backups on her side.

She carefully positioned herself far enough away so that he could step out of the elevator without getting too close to her. She didn't want to either be forced to back away from him, or to invade his personal space. *Please just don't let him open fire right away...*

The elevator doors slid open. Roger burst out, then halted as he saw her. The surprise was clear on his face.

"Roger," Alex said calmly. "You were looking for me?"

"McCarthy must have been shitting in his pants," he snarled. "Had to call his mommy, huh?"

Alex could smell the alcohol on him from a yard away. She kept her voice low and calm. "Roger, it seems you may have had your interview while you were impaired."

She couldn't believe Chad McCarthy had interviewed Fullerton in this condition. CJ would have chewed her sergeant up and spit him out for that. Actually, McCarthy wouldn't have done the interview at all if CJ had been there.

"I'm not fucking impaired. I'm pissed off. What the hell are you doing, trying to ruin my career?"

"Roger, why don't you let me get somebody to drive you home? You can sleep it off, and reschedule the interview for when you're feeling better."

He gave a bitter laugh. "What, do you think I'm a fucking moron? I oughta…"

At that moment, the door to the ladies' room opened. Jo Adamcyzk stepped out into the hall.

Fullerton jerked his head around as his right hand dove under his left shoulder. *Oh, hell.* He was carrying his backup gun.

Alex waited an extra split second until she saw the butt of his semiautomatic in his fingers.

"Gun!" she shouted. "Roger, don't…"

She moved into him, trying to get a grip on his right arm before he could clear his holster.

He shoved her hard with his left arm, and Alex staggered backward.

At the same instant Frank and Chris both yelled, "Drop the gun!"

Fullerton saw Frank first because he was already looking toward Jo Adamcyzk. Jo dove toward the corner as Frank eased out enough to point his gun at Fullerton.

"No!" Alex yelled.

The next moment, Fullerton fired, just an instant before Chris Andersen plowed into him from behind. Alex jumped toward Fullerton, focused again on his gun arm.

Chris had him down on his belly, and Alex, keeping clear of his line of fire, stepped hard on his right wrist. He gave a little scream and released the weapon. Alex scooped it up and pulled her own revolver, pointing it at the back of his skull.

"You twitch and I'll blow your head off!" she rasped.

Chris got to her feet, her foot firmly planted in the small of his back. "Son of a bitch," she panted.

"I've got him. Cuff him!" Alex barked at her.

Chris put her weapon away and pulled out her handcuffs. He yelped again when she pulled his right hand behind his back and she muttered, "Shut the fuck up."

They got him to his feet and Alex did a brief but thorough pat down, ignoring his mixture of curses and painful grunts.

"You broke my goddamn wrist!" he spat.

Chris pushed him up against the wall and growled, "I don't want to hear one more single fucking word from you."

Alex took a deep breath and called out, "You guys okay?"

From down the hallway, Jo's shaky voice responded, "Morelli's hit."

Chris cried out, "Jesus!"

"Stay with Fullerton," Alex ordered her firmly, and went down the hall.

She found Jo with her weapon out, standing protectively over Frank. She looked as shaken as she had sounded.

"Adamcyzk," Alex said, keeping her voice even. "Go call nine-one-one, then call the watch commander downstairs and give him a report. Tell him Fullerton is in custody, to send the paramedics up here as soon as they arrive."

"Yes, ma'am," Jo said and ran toward the bullpen.

She knelt by Frank. "How are you doing?"

Frank was propped up against the wall. His olive skin was pale and his mouth was tight with pain, but he said, "Don't think it's too bad, Cap."

"Let me see it, okay?" Alex asked gently.

She eased his jacket off his right arm. There was blood on his shirtsleeve and the side of his shirt. She unbuttoned his shirt and saw the wound in his side. The bullet had skittered across his ribcage, but it didn't seem to have penetrated his chest. The bleeding wasn't very profound.

"Can you move your arm?" she asked.

He flexed his fingers, then made a fist and was able to lift his arm, grimacing as he did so.

"Any trouble breathing?" Alex asked. "Take a deep breath."

He did, and then released it without difficulty.

"You're right," she said reassuringly. "It's not bad. It looks like what they used to call in the those old westerns 'a flesh wound.' You'll be okay, Frank." She made an effort to sound relaxed and in control.

"If you say so, Cap," he said, and flinched. "Do me a favor, huh? Go back and check on Andersen?"

She nodded and patted him briefly on his uninjured shoulder. When she went around the corner, she saw Fullerton up against the wall between the two elevators with Chris on one side facing him, Jo on the other.

Alex walked calmly toward them. To her relief, Fullerton's face looked unmarked. At least Chris hadn't used him for a punching bag.

"Paramedics will be here in a minute," Jo reported.

"How is Frank?" Chris demanded, her voice a little unsteady.

"He's going to be fine. It's minor," Alex reassured her.

"Really?"

"Really."

A look of profound relief crossed Chris' face. "That's a good thing for you," she muttered to Fullerton.

"Bitch," Fullerton responded.

Alex stepped closer to him and said, "Shut up, Roger. You are under arrest. You have the right to remain silent, so I strongly recommend you use it. You have the right to an attorney and to have one present during questioning. If you cannot afford one..."

She finished reciting his Miranda rights, then said to Chris, "Get him downstairs. I'm sick and tired of looking at his drunken face."

"A pleasure." Chris jerked him by one arm. "C'mon, dickhead, let's walk down."

The paramedics came out of the elevator and Alex got them to Frank. Then Jo said to her, "Captain, I'm so sorry. This was all my fault."

Alex turned to her. "Listen to me very carefully, Detective." Her tone was firm. "That was just bad luck, pure and simple. You're allowed to use the ladies' room, and you had no idea what was happening. If it's anybody's fault, it's mine. I should have checked the restrooms, we just ran out of time."

Jo shook her head. "I still feel responsible."

"Well, get over it. Fullerton was a time bomb, and it could have happened regardless of what you did or didn't do. When it did happen, you kept your head. You got under cover and when Frank was hit, you were ready to protect your fellow officer. You followed orders and you did fine under fire. All right?"

"Yes," Jo said, and she seemed to relax a little. "Thank you, Captain."

It was a mess. Frank had been hurt and one of her detectives was going to face criminal charges. On the plus side, Alex told herself ruefully, Fullerton was going to be permanently out of her hair, it looked like Frank was going to be okay and she knew that Jo Adamcyzk wouldn't panic the next time somebody took a shot at her.

But mostly she was happy about Chris Andersen keeping herself under control. When she had every reason to shoot Fullerton, she'd tried to take him down without using deadly force, and she'd managed not to beat the hell out of him when Alex knew how much she wanted to, something Alex hadn't been quite sure of before. *You'd be proud of me, CJ, seeing the glass half-full like this.*

* * *

When Alex got to Frank's house that evening, there were already a couple of cars outside, parked at the curb. She was a little surprised. She'd called Jennifer Morelli to see if Frank was up for company, but Jennifer hadn't mentioned other visitors.

Jennifer greeted her at the door, saying, "Alex. Please come in and join the crowd. They're back in the family room. You want coffee or something?"

"No, thanks," Alex said, hugging her hello. "How's he doing?"

"Oh, he's fine, the big ham. You'd have thought he was in a two-hour firefight, instead of one little nick in the side."

But Alex could see the worry behind her eyes.

"Hey," Alex said gently. "I know how hard it is to get that phone call, Jennifer, and I'm truly sorry."

Jennifer gave her an assessing look, and said, "You really do know, don't you? You went through it. After all, you're married to a cop too, aren't you?"

Alex looked at her, a little startled, and then laughed a little bit. "You know, I never thought of it that way before."

Frank was propped up in his recliner, his right side bulky with bandages. On the couch were Chris and Beth. In the other chair, to Alex's surprise, was Jo Adamcyzk. All three women stood when Alex entered, and Beth went over to hug her.

"Oh, Captain Ryan," she said quietly. "How are you doing? We've been so worried about you."

Alex looked over her shoulder at Chris, who had the grace to look embarrassed. What on earth had Chris been telling Beth about her? That Alex had been a complete zombie bitch for the last eight months? Not that that wasn't pretty much true.

"I'm okay," Alex said to Beth. "And stop calling me Captain Ryan. You don't work for the department anymore. Call me Alex."

Beth blushed a little. She'd been a clerk in the Colfax PD evidence room when she met Chris and she was always careful to treat Chris's boss respectfully.

Alex smiled at the three detectives, and added, "And that first-name basis stuff does not apply to you guys during working hours."

They all laughed and Alex sat in the other chair. "How are you feeling?" she asked Frank. "You achieved the best possible medical report: 'treated and released.'"

Chris snorted and said, "He achieved the perfect vacation. 'Oh, gee, sorry, Captain, I can't work for five days, I have to stay home and drink beer.'"

"Hey," Frank protested, "I'm not allowed to drink. Painkillers and antibiotics."

"Ha! Painkillers, my ass," Chris continued. "Probably hurts about as much as a hangnail."

Frank pulled an exaggerated look of distress and touched his side with his free hand, moaning, "Oh, that's so cruel. I'm in agony."

"Stop," Beth said to Chris. "You're being mean. The poor man was shot, after all."

"Thank you, Beth," Frank said, with dignity. "At least somebody understands my deep distress."

"I'll give you some deep distress," Chris muttered.

Beth reached over and grasped Chris's hand. "Behave," she murmured.

Chris cocked an eyebrow and said, "That's not what you usually want."

As Beth blushed, Frank sputtered, "Oh, jeez, knock it off already, or I'll start calling you Hans in front of suspects."

Jo asked, "Hans?"

Chris made a face and said, "Hans Christian Andersen. It's Frank's lame idea of a joke."

"It's not his fault he's lame," Jo responded quickly. "Cubby fans don't have much of a sense of humor, for obvious reasons. Did I mention his team hasn't won a Series since before World War One?"

"Hey, knock it off!" Frank gave a mock growl.

"Or what, Harlem Avenue? You gonna slug me with that grievous injury hampering you?"

"Nah," Frank replied easily. "I'll get my partner to do it for me. She's tougher than I am anyway. Sic 'em, Hans."

Chris held up both hands, palms out. "Hey, I'm a Rockies fan. You do your own dirty work."

"Colorado Rockies," Frank sniffed. "A bunch of johnny-come-latelies."

"Don't you start with me," Chris warned him. "Even the Rockies have been to the World Series since the Chicago Cubs have."

"Ow," Frank said. "Now that really hurt."

Suddenly Chris shook her head angrily. "Not as much as that asshole Fullerton hurt you. Another cop, for God's sake. Pisses me off."

Frank's tone grew serious. "Yeah. I know. Somebody you depend on…"

Alex interjected, "Somebody you think has your back turns out to be someone you can't trust. I'm sorry, Frankie. It was me he came up there to get, not you."

"Don't you apologize for him, Cap," Frank said. "You didn't do anything wrong. It was him. He was never right, not from the start. He was always bitching about something." He slid his eyes toward Jo, and lightened the mood with, "Kinda like a White Sox fan."

"Really funny," Jo said. "And speaking of which, I brought you a present." Jo pulled a plastic bag from beside her chair. "Something to cheer you up."

"A National League Pennant for the Cubs?" Frank asked.

"No. Better."

Jo produced a White Sox baseball cap and tossed it into his lap.

"Hey, put it on!" Chris urged him, laughing.

Frank recoiled in horror. "Oh, my God, get that outta my house!" he exclaimed. "Jeez, are you trying to get me whacked? I show up in my neighborhood with that and I'll end up like Jimmy Hoffa."

"I thought he got iced in Detroit," Jo said with a smirk.

"Yeah, for all you know about it," Frank deadpanned.

Now they were all laughing together. Alex felt another layer of unhappiness peel away from her in the company of people she knew and respected, people she liked.

Underneath it all was something she'd had precious little of in the last months: hope. Hope that they could find David's killer, hope that she could bring CJ home again and above all, hope that she would, some day in a future not too far away, be happy again.

CHAPTER FIFTEEN

First thing the next morning, Alex called Chris Andersen into her office. "Since Frank won't be back until next week, I want to talk to you about your caseload," Alex began.

"Okay. It will be a short conversation, though. I've got that liquor store burglary with no leads and no forensics, an assault case that my grandmother could have solved in fifteen minutes, a criminal mischief at the local middle school and the Castillo murder. I don't need any help on any of them except for the last one. I'm waiting on a warrant on the assault case and I can get uniformed to go out with me when I pick the guy up when it comes in. Everything's under control."

Alex was struck again by the similarity between Chris and a young Alex Ryan, both made of hard work and dedication. She briefly switched topics to, "It was good to see Beth last night. I meant to ask her how school was going."

The expression on Chris's face softened immediately. "She's doing great," she replied proudly. "She's starting her hospital rotations soon—you know, going through emergency, pediatrics, stuff like that. Her grades are perfect and one of her instructors told her that after she gets her license as a practical nurse, she should consider continuing in school to become a registered nurse. I'm so goddamned proud of her."

Alex smiled at her. "Good for you. And good for her. She's a very nice young woman."

"Yeah. A lot younger than I am," Chris said ruefully.

Alex laughed and said, "Come on Andersen, you're not quite over the hill yet. What are you, thirty-one, thirty-two? You'll do fine together."

Chris lifted an eyebrow at her. "Are you trying to sell me on the virtues of younger women?"

A couple of weeks ago the remark would have stung. Alex said, "I certainly could, but I think we'll need to be out of the office and on our second beer first. Now, what's the status on our murder case?"

Chris sighed. "Not much new there. The interview with our district attorney wasn't helpful, although he did try very hard to convince us he was romantically involved with some other woman, Sue something or other, and therefore was no longer interested in getting rid of St. Clair or getting back together with his ex-wife."

"Well, that would be nice," Alex said dryly. "I think he's been trying to convince me to marry him again since the judge signed on the final dissolution decree. God knows why. He thinks it would be good for his career, I guess. What does this Sue something or other do for a living?"

"Investments, I think Bradford told us."

"Oh, good," Alex said. "He'd like that, a woman as worried about money as he is. Have you checked on his whereabouts for the two dates last year?"

"Yes. He was at some local political rally on the Fourth of July, about three hundred people saw him there all afternoon. He was actually at the office on March sixteenth last year, waiting with some of his staff for the jury to come back on the pizza delivery murder case. Alibis all round."

"And you haven't turned up anything on Stephanie Morrow?"

"Nothing other than a case filed with the Division of Real Estate a couple of years ago. Some client complained about her, a dispute about an escrow account. They didn't jerk her license or anything. There was a…what did they call it?"

"Settlement?" Alex suggested. "Stipulation?"

"Stipulation, that was it. She paid the client some money, basically. That's it. No criminal record or arrests on her, just some traffic stuff. There's obviously no criminal record on our district attorney."

Alex smiled. "You actually checked him out?"

"Hell yes, I did. And I can't find any arrest record on Laurel Halliday, either, here or in Georgia."

Alex folded her hands on her desk and asked, "How did your search for someone from my past arrests go?"

Chris pulled a face. "Okay, so not one of my better ideas," she sighed in resignation. "There's nobody who just got out last year after a long sentence from your days on patrol or as a detective, and the people you've arrested in the last three years or so are all either in prison, jail, or dead. Have you thought of anybody else who might have a particular grudge against you?"

"Honestly? No one." Alex swiveled her chair and looked out the window, thinking.

"What is it, Captain?" Chris asked after a moment.

"Just before all hell broke loose with Roger, I had a thought. I want to know what your reaction to it is."

"Of course."

Alex summarized her theory that the driver in March, and the shooters in July, had been hired to go after her. "If I'm right about that," she concluded, "the alibis on our suspects don't mean much."

"I agree," Chris said. "But it does sort of limit the pool of candidates. It's hard to think of Stephanie Morrow knowing some punk who would boost a car and take a friend along to shoot at your family."

"Yes," Alex agreed, remembering that CJ had made the identical argument. "But it's not too far-fetched to imagine Tony finding somebody, now is it?"

Chris digested that for a moment. "I see your point," she said at length. "Do you really think your ex-husband is behind all of this?"

Alex sighed. "I can't believe he is," she admitted. "He's always been self-centered, and God knows he really hated CJ. But murder? I lived with the man for two years and it's hard for me to believe he's capable of that. Of course," she added wryly, "I didn't know him nearly as well as I should have. Or maybe it was myself I didn't know."

Abruptly Chris said, "You don't think Fullerton had anything to do with this, do you?"

Startled, Alex said, "Why, do you?"

"No, not really. The timing is all wrong. It's just weird that you have all these people lining up to try to kill you."

Alex smiled ruefully. "Must be my charming personality."

Chris laughed. Alex asked, "When are you going back to see Stephanie?"

"I could go this afternoon. Want to ride along?" she suggested. "Just having you in the room might make the follow-up interview more interesting."

"That," Alex replied thoughtfully, "is a very good idea."

* * *

On the way to Stephanie Morrow's office that afternoon, Alex's cell phone rang. Since Chris was driving, Alex took the call.

"Hey, *chica*," Rod Chavez said. "How's it goin'?"

"Rod, good to hear from you," Alex said, with a tiny stab of guilt. She should have called CJ's oldest friend from the Roosevelt sheriff's office after she found the note sent to CJ.

"Glad to hear you soundin' so chipper," he responded. "You didn't get a call from her, did you?"

"No. But I have a lot more information than I did a week ago," Alex explained.

"Yeah? Can you share?"

She took a brief sideways glance at Chris, then said, "Let me give you the condensed version."

When she'd finished, she heard him give a low whistle. "Damn it, Alex," he said. "I knew it had to be somethin' like that! CJ would never have just taken off. We should have figured this out sooner."

Alex, remembering her last session with Elaine Wheeler, said, "In a way, I always knew she left for a good reason. It was just hard to see, when…"

She stopped, still very aware of Chris in the car, but Rod finished for her, "When you were hurting. I get it. Now, what can I do to help?"

The offer touched her. He had been very protective of her while CJ was gone, calling her every week.

"If I think of something, you'll be the first one I call," she promised him. "But you tell Ana I'm expecting the best welcome home party she's ever thrown when we get this guy and CJ can come home again."

"Yeah," he said, and she realized that he was a little choked up. It made her tear up a bit too.

"Hey, knock it off, tough guy," she said. "I'll call you when I know something, all right?"

"Alex, you take care."

On the first visit, Frank and Chris had simply shown up at Stephanie's office, but this time Chris had made an actual appointment. Both methods worked, for different reasons. Surprise could be useful, not letting a suspect prepare for the interview, but letting a person worry about the upcoming meeting was effective, too.

Stephanie's assistant was a drop-dead gorgeous woman who looked to Alex to be about seventeen and a new graduate of some modeling school, but she was probably in her mid-twenties. The nameplate on her desk read Judy Soames.

She actually ushered them into Stephanie's office, decorated in what Alex supposed was Swedish modern, all sleek, light wood. Stephanie was on the phone, but waved them in as she continued to harass some appraiser about his report.

When she hung up, she said to them, "I hope this harassment session is going to be short, Captain Ryan. I've got a closing tomorrow that's going south, and an idiot who apparently can't write a report in the English language."

Alex saw something in her face. Distress? Apprehension? Resignation?

"Ms. Morrow," Chris said. "I'm sure you remember me, Detective Andersen. I believe you've met my boss."

Stephanie looked from one to the other and said, "Yes, we've met. So fucking wonderful to see you again." She looked less polished today than she had at the cocktail party when Alex first met her. Her hair and makeup were still perfect, but her expression was harried and the lines around her mouth were tightly drawn. Alex could see for the first time how she would look in twenty-five years or so, when she turned sixty. *She's going to need that face-lift*, Alex thought wryly.

Alex suppressed her natural tendency to take control of the interview, and sat back to let Chris work.

"Ms. Morrow, we just came back by to see if you could remember anything else that would help us with our case," Chris said, deliberately casual.

"As I have been telling your boss here for a year or so," Stephanie snapped, "I don't know anything about the stupid accident, and I don't know what the hell happened to CJ. I'm running out of different ways to say I had nothing to do with any of it."

Unmoved, Chris opened her notebook, and seemed to be reading her notes. "You stated that you hadn't seen Ms. St. Clair for more than four years when you met her again at the party on March sixteenth last year," she said.

"That's right."

"And you also stated that you had no idea that she'd been married in the interim," Chris continued, her tone ignoring the fact that the other party to the marriage was seated next to her.

"Detective, how would I know anything about what she was doing? I said I hadn't seen her."

Chris said mildly, "That doesn't mean you weren't making yourself aware of her activities."

"What the fuck are you—" Stephanie glared at Chris a moment, then suddenly looked at Alex and seemed to slump in defeat. "Oh, the hell with it." She picked up her phone, jabbed a button and said, "Judy, will you come in here a minute?"

A moment later the blond and elegant Ms. Soames came into the office. "Yes, Stephanie?"

Stephanie gestured toward the two detectives. "Judy, this is Captain Ryan and Detective Andersen. They're from the police."

Judy blinked bright blue eyes at both of them.

Alex asked calmly, "Why is Ms. Soames here, Steph?"

Her use of the nickname was deliberate, invoking CJ into the room with them. Stephanie met Alex's eyes.

Quietly, Stephanie said, "Tell them what we talked about last night."

"What?" Judy looked startled.

"I'll explain it to you later. Just tell them, okay?"

"Oh. Um. She—Steph—asked me to move in with her." She blinked again and added, "I said yes, of course."

Chris made a little sound in her throat, then cleared it, and said, "You're dating?"

Judy said, "We've been in a relationship since last summer." She turned a flirtatious look Stephanie's way and added, "She's awesome."

Alex turned back to Stephanie and said mildly, "This doesn't necessarily let you off our suspect list."

"Suspected of what?" Judy demanded. "Steph, what are they talking about?"

"I said I'd tell you later," Stephanie said wearily. "Look," she was addressing only Alex this time, "check out anything you want. I've moved on, okay? I don't care who CJ is sleeping with, or what she does. I didn't try to kill you, or get her away from you.

"Why would I want to when I've got her in bed with me every night?" She gestured at Judy, who preened happily.

Beside her, Alex actually felt Chris shudder a little. Abruptly, Chris stood up and said, "We'll be in touch, Ms. Morrow."

They were halfway back to the office, driving in silence, when Alex said, "So. My sense is that she's telling the truth. What's your take on it?"

Chris said nothing for a moment, then responded, "You know there was a time, not that long ago, when I would have spent quite a bit of time trying to get her into bed."

Surprised, Alex asked, "Who? Judy or Stephanie?"

Chris made a face. "Either one, frankly." She glanced at Alex and blew out a breath. "Any woman I saw who might be interested."

Alex knew Chris was thinking about Chris's unsuccessful effort to seduce her just after Chris was promoted to detective two years ago. In a calm tone, Alex said, "Are you over that?"

"It's weird," Chris mused. "It's like I can look, and enjoy the scenery, but I don't really want to touch anymore. I just want to go home to Beth, and be with her. I never, ever, in a billion years, thought I would turn into one of those fully domesticated lesbians."

Gently amused, and reminded of Vivien, Alex said, "It's not so bad, now is it?"

Chris glanced at her again and said, "Don't tell anybody, especially Frank, but it's pretty goddamned wonderful. And to answer your first question, I do actually think Morrow is telling the truth. But I'm going to check out Judy Soames anyway, make sure this wasn't some kind of setup. This case has got me thinking. I don't trust anybody."

Alex said dryly, "That's actually a good quality to have on the job, Detective."

CHAPTER SIXTEEN

Alex glanced at her clock and noticed it was after two p.m., which explained why her stomach was complaining that it hadn't had any lunch yet. The sensation of actually wanting to eat on a regular basis was still surprising. She was considering whether to go out or order something from the deli across the street to pick up, when her office phone rang.

"This is Roger Edgarton," her caller said in his basso profondo. "I have some of the information you requested about Laurel Halliday I hope you will find useful."

Alex picked up her fountain pen. "I'm ready."

"Miss Halliday left her position at Oglethorpe University for a very interesting reason," he began. "She originally came from a middle-class family, and had a brother, four years younger. You may have heard of him. His name was Jackson Monroe Halliday."

The name sounded vaguely familiar to her, but she couldn't quite place it.

"He dropped his last name when he submitted his book to his publisher," Edgarton prompted her.

Jackson Monroe.

"Oh, my God," Alex remembered. "*Foe without Hate*. The biography of Robert E. Lee. It was on the *New York Times* best-seller list, right?"

"Several best-seller lists, and the book won a Pulitzer for its author. Posthumously."

"I remember now," Alex said. "Monroe shot himself before the book was published."

"Yes. The rights to the book had been sold to a Hollywood studio as well, so his estate was worth several million dollars. And that estate went to his only relative, his sister. When she received word of the inheritance, she simply quit her job and walked away."

Alex was scrambling to put this piece into place. A copy of the book was in CJ's bookshelf at home, next in line to be read. Did she know Laurel's brother had written it?

Alex said, "So the question is: where is she now?"

"That's apparently not a simple question," Edgarton rumbled. "She did make a few appearances in and around Georgia, publicizing the book. There was one interview early last year in California and one in New York. She still has an apartment in Atlanta but she's apparently gone often, traveling extensively now that she can afford to do so. So I suppose the answer is: she's around here in Georgia somewhere."

"I see." Alex felt deflated. "I'd like to thank you for all of this, Mr. Edgarton. And I want you to know that we're still working this case vigorously. I still hope to see you very soon."

"I will look forward to that, Miss Ryan."

Alex looked at her notes for a few minutes, playing with the fountain pen in her fingers. What did any of this mean? Laurel was still in Georgia, wealthy and promoting her late brother's book, Stephanie was seriously involved with another woman, and no one from Alex's professional past seemed interested in coming after her.

But someone had sent CJ that note. Someone desperately wanted them apart, and was willing to try murder to achieve it.

She tried not to think about Tony, but her thoughts continued to circle back to him. He had alibis for both attempts on her life last year, but it didn't matter if he'd hired someone. It would be so easy for him to find some defendant with the talents necessary to hire, bribe or threaten into helping him.

She put the pen down and closed her eyes to think. Maybe she should look for people arrested during the period just before the first attempt who seemed likely to be able to help him. The problem was that it could have been someone from any time period, and the district attorney prosecuted people from jurisdictions other than just the suburban city of Colfax. It could have been a perp from Sherill Heights or Bear Creek, or even someone arrested by the sheriff's office in the unincorporated part of the county.

Alex hated to give the task to Chris, already working the caseload she shared with Frank alone, so she sighed and began logging on to her records program. She reminded herself to call Rod Chavez later, and give him a similar job with his database from Roosevelt County. In fact, she mused, since the sheriff's office also ran the jail that all of the municipalities used, he would have access to more information than she would, at least booking information. She smiled a little to herself. *And that's what he gets for offering to help.*

What they were trying to find might not be there... What exactly it would mean if she did find what she was looking for, she put off thinking about.

CHAPTER SEVENTEEN

When Alex looked up from her computer screen, she saw to her surprise that it was dark outside. The switch to daylight savings time had happened last Saturday, so darkness meant it was really too late for her to still be at work. *Oh, well,* she thought, logging off, *at least it sets a good example for my detectives, seeing me in here slogging away as they leave for the night.*

To her faint surprise, she saw Chris still at her desk, staring at her own monitor. Alex got up, stretched, and walked out to her.

"I can't afford this much overtime for you," Alex greeted her.

Chris looked up, startled. "Oh, Captain. Don't worry, I wasn't planning on putting in for this."

Alex said sternly, "You clock every minute you work, Detective. The Feds have rules about that kind of thing. And besides, I thought you had someone to go home to now. I don't want to start getting threatening phone calls from Beth."

Chris laughed, and Alex joined in. The thought of Beth making threats to anyone, much less Chris's boss, was equally amusing to both of them.

Chris said, still chuckling, "Beth told me nicely to stay away. She's studying for a final exam in—what was it? Oh, yeah, pharmacology." Chris shook her head, adding, "You should see the kind of stuff she has to memorize. Medications. Calculations for intravenous drip rates. Jesus. Anyway, I'm not allowed home before nine p.m." She grinned. "She says I'm too distracting."

Alex said dryly, "You can spare me your smugness. How about I buy you dinner, then send you home? It ought to be safe for you by then."

There was a moment's pause. The memory of what happened between them hung suspended for a moment, then Chris said quietly, "I'd like that. You know you can trust me, right?"

Yes, Alex thought. She hadn't always thought so, but she knew it now. Even with CJ gone to wherever she was, she knew she could trust Chris. And herself, as well. "Of course," Alex said. "I think we can be friends, Chris. All right?"

Chris began to log off. "I have this tremendous craving for homemade pizza," she said cheerfully. "Can we go to Romano's?"

"You're as bad as my nephew," Alex said. "Yes, you may have pizza."

Ten minutes later, as they were waiting at their table in the restaurant, Chris said, "Can we talk about work for five minutes? I promise after that we can talk about anything else."

"Sure. What have you got?"

"I guess you could say I've got good news and bad news. The bad news, I suppose, is that Judy Soames checks out. She is who she says she is, and it looks like the relationship is real. They haven't been hiding it. I guess since Morrow is the boss, she can sleep with her employees at will. Anyway, it looks like she was telling us the truth. But here's something interesting: Soames's father has a record."

"Really? For what?"

"Apparently Mr. Soames makes a living by stealing other people's stuff. He's got one criminal mischief and two second degree burglary convictions, along with half-a-dozen other arrests. He's seen the inside of Cañon City fairly recently, though he's out on parole now."

"Any weapons charges? Auto theft? Assault?"

Chris sighed. "No. I guess the news wasn't that good. I mean, he knows some people who know some people, probably, but I can't see him as the bad guy we're looking for."

Alex said, "And why would the father of the new girlfriend help Stephanie get her old girlfriend back by killing me?"

"I didn't think that theory was going to fly," Chris said. "Oh, well. Just being thorough."

"I've been working on being thorough, too," Alex admitted. "Remember my thought that Tony has access to some defendants who would be able to pull these jobs for him? I've started looking through the arrest records for a year ago, and I've got a colleague, Rod Chavez at the Roosevelt SO, doing the same for other jurisdictions."

Chris said, a touch defensively, "I can do that, you know."

"I know. But you're busy and we can help. I'm a real detective, got the badge and everything."

"You're so funny. Look, I have to tell you. If Tony Bradford really does have a new girlfriend, then he doesn't have anymore motive for coming after you or getting rid of St. Clair than Stephanie Morrow does. I can see the new girlfriend maybe trying to get rid of you, the ex-wife, but it makes absolutely no sense to get St. Clair out of the picture."

Alex sighed. She had thought of that, but she felt as if she were searching in the dark. "Maybe, while we're running all these useless checks on everyone, we should do a background on Tony's new girlfriend," she suggested.

"Good idea, Captain. You really are a detective."

Alex said, "You don't have to call me Captain when we're off duty, okay? It's Alex."

"Okay," Chris said softly. "Look, maybe when this is all over, when we get this guy and St. Clair comes home—maybe the four of us could, you know, hang out a little. Beth really liked St. Clair a lot, and we don't really have a lot of, um, friends who are couples. Gay, I mean. And I'd like a chance to prove to St. Clair that I'm not really a terrible person. Do you think that would be all right?"

Alex smiled. Chris really had come a long way. "I think that would be good," she said.

Chris exhaled a long, relieved breath. "Another thing," she said. "I never really, well, thanked you."

"What for?"

Chris looked away a moment, then said, "It was you who told me it was worth the trouble to find one woman to be with, and stay with. Remember telling me that?"

Alex remembered it vividly. It was part of telling Chris that she wasn't interested, she only cared for CJ. "I do," Alex answered.

"You may not believe this, but it was that same night I asked Beth out for the first time."

"Really? I'm surprised."

"You know what? I was, too. But you were right. It's a lot more work to be with just one person, but it's a lot more—I guess you'd say, rewarding, too." She dropped her head into her hands and grumbled, "Jeez, I really am completely whipped."

Alex said kindly, "You know what? You're not. You're in love, and there's not a damn thing in the world wrong with that. In fact, you might say that there's nothing better."

"Yeah?" Chris said ruefully. "And what about you, Alex? After all this, are you still in love, too?"

"I am," Alex said. "Even after all this, I really am."

* * *

"I can't believe it," Nicole said for the third time. "It just seems so outrageous."

"Which part?" Alex asked. "The note, or the fact that Tony has emerged as the number one suspect?" She shifted the phone to her other ear as she propped herself up on her couch.

"The note," Nicole answered promptly. "I can't believe someone tried something like that, and I really can't believe it worked. What the hell was my sister-in-law thinking?"

"She was trying to do the right thing," Alex said quietly. "And she didn't have a lot of time to think about it. I wish she hadn't gone away, but at least I understand why now. The best news is that I'm pretty sure Roger Edgarton, her trustee, knows where she is, or at least where I can locate her. If we can solve this, I can go and find her."

"And you really think it's Tony?" Nicole demanded.

"Honestly, I don't know. He's certainly the leading candidate, but I don't know." She blew out a deep breath. "Christ, Nic, I can't believe he would do this to me. I know he hates that I'm married to CJ, but I just can't quite believe this about him. And why now? CJ and I have been together for three years. If he were going to do this, why after all this time?"

"Maybe the new girlfriend is the motive," Nicole suggested.

"Maybe, but I can't make any sense out of it," Alex said grimly. "I want you to know this, though, Nic. I'm going to figure this out, for both of us. I promise you that."

As she lay in bed after turning out the lights, Alex found herself having a mental conversation with CJ.

I really wish you were here so I could talk this over with you, Alex told her. *You read people so well, and I just feel confused. And you'd know more about Laurel and Stephanie than anybody here would know.*

Alex rolled over in the bed. *Are you thinking about me tonight, sweetheart? Do you miss me the way I'm missing you?*

It was a physical ache, this loneliness. She'd missed her mother, she'd missed her father, too, but as much as those losses hurt, it was nothing like this. Even knowing why CJ left, understanding the reason, didn't fill the pain of the emptiness that enveloped her, like a black hole that let no light escape.

She was afraid, too, afraid that too much time had passed. What if Elaine Wheeler was right and they could never get back what they'd had before? Alex tried to imagine something worse than losing CJ forever, and knew there would be nothing she dreaded more than that. And what if she couldn't solve this case, figure out who was threatening them so that CJ could come home?

Don't give up on me, sweetheart. I'll get you back, somehow, some way, even if I have to go to Savannah and threaten to kill Roger Edgarton to do it. Just don't give up on me.

CHAPTER EIGHTEEN

Alex tapped on Deputy Chief Paul Duncan's door and asked, "Are you ready for me?"

He looked up at her, his two index fingers poised over his keyboard. She thought, not for the first time, how challenging it must be for a generation of cops who hadn't dreamed of ever having to deal with a computer to cope with the fact that it was impossible to do the job without them these days. He seemed to be relieved at the interruption and said, "Alex, come in."

When she was seated, he gestured toward the window. "Third day raining. Had enough of that yet? If I wanted it to rain every damn day, I'd move to Seattle."

Alex recognized the weather as an opening topic of discussion for his attempt to reconnect with her after their last, less than cordial, conversation. "We'll be glad of it come July," she said. "No such thing as too much rain in Colorado."

He grunted. "That's because we sold all our damn water to California."

Lack of water was another familiar topic in Colorado, so Alex played along. "The good news is the snowpack is at a hundred and sixty percent, or something like that. It shouldn't be too dry a summer."

Paul grunted again, and Alex could see him working himself up to whatever he'd brought her over to talk about. "I understand you put the Castillo murder back on the front burner," he said at length.

Alex knew she shouldn't be surprised. Word always got around. "Yes," was all she said.

"Any particular reason?"

"We got a new lead," she said.

He glared at her. "You want to be a little more forthcoming, Captain?"

Alex folded her hands and looked him in the eyes. "I'll be happy to explain my reasons and my theory to you, Chief," she replied, "but I'd like to make certain we're having a professional conversation. Our last professional conversation diverged into my personal life."

He sat back and drummed his fingers on his desk. "This murder is very personal to you," he said, his voice a touch defensive. "You were there, it was Nicole's husband who died."

"I'm very aware of that," Alex said coolly. "I've assigned the case to Morelli and Andersen, and I'm treating it like any other case on the Investigations caseload. As a supervisor."

"You want to tell me what you've got?" Paul still looked unhappy.

Alex summarized it for him, from her discovery of the note to the most recent developments. By the end of the story, he was drumming his fingers again.

"You have any idea what kind of political insanity an accusation of murder against our current district attorney would cause?" he demanded.

"A rough idea, yes. Believe me, I'll let you know if I think we're anywhere close to getting a warrant. We're a long way from that now."

"Keep me informed. I mean that."

"Of course, Chief," she said calmly.

He grimaced at her tone and said, "Look, Alex…"

"Is this conversation about to become personal again?" she asked.

"Yes," he sighed. "I owe you an apology."

"I agree," Alex responded dryly.

"Jesus, you sound like Betty," he mumbled. "She tore me a new one when I told her what I said to you."

"I've always respected Betty's opinion," Alex said, but she relaxed her tone a little.

"I shouldn't have said anything about St. Clair to you. I was out of line."

"I agree with that, too," Alex said. "Whether you approve of my relationship or not is really irrelevant to me at this point in our lives, but I want you to remember that CJ is my wife. I need for you to respect that. I'm willing to give you the benefit of the doubt because I know you really care about me. Let's forget about it, all right?"

He paused, gazing at her uncertainly. "Betty says you haven't called her," he said finally.

"That's true," Alex admitted. "I've been busy. But I'll talk to Nicole and call her tomorrow. You can tell Betty that."

* * *

Chris poked her head into Alex's office just after lunch. "Hey, Captain. Just wanted to tell you I'm going out to work on that background check on Bradford's new squeeze, Sue Davis."

"You have an address?"

"Yeah, she's got one of those pricey condos over in Greenwood Village. She's renting, looks like."

"Do you have a Colorado driver's license on her?"

"Nope. I'm hoping to get a look at her rental application and get ID information, maybe a prior address. I know she's not registered as a certified financial planner, and she doesn't have a broker's license."

"Okay. Good luck and be careful."

Chris grinned and said, "Always."

The rain was still hanging around this afternoon, splattering irregularly against Alex's window, a random counterpoint to the clicking of keys on her keyboard. When her telephone rang, she scooped up the receiver without her eyes leaving the monitor.

Rod Chavez said, "I am really, really good."

"I've heard rumors about that, but I've got no proof yet," Alex retorted. "What's up?"

"I think I've found your guys," he announced.

"What?" She felt her heart rate spike suddenly. "The shooters? You're kidding."

"I am not. I'm sending you an email now. Look at the attachments and call me back to tell me how brilliant I am."

She opened his email, read the documents on her screen, arrest reports and booking information, with an increasing sense of incredulity. She finally punched in Rod's number at the sheriff's office and when he picked up, she said, "Oh, my God."

"I know. Is that not amazin'?"

"What's amazing to me is how obvious it is," Alex said ruefully. "I should have looked for this days ago."

"Don't sell yourself short, *chica*," Rod said reassuringly. "Like a lot of what we do, it's only obvious if you know exactly where in the haystack to look for the needle."

Alex scanned her screen again. "Assault with a deadly weapon, auto theft on suspect one, weapons charges and two assaults on suspect number two. They were even arrested together, so clearly they're associates."

"Cousins, actually," Rod said. "Arrested last February twenty-first. Deferred prosecutions were entered July seventeenth. Not even a guilty plea and suspended sentence, Alex, deferred pros. Jeez. They stay out of trouble and in a year, their records are clean as a whistle. And the cases were solid against them, there was no reason for the deferred prosecutions. This stinks really, really bad, Alex. They were arraigned and out on bail in plenty of time to get a nice offer from the DA. They're arrested just three weeks before your car accident, and the prosecution deal is entered less than two weeks after David's murder."

"My God, this must have taken you hours to come up with, Rod."

"Nah, not that bad. So what's next?"

"As soon as my detective comes back from an interview she's doing, I think it's time to pay our two suspects a visit," Alex said.

She looked at the faces of the two men on her screen, and wondered which one of them had actually fired the bullet that had pierced David Castillo's heart.

CHAPTER NINETEEN

Alex was waiting for Chris Andersen when she got back. "How did it go?" Alex asked her.

"I don't know much yet. I did manage to get a copy of Sue Davis's apartment application, so my plan is to run down the information, prior address and the rest. Why?" Chris asked, suddenly looking at Alex squarely. "What happened here?"

Alex replied, "Rod Chavez, my friend at the Roosevelt SO, may just have come up with the lead we were looking for."

Chris leaned over her shoulder as Alex pulled up the information Rod had sent her on her computer. "Jesus," Chris murmured as she read. "These guys look awfully good for this."

"I thought so, too," Alex said, feeling her excitement return. *We're getting closer, sweetheart.*

"I think my next job is to find out where these two fine citizens might be and go out and have a little chat with them," Chris said happily.

"I agree, but I don't want you going out alone. Grab somebody else to go with you, or come and get me if you can't get anybody else. I don't want you going out there by yourself. These guys are dangerous, and more importantly if they are involved in David's murder and the attack on me, they don't have a lot to lose. Are we clear?"

"Very clear, Captain," Chris responded solemnly. "Don't worry, I have no desire to become a martyr."

"Glad to hear it. Keep in touch."

* * *

On the plus side, Alex thought, at least the sun is shining today, the rain having finally moved east to bless Kansas. On the less positive side, she had been stuck in a command staff meeting for two hours now, listening to Chief Wylie drone through PowerPoint slides about some new federal grant for anti-gang activities. That the chief had scheduled the meeting for three o'clock in the afternoon had compounded the boredom factor.

Alex shifted uneasily in her chair at the conference table. Gangs were certainly a problem in the more concentrated urban areas of Denver, and activities had spread to some of the suburbs like Aurora, but the topic wasn't very relevant to their day-to-day policing in Colfax. Her counterpart in charge of the Patrol Division, Captain John Robards, was concentrating his attention on Chief Wylie so completely that Alex knew for certain that John was bored out of his mind. Paul Duncan, at the other end of the table, had been fiddling with his pen for the last half an hour.

She had her eyes on the screen, but her mind was far away. She'd been mentally rearranging the pieces of the case all day, trying to see beyond the obvious.

It has to be Tony, she kept thinking. *I don't know why, exactly, but it has to be.* The deal cut with the suspects was too obvious for anything else. If Chris came up with something, anything tying the two suspects Rod Chavez had identified to the attacks, it *had* be Tony. But what was his motive? He certainly had plenty of animosity toward CJ that he hadn't kept secret, but before CJ left it had seemed to Alex that CJ and Tony had finally come to some kind of truce, mutual tolerance, at least. Why would Tony do this now? She continued to ask herself the same question. And for all of the difficulties surrounding their divorce, and Alex's later relationship with CJ, she'd never in her wildest imagination thought that Tony would try to kill her.

Their marriage had been a brief and unhappy one. Alex married him because he seemed to genuinely love her, but it hadn't taken long for her to discover that he viewed her primarily as an important asset to his budding career. "Married guys look more stable, more like promotion material," he'd explained to her once. For her part, Alex admitted that she'd been trying to do the right thing by marrying him. Well-raised Catholic girls were supposed to get married. To men.

But it hadn't worked. Tony had been deeply unhappy when she asked for a divorce after only two years together. The higher her rank in the department, the more he seemed determined to convince her that she'd made a mistake, that they still belonged together.

Then she'd met CJ and everything changed. To describe Tony as unhappy about her relationship with a woman was an understatement. He despised CJ, hated their relationship, and had since had several attempts at breaking them up.

If this is Tony he would have gone after CJ, Alex thought. Not me.

Maybe she wouldn't know the motive until they finally put the case together and interrogated him. The only reason for the timing she could think of was the appearance of his new girlfriend, Sue Davis. That had to be it, somehow, she thought. The girlfriend's involvement must somehow have triggered Tony's desire to take more drastic steps. But why?

She hadn't heard yet from Chris about her follow-up on Davis. She sneaked a glance at the clock on her phone, carefully set on silent, and saw that it was just about five. She also saw two missed calls from Chris.

Wylie seemed to be winding down, thank God. As soon as he finished, Alex made her farewells, and went into the hall to call Chris.

"What have you got?" Alex asked.

"Good news and bad news," Chris began.

Alex had stopped in the hallway since she couldn't get cell phone reception in either the elevator or the stairwell. Now she paced up and down as she talked. "Give me both barrels," she said to Chris.

"The good news is that I think Chavez's suspects really are our guys, for a variety of reasons I can tell you about later, including the fact that they suddenly had some extra cash after the traffic incident in March."

"Did you talk to them?" Alex demanded impatiently.

"That's the bad news. I couldn't."

"You can't locate them?"

"Oh, I can locate them, all right," Chris said, and Alex heard unhappy resignation in her voice. "They're dead, Captain."

Alex stopped pacing. "What?"

"They found both of them shot on July twenty-seventh last year," Chris reported unhappily. "In a vehicle, dead on the scene. Sherill Heights caught the case. I talked to the primary detective on the case. He put it up to a drug deal gone bad. No witnesses, and no suspects."

"Oh, my God, Chris," Alex exclaimed. "Our perp hired them, and after David's murder he or she made sure they couldn't talk."

"That's my read too, Captain. Our guy didn't need them anymore, since he'd gotten rid of St. Clair by then, so he made sure to cut loose the deadweight."

Alex's mind was racing. "Any information on the weapon used?"

"Twenty-two, not a known gun. But I checked, and District Attorney Bradford owns a Colt twenty-two caliber revolver. You don't think he'd be stupid enough to use his own gun, do you?"

"Hell," Alex said forcefully. "We have to get a warrant now."

"I thought you'd say that. Do we have a clue where the gun might be?"

Alex thought a moment. "He keeps it at his house, at his desk. Or at least he used to. I just wish I knew why—" She stopped suddenly for a moment, then said softly, "Oh, my God."

"Captain?" Chris asked into the silence.

"Chris," she said abruptly, "did you check out the background information on Tony's girlfriend yet?"

"No, I've been running down Chavez's two guys all day."

Alex told her what she wanted her to do. Chris said, "I'll go over there now. It'll take me a little while in rush hour traffic."

"Call me on my cell as soon as you get anything. I have an appointment with the district attorney in ten minutes."

"What?" Chris demanded sharply. "I don't think that's a good idea, Captain. He's looking pretty good as our perp."

Alex said, "He called me this afternoon as I was getting ready to go into this meeting and wanted to talk about the charges against soon-to-be former Detective Fullerton. Don't worry. I'm meeting at his office, not his house."

"Yeah, but it's after hours," Chris still sounded unhappy.

"Chris, relax. He's not going to shoot me himself, and certainly not in his office. Maybe I'll get some information that will help us. Call me as soon as you know something, I mean it. I'll take the call even if I'm still with him. If I don't pick up, then you can worry, all right?"

"If you say so," Chris grumbled. "I'll call you soon."

As Alex walked across the street to the DA's offices, she tested her earlier moment of insight with logic. She hoped that Chris might be able to confirm her suspicions very soon.

It frustrated her that there was a clue she should have seen from the beginning, the one CJ had given her if she'd only known what she was looking at when she saw the note.

Or, rather, the envelope.

Still deep in thought, she took the elevator to Tony's office, on the fourth floor. He had the corner office and his door was open. She stepped into the doorway and saw him at his desk, sitting as if he were waiting for her.

He looked up and said stiffly, "Alex."

She took another step into the office, and the door was pushed shut behind her. She turned to look into the barrel of the gun aimed at her chest. Tony's twenty-two, she thought, momentarily light-headed from shock. She lifted her eyes from the gun to the woman holding it.

"Captain Ryan," the woman said. "So nice of you to join us. Put your gun on the floor, and do it very, very carefully."

Alex eased her Glock from her holster and put it flat on the floor.

"Good," her captor instructed. "Get up, Tony."

"Why are you doing this?" Tony demanded, his voice was shaking.

The woman snapped her eyes to Tony before returning to watch Alex. "Shut up and get over here."

He got up and came around the desk, and she backed up a couple of steps to keep them both covered.

Alex glanced at Tony. He was pale and sweating. *She's had him here for a while*, she thought. His call to her had apparently been a setup to get Alex to the office.

"Put your handcuffs on him," the woman ordered Alex. "And do a good job, because I'll check."

Tony turned pleading eyes to Alex. She said to him, "Turn around."

She cuffed him behind his back, loosening the cuffs a little to keep them from digging into his wrists. When she was finished, the woman pulled on the handcuffs to test them, then pushed Tony down onto the carpet, first onto his knees, then onto his stomach.

"If you move," she said to him, "I'll shoot you dead. Believe me, I will. I don't need you anymore."

Tony made an awful noise, half groan, half choking.

The woman said to Alex, "Sit down. Put your hands on the arms of the chair and leave them there."

Alex did as instructed, and the woman moved around to sit in Tony's desk chair. The woman wiped Tony's revolver clean and left it on his desktop, holding Alex's much larger Glock semiautomatic on Alex and Tony as she sat behind his desk.

"Now," the woman said in a friendly voice, "that's better. We can have a little chat."

From behind her, Tony moaned, "Sue, baby, why are you doing this?"

"I told you to shut up!" the woman said, suddenly furious. "I've had to put up with getting fucked by you for months. We're done now, so shut up!"

"Sue—" he whined again.

Alex interrupted. "It's not Sue, is it?" she said calmly. "You've changed in the last decade, and your hair is a different color, but I do recognize you. You used Sue Davis as an alias but I know your name. It's Laurel Halliday, right?"

Her mercurial mood changed again and she smiled. "Yes," she said, almost friendly. "I'm not surprised Belle showed you pictures of us. You saw how happy we were together."

The general rule in crisis situations, Alex knew, was not to engage in dialogue with people who were mentally ill or had personality disorders. It gave them a sense of power and control, and that was the last thing Alex needed the woman to have, not with Alex's own gun pointed at her.

But sooner or later, something would happen. A cleaner would knock on the door, or a late-working staff member might stop by. At worst, Chris Andersen knew where she was and would eventually come looking for her. All Alex had to do was keep them all here alive and unhurt long enough for something good to happen. That meant that she had to talk, and let Laurel talk as well.

She tried to breathe away the knot in her stomach. Then, testing the limits of what Laurel would tolerate, she sat back a little and deliberately crossed her legs, leaving her hands motionless. Laurel's eyes narrowed but she didn't move the gun.

"You were smart about it," Alex said, trying to sound as relaxed as if she were safely in one of her own interrogation rooms. "Getting the two young men to do your dirty work for you was a very good idea."

"You think so?" Laurel sneered a little, and Alex wondered how a woman so pretty could make her face look so ugly. "They certainly botched the job badly enough."

"That depends on what you were trying to accomplish," Alex continued. "If you were trying to scare CJ, you certainly accomplished that."

"Don't call her that!" Laurel spat at her. "Her *name* is Belle. You don't even know her name, do you? What the hell she saw in you, I'll never know. What are you? You're not beautiful, you're not rich, you're a civil servant, for the love of God. Obviously you were just someone to fuck her while she was waiting for me to come back to her."

Grandiose expectations, exaggerated self-importance, thinks the world revolves around her. Narcissism? Alex knew she was guessing at a diagnosis without enough professional expertise.

"But she uses CJ in Colorado," Alex said. "And that's where you made a mistake. The envelope you sent her said 'Lieutenant C. St. Clair' on it. Anyone who'd met her here would have used both of her initials. Christabelle Johnson, old family names. Belle is from Christabelle, that's why you used just her first initial."

Apparently, making a mistake didn't fit into Laurel's world view, so she ignored Alex's remark and said smugly, "She certainly jumped when I told her too, didn't she? She was always so compliant." She smirked at Alex and said, "You should have seen her when she was nineteen. My God, she was gorgeous and so very innocent. She was a virgin when I first took her, did you know that? Sweet as strawberry pie. I believe she thought I'd invented sex." Laurel gave a pleasant laugh. "She would do anything I asked her, anything I could think of to do to her. She could not get enough of me."

Alex felt her fingers tighten on the chair, forcibly reminding herself that Laurel was trying to provoke her. *Stay calm. Breathe.* "You haven't been together in almost twelve years," Alex said, to see what that would get to her.

"She always knew I'd come back for her," Laurel said with casual assurance. "I had a few other women to get out of my system first, but she has always belonged to me. You think she's yours, but she never was. Belle has *always* belonged to me."

Alex studied Laurel, trying not to look at or think too much about the gun pointed at her. She truly was a lovely woman, blond hair with honey highlights, an almost delicate face, beautiful skin. But her eyes glittered with—what was it? Jealousy? Greed? Lust? Hatred? All of them, perhaps.

"Why?" Alex asked her. "Why, after all this time?"

Laurel showed her even white teeth in a grimace of frustration. "She disappeared on me. She was so upset about losing me after I broke things off with her that she just left Georgia and went away."

Interesting revisionist history there, Alex thought.

"I couldn't find her," Laurel continued, "not until I acquired quite a lot of money. Then it was just a matter of hiring someone to track her down."

Alex said, carefully, "It's really your brother's money, isn't it?"

The flash of anger was back. "It's *my* money now, you know. God knows I earned it. I did the research for him, did you know that? I practically wrote the damn book for him, but who gets the big contract? Jackson was never going to take advantage of what money could buy a person. And did he put my name on the book? He did not. So I made sure the money ended up where it belonged."

Alex felt her hands tighten on the chair again. "He committed suicide."

Laurel laughed. "Oh, I assure you he did no such thing. But my experience with police officers is that they're just pretty damned stupid."

Ignoring the jibe, Alex said flatly, "Are you saying you killed him?"

She shrugged casually. "Ungrateful bastard. He deserved it. And he was in my way, after all."

"Just like those two boys you shot last July," Alex ventured carefully. Now that she had Laurel in a confessional mood, she wanted to get as much as she could. Thankfully, Tony would be able to confirm these revelations.

"They were incompetent idiots." She spat out the words. "They deserved what they got. They never had any idea I would just shoot them, the morons. I paid them good money to get you out of my way, and they murdered some poor idiot instead and you come out without a scratch." She snorted. "Can you believe they were apparently so high on something that afternoon that they forgot that I told them that 'Alex' was a woman? Fucking idiots. They shot the only man there and thought they were following instructions. It was actually a pleasure blowing what little brains they had out of their heads."

Anger pounded through Alex's head, but she forced it down again. "You must have had a lot of influence on Tony to get access to his files, and then convince him to give them deferred prosecutions."

There was a strangled moan from the floor behind her.

Laurel laughed again, unpleasantly. "All he did there was to give me access to his staff. He didn't even know about my two new employees. I just had to use my—influence, let us say, on one of his assistant district attorneys. It was ridiculously easy."

"Influence," Alex said, still drawing her out. *Why hadn't Chris called?* "Did you bribe the guy, threaten him with Tony's displeasure, or make promises?"

"None of those. Haven't you figured out yet that all men think with their dicks? I just let him fuck me a couple of times."

Tony groaned, "Sue, for God's sake!"

Laurel jumped up from behind the desk and lifted the gun his direction. "If you don't shut the fuck up, I'm going to shoot your miserable excuse for a cock off. If I can find it. Now shut up!"

Alex looked at Laurel's gun hand, her finger tight against the trigger. She drew a deep breath.

At the movement, Laurel swiveled the gun back to her. "Don't you start thinking I won't kill him," she threatened Alex. "I don't need him anymore, so I would just love to shut him up on a permanent basis. And I'll be sure to use your gun to do it."

Alex said slowly, "It must have been tough on you, being a lesbian, sleeping with all these men to get what you want."

Laurel, somewhat mollified, sat down again, still keeping the gun trained on Alex. "What it was mostly was goddamned boring. I just don't get the attraction, you know? It's always about their dicks. Get it hard, slam it in, or suck it off. And they always think because they're getting off, that you are too. God, they're idiots. I actually feel sorry for straight women. Now, fucking with a woman, on the other hand…"

Laurel raked her eyes up and down Alex's body, and Alex suppressed a shudder. "Sorry we don't have time, or I'd be happy to demonstrate just why women are so very much better."

Tony made a choking sound, and this time Laurel laughed at him. "Getting off on that one, aren't you, dickhead? Well, think about this one for a minute. She and I have both fucked you, and we both prefer women. Figure it out."

Alex wanted Laurel's focus away from Tony. She knew that Laurel really believed him to be expendable, and he was in more danger at this moment than she was herself.

"So if things are working out so well for you," Alex said conversationally, "what are you doing now?"

Laurel gave a little sigh of frustration. "One way or another, you selfish bitch, you have been a real pain in the ass. First you wouldn't just die like a good little girl so I could show up and reassure Belle that she hadn't lost anything worth having, and now you're sending one of your minions out to check up on me. That won't do at all."

Chris's visit to her condo yesterday, Alex thought. Laurel found out about it and realized we were closing in. As if on cue, she felt the cell phone vibrate in her pocket. She ignored it.

"I see," Alex said. "So you're going to kill us, Tony and me, is that it? Or is this going to look like some murder/suicide set-up?"

Chris will know better. Once she identifies Sue Davis as Laurel, she'll know who the perp is. Of course, that won't do me much good. She had a flash of sorrow at the thought of CJ coming back for her funeral. *Can't let that happen.*

"I'm not ready to kill you. Not quite yet," Laurel said.

Then Alex finally understood. She slowly uncrossed her leg, then crossed the other one instead. "I know what you want," she told Laurel.

The glittering eyes narrowed dangerously. "I'm sure you do. She belongs to me, and I'm going to have her back. Now, where in the hell is she?"

"What's the matter?" Alex said. "Did you lose track of her again? That was careless of you."

The gun edged closer. "Don't fuck with me. You like to go running, right? You would be amazed about how much information I know about you from lover boy over there. How far do you think you'll be able to run if I put a couple of bullets in your knees? Where did she go?"

Alex's stomach tightened in fear, but she said mildly, "It was your idea to send her away."

"Fuck you!" Laurel exploded. "She was supposed to *leave you*, not fucking *disappear!*"

Alex said, "You've been looking for her, I imagine."

"You were supposed to lead me to her. Why the hell do you think I've been hanging around here for months, screwing lawyer dick over there, waiting for you to slip up? I'm tired of waiting, you stupid cunt. How much do you think Belle would like you if I just cut up your face?" She fingered Tony's letter opener with her free hand. "I might actually enjoy that."

"You don't know her very well," Alex replied as calmly as she could, "if you think that would make any difference to her."

Laurel surged over the desktop toward her, spittle gathering in the corner of her mouth. "Don't *you* tell me I don't know her!" she was yelling. "*Nobody* knows her except me, understand? No one! She belongs to me, and you're going to tell me where she is!"

"No," Alex said, her voice still cool. "I'm not."

"The hell you're not!" she screamed. "You want me to shove this gun between your legs and pull the trigger? Tell me!"

She pushed the gun almost into Alex's face. *No more time*, Alex thought. No time to wait for Chris, or anything else.

She looked at her own gun, inches away from her nose. Laurel should have stayed with Tony's revolver, she thought.

Alex pushed the gun barrel away and dove for the floor, pulling her backup weapon from her ankle holster as she rolled.

Laurel frantically pulled the trigger of the Glock, but nothing happened. Apparently Laurel had never used a semiautomatic with a safety before.

The safety was still on.

Alex rolled onto her back, bringing her gun hand up as she watched Laurel fumbling with the safety catch. "Put the gun down!" Alex yelled at her.

Laurel's thumb found the safety and pushed it off. She aimed the gun at Alex.

Alex fired first.

Behind her, Tony screamed into the carpet.

Alex watched Laurel stagger back toward the desk chair, gripping her right arm. The Glock dropped with a heavy thud onto the desk. Laurel tried to use her right hand to find the gun again, but her muscles didn't seem to be working. Alex got to her feet and snatched both guns from the desktop, getting them out of Laurel's reach.

Laurel was screaming, incoherent bellows of pain mixed with obscenities. Alex scooped up Tony's phone, keeping her gun on Laurel, and punched in nine-one-one.

CHAPTER TWENTY

As Alex prepared to make the turn to merge onto the Valley Highway, she stopped at the traffic light and punched in the code for her sister's home telephone number.

"Alex," Nicole answered. "It's late for you to be calling. Everything all right?"

"Yes," Alex answered. "Do me a favor, will you? Don't watch the ten o'clock news when it comes on in a couple of minutes. I'm on my way to your house."

"What?" Nicole's voice was sharp. "Why? What's happened?"

"It's not bad news, Nic," Alex said gently. "But I want to tell you in person. The newscasts never get it quite right."

"Get what right? Alex, what happened?"

Alex sighed into the phone. "Nicole, for once would you just do as I ask you? You can wait twenty minutes until I get there. Charlie's asleep, right?"

"Of course," Nicole said, and Alex could hear her trying to calm down. "You're sure everything is all right?"

"I'm sure. I'll see you soon."

Alex rolled down her window and let the cool air wash away some of her fatigue. It always amazed her how quickly a shooting incident could happen, and how long it took to clean up afterward. She decided at that moment that she would be sleeping in Nicole's guest room tonight. After this conversation, she knew she wouldn't have the energy to drive back home to the condo again.

And if she stayed at Nicole's tonight, she could have a drink when she got there, which was sounding like a better and better idea.

* * *

Nicole had the gas fireplace going, and it felt good after the chilling ride to the far south suburbs. Nicole took her jacket and asked, "Are you staying tonight?"

"Yes, I'd like to."

"Good," Nicole said, and without another word got them both a scotch on the rocks.

They sat in front of the fireplace a couple of minutes without talking. Alex took a drink and felt the liquor wind a dark path to her stomach. Finally, Nicole said quietly, "There's blood on your shirt cuff."

Alex looked down in surprise. "Sorry. I didn't see it."

"I assumed not," Nicole said, a little dryly. After a moment, she added quietly, "This is about David, isn't it?"

Alex turned to her in surprise. "Yes. How did you know?"

"Sisterly intuition, I suppose. Did you find the man who murdered him?"

"We found the person responsible, yes."

Nicole's face twisted a little in pain. "Is he in jail?" she asked. "Or," she looked down at the tiny bloodstain again and choked out, "Or did you kill him, Alex?"

Alex set her glass on the coffee table and took Nicole's hand. "There were two men who did the actual shooting," she began. "The person who hired them to go to the park that day killed them herself a couple of weeks later. They've been dead for months, Nic."

"And the person who hired them? A woman?" Nicole's voice rose. "It wasn't—it couldn't have had anything to do with David."

This comfort, at least, Alex could give her sister. "It had nothing to do with him," Alex reassured her. "David didn't do anything wrong, Nic. It was me they were trying to kill that day. If it's anyone's fault, it's mine."

Nicole stared at her, the reflection of the flames dancing on one side of her face. "My God," she said. "My God, Alex. Was it someone you'd arrested in the past, or what?"

"No," Alex said. "It's a lot more complicated than that."

Nicole said, "In that case, I'm going to need another drink."

When she returned to the couch, Alex could see that she had composed herself a little, as if steeling herself for the rest of the story. "Tell me," she said quietly.

Alex sighed. "The woman who hired them—the same two men who ran me off the road last year, by the way—was CJ's former lover. She wanted me dead so she could come back into CJ's life. When the two attempts didn't work, she killed her accomplices and sent the note to CJ, telling her to leave me or she'd make another attempt. That's why CJ left, Nicole. She really was trying to keep me safe."

Nicole stared at her. "That's insane."

"Yes. Well, the woman behind all of this is some kind of crazy."

"Why didn't you want me to watch the news tonight?"

Alex leaned back against the sofa and closed her eyes a moment. "Because I had to shoot her," she said. "We were in Tony's office, and there were a couple of local film crews outside when we finally got out of there. I just didn't want you to hear about it on the news."

She explained everything that had happened. Nicole sat a long time, listening and staring into the fire. When she was finished, Nicole asked softly, "Is she dead, Alex? Did you kill her?"

Alex couldn't tell if Nicole was hoping for a yes or a no. She replied, "They teach police officers not to use our weapons unless we're prepared to kill someone. You always aim for the middle of the torso, if you can, it's the biggest target. But she was moving, and I was on the floor—well, anyway, my bullet shattered her upper arm, apparently severed an artery. She's going to live, because we got her to the hospital right away, but the doctors don't think they can save her arm. She's in surgery now."

Nicole looked deeply into her whiskey. "What will happen to her? We'll have to go through a trial, I suppose."

"It's possible, but not very likely. And I don't know what the shrinks are going to say, but she's really crazy, Nic. She may or may not be competent to stand trial. If she's not, they'll commit her to the state mental health institute at Pueblo. She could end up at Pueblo anyway, if there is a trial and she's found not guilty by reason of insanity." Alex added, "And don't worry. Even if she does go to trial, she pretty much confessed to everything she'd done, not just to me, but to Tony as well. She took his gun and apparently used it to kill her two co-conspirators. We're beginning to gather the rest of the evidence we would need to convict her if there is a trial. She will not walk away from this, I promise you that."

Nicole finished her drink and sat back. "What a waste," she finally said. "David died because some insane woman thought CJ still loved her."

Hesitantly, Alex said, "I have to say something to you. I was afraid to tell you all of this."

"Why? Because it would bring everything back?"

"Partly. But mostly because I'm afraid you would, I don't know, blame CJ for this somehow. If she weren't in my life, if I hadn't married her, David wouldn't be dead right now."

Nicole looked at her steadily. "I never want to hear that again," she said firmly. "This wasn't your fault, this wasn't CJ's fault, it was no one's fault except for this woman and the people she used. Although," she added bitterly, "you'll forgive me if

I save a sliver of blame for your idiot of an ex-husband. How could he be so stupid? Who dates a woman for months and months and can't figure out that she's crazy?"

Alex tried a smile. "Clearly, he has lousy taste in women."

Nicole glared at her. "Stop that. He deserves whatever humiliation he gets from this."

"Nic…" Alex gently touched her arm. "Don't worry. He had what was about the worst couple of hours of his life today. He was almost as hysterical as Laurel by the time I released him from the handcuffs. The fact that I was the one who saved his sorry ass is probably the worst part of all, at least for him."

Nicole said sadly, "It's all terrible. Don't misunderstand, I'm glad you caught her, but it doesn't change anything. David's still gone. Everyone's suffered from this, you and me and Charlie and CJ. Oh, my God, Alex. Does this mean she can come home?"

"Yes," Alex said. "If I can find her. And if she wants to come home."

"What? Why wouldn't she?" Nicole demanded.

"I don't know. Lots of reasons. Guilt, for one thing. She was under a lot of pressure when someone threatened me and she wasn't thinking clearly. She probably regrets that. She may be angry with me for not resolving this earlier, for leaving her alone, wherever she is. Or maybe—she might have a new life, Nic. She might have someone new."

"You don't really believe that could be true."

"No. I don't know. I don't know what to think. I won't know anything until I find her."

"It will be all right, honey," she said, but Alex heard Nicole's voice starting to shake. "It will be."

Alex saw her face crumple. Alex moved in to take Nicole into her arms as the tears started. Alex had known this was coming, the reaction to the finality of David's death, now that the reasons were known. She'd spent many hours since last July trying to comfort her sister, and Alex wondered if this would be the last time Nicole would cry like this for David.

Probably not, she thought in the next moment. Sorrow has a long lifetime.

* * *

"So," Elaine Wheeler said, "what are you going to do now?"

Alex looked for a moment at the chessboards neatly lined up on the glass bookshelf in Wheeler's office, and wondered why today one of them seemed to be frozen in mid-game, the pieces in a pattern she didn't recognize.

"I'm going to Georgia," Alex answered her. "I don't know how long I'll be gone, but I've asked for two weeks' leave. If it takes longer than that, then I'll just have to take more. I'll call you when I get back. I'm going to see someone who I believe knows where CJ is, and I'm going to find her and bring her home."

"Even if she doesn't want to come home?" Wheeler asked, and Alex thought she was trying to keep her voice gentle.

"No," Alex said, trying not to choke on the word. "Of course not. If she doesn't want to come back, of course not. I want her back, but I want her to be happy. If she's happy somewhere else, then…" She couldn't finish.

"I just want you to consider the possibility," Wheeler said.

"I've considered it," Alex said. "Maybe she's moved on. Maybe she'll be too angry with me to come back. But I don't believe it. I can't believe it. She left everyone, everything she knew, for my sake. All I can really believe is that she will walk back into my arms. If she doesn't, then we'll…we'll just deal with that if it happens."

"But you do remember what we talked about before? Even if you find CJ, even if she comes back with you, that's not necessarily the end of the issues between you. We talked about that before."

"I'm very aware of that," Alex answered. "And I am angry with her for leaving. Why didn't she just tell me about the threats? We could have figured it out together. She just took off alone. Didn't she have any faith in me as a detective? Instead she just hides some note in a file and leaves me to figure it out on my own—"

Alex realized her voice was rising and took a moment to take a breath. "I was thinking about asking you something. I know you said you don't normally do marital counseling, but I was wondering if I could call you when I get back and bring CJ here...if she comes home with me. To meet you. Maybe the three of us could talk for a session, at least. Would that be all right?"

Wheeler looked as if she were considering her answer, then with a slight smile she nodded. "Of course. You know I won't break patient confidentiality, but if you want to include CJ in our session so she can understand more about what has been happening with you, that would be up to you. If she wants to see me separately after that, we can discuss that, too. It's fine with me."

"Good. I'd like that, I think."

"And how are you feeling about your trip?"

Alex considered. "About equal parts terrified and hopeful. I don't think it's going to seem real to me until I'm actually in the same room with her again."

Wheeler leaned forward. "Then I hope it goes as well as you're hoping, and the things you fear won't become reality."

"Me too," Alex answered fervently.

CHAPTER TWENTY-ONE

"Mr. Edgarton can see you now," the young woman said to Alex.

Alex was momentarily startled by the soft drawl, almost exactly the same cadence that CJ used. Edgarton's legal assistant was a petite brunette, so Alex wasn't in danger of seeing CJ in her, but the similarity of dialect was disconcerting.

Alex gathered her briefcase and followed the woman into Edgarton's massive office. The law firm was located near Savannah's historical district, which was filled with antebellum mansions and old commercial buildings. Alex had seen a plaque designating the area as a National Historic Landmark, and wished she had time to explore the city CJ grew up in.

Later, she told herself. I'll come back here, someday, with CJ, and let her show me her home. Soon. As soon as I find her.

Roger Edgarton rose from his desk to greet her just inside the door. "Good afternoon," he said. "I'm sorry you had to wait."

"Alex Ryan." She took his hand. He covered her hand with both of his and looked down at her with what she thought was both curiosity and compassion.

"I cannot tell you, Miss Ryan," he said in his deep voice, "how very pleased I am to meet you at last. Belle speaks of you constantly."

Alex felt her throat closing up a little, but managed, "Thank you."

He led her to a rectangular seating area, two oxblood leather couches flanking a wooden coffee table, with matching leather club chairs at either end. She noticed that he took one of the chairs and eased himself into it. She assumed the chairs were easier for him to get out of than the lower, butter-soft couch she sank into.

Edgarton had to be seventy, easily. He had completely white hair, neatly clipped short and parted to show his pink scalp. His cheeks were pink too, so perfectly shaven she assumed he must have someone do it for him every morning. Despite the April heat, he was dressed in a navy suit complete with buttoned vest, and a striped tie. If she had been casting a movie that called for a Southern lawyer, she would have hired him in an instant.

Proudly displayed on the wall over his head was a series of photographs in matching frames. Various young women, and one older woman, in a variety of poses: backyard barbeques, football tailgating parties, dog shows displaying ribbons. Every photo prominently featured at least one handsomely ugly bulldog, fawn-colored, and all of them looking immensely self-satisfied. Alex couldn't help but remark on them.

"I'm guessing you own bulldogs," she ventured.

He smiled, showing teeth that were too white and even to be anything but very expensive dentures.

"Ah, our pride and joy. My wife and I have bred them for many years. Several of them have actually served as the official mascots of the University of Georgia Bulldogs."

"They're very striking animals," Alex said.

Nodding toward yet another photo, Alex said, "And are those young women your daughters?"

"Yes, indeed. Alice and I have three lovely daughters and five grandchildren."

"A nice family," she said. She was impatient, eager to get on with their business, but recognized the need to observe the necessary formalities.

He settled back in his club chair and said, "I suppose we should dispense with the awkward but necessary business of establishing your bona fides."

It took her a moment to realize he was asking for her identification. She opened her briefcase and took out several items. "My police credentials and driver's license," she said, and produced both. "Here's my passport as well."

He examined them closely, and then she gave him a final piece of evidence.

"I thought this might help," she added quietly.

He studied the photograph for a long moment, seeing the picture of Alex and CJ together, a copy of the one from the back of CJ's photo album. He looked up from the picture to Alex's face and smiled again.

"Yes," he said. "I can see that not only are you really who you say you are, but you are Belle's choice as well. She looks very happy in this picture."

"She was happy," Alex said with certainty. "I hope very much that she will be again."

The outer door opened, and the legal assistant entered bearing a tray with pot, saucers and a covered plate. Afternoon tea? Alex thought, This is going to take longer than I thought.

After the teacups were filled and a variety of delicate little cookies was revealed on the plate, Edgarton sat back again in his chair and regarded her over the rim of his cup.

"Belle contacted me shortly after she left Denver," he began, and Alex quelled her impatience. He needed, for whatever reason, to tell her this story, and perhaps she needed to hear it as well.

"She was, well, not to put too fine a point on it, very upset. She wasn't sure at that time where she was going. I, perhaps not surprisingly, urged her to come home, but she, also not surprisingly, refused. Her family has been extremely discourteous to her. How much of that has she told you?"

Alex wasn't sure if this was a test or not, but she answered honestly. "Some of it. I know about the trust fund her grandfather left for her, that you are the trustee, and I also know her parents threw her out when she told them she was a lesbian."

He sipped some tea gravely and said, "She was twenty-three, and the only daughter of a man I regarded as my closest friend in the world. He and I had known each other since we were boys, and I watched him just disintegrate after she left. Belle was very much the pride and joy of her father's life. I will tell you frankly that I care for her almost as much as if she were one of my own daughters, and she was a kind, high-spirited, outgoing and loving young woman. Losing her was most disturbing to her father. When he passed away, I called Lydia, Belle's mother, to urge her to permit Belle to return for the funeral. She adamantly refused to permit it, and Belle, wisely I think, chose not to force the issue."

"I know," Alex said. "We talked about it quite a bit. In the end, she thought it would dishonor her father's memory if she came and her mother made a scene." She omitted a description of how upset CJ had been. Alex had held her as she cried herself to sleep for several nights in a row.

He made a distasteful noise and set down his cup and saucer. "I can reassure you that Lydia St. Clair is, and was, more than capable of making quite a histrionic display. Belle chose sensibly. When she is ready to return to Savannah, please tell her I will arrange for her to visit her father's grave, and I have the program from the funeral as well, should she choose to see it."

"That's very kind of you," Alex said, feeling as if she were beginning to talk as formally as he did.

He waved a blue-veined hand dismissively. "Well, as I said, she's practically one of my own daughters." His dislike of CJ's mother was tacit but clearly understood. "I cannot, I fear, claim the same relationship with Clayton."

"Her brother is still in Savannah?" Alex asked.

"Yes. He is a local dentist. I regret to inform you that he has, I'm afraid, taken after his mother in his unceasing desire to climb higher on the social ladder. There are a number of rumors around him, specifically concerning his, ah, inclination toward young women. He is on wife number three, I think, and he's not quite forty yet."

Alex digested this a moment, dryly amused. When she glanced up to see Edgarton looking at her curiously, she explained, "Sorry. I was thinking about what a judgmental prick...ah, prig he's been about his sister, when he apparently has some issues of his own."

"Indeed." He seemed to appreciate the irony as well. "I fear his ways are coming back to haunt him. He's having quite a bit of difficulty with his own daughter."

Alex felt a little jolt. "I didn't know CJ had a niece," she said.

"Yes. They've never met, obviously, but Belle is most meticulous about birthdays and Christmas. For obvious reasons, I have acted as an intermediary. Clayton disapproves of his sister as much as his mother does."

Alex shook her head wonderingly. There were still a few things she didn't know about CJ, it seemed. She was having trouble controlling her impatience, and, as if sensing that, Edgarton rose and crossed for a moment to his desk, returning with an envelope.

"It is my understanding," he said softly, "that you have resolved the issues that led to Belle leaving nine months ago."

Nine months. Alex did the math and realized with a start that it had been exactly nine months. "Yes," she said simply. "You read the online news reports I referred you to, I assume."

"I did," he said. "And I believe my client's instructions clearly indicate that I should give you this." He handed her a sealed envelope.

It had her name written on it, in CJ's handwriting. Just seeing the words made her feel better.

Edgarton explained, "She sent this to me about a month or so after our initial phone call, and asked me to hold it until you arrived and were able to prove that the situation was resolved."

Alex weighed the envelope in her hand. Was there a letter, an explanation? Or would there be another plea for Alex not to seek her out?

She decided, in the moment before she opened the envelope, that she would have to ignore any request from CJ to leave her alone, if that's what it was this time. She was going to see CJ again if it was humanly possible to do so. If CJ wanted Alex to go away, she would have to tell Alex in person.

Edgarton was watching her, and said at length, "Would you like some privacy, Miss Ryan?"

"No," she said. "It's all right." She tore open the envelope. There was no note, no letter, just a single piece of cardboard. A postcard, she realized after a moment.

On the front of the postcard was a photograph of a one-story, adobe-style building with a sign that said "Palace of the Governors." Alex turned the card over.

The tiny print at the top of the postcard on the address side read, "The historic Palace of the Governors in Santa Fe, New Mexico is the oldest continuously occupied public building in the United States."

There was nothing written in the address section, nor in the space for the message except four numerals separated by a hyphen: 10-20.

CJ, unsure of what was happening, had been very careful. Alex handed the postcard to Edgarton and kept her voice from shaking as she said, "Thank you. I wonder if your assistant could make a plane reservation for me to fly to Albuquerque as soon as possible. I'll need to rent a car and drive up to Santa Fe, I think."

He looked down at the postcard. "Belle is in New Mexico?"

All these months, and CJ had been less than a six-hour drive from Denver. Perhaps she'd wanted to be close, just in case, Alex thought, warming herself with the possibility.

"Yes, she's in Santa Fe," Alex said with certainty.

Edgarton looked puzzled. "How can you be certain of that?"

Alex responded, "The numbers on the card are a ten signal, the radio code most police departments use. A ten-twenty means location. She's telling me where she is."

Alex felt a sudden surge of exhilaration.

She wants me to find her.

CHAPTER TWENTY-TWO

As she sat in the corner of Collected Books, Alex stared at everyone as they entered, ignoring the book on the architecture of New Mexico she held in her hands.

A full week here, and no trace of CJ. No one had heard of her at the Palace of the Governors, now primarily used as a museum. The local police department had no record of her either, which didn't surprise Alex—CJ surely knew how to keep a low profile. No hotel had her registered as a guest. Alex had been to every place she could think of to check. She'd been reduced to staking out the bookstore nearest to the plaza, hoping CJ's insatiable craving for reading material wasn't being fulfilled by her downloading books onto an e-reader.

Every moment since she'd left Georgia, Alex had been thinking about CJ. Had CJ been expecting to see her every day for months? Had she perhaps given up hope that Alex would ever come and find her? Alex had spent so much time recognizing and responding to CJ's emotions over the past three years that not knowing what CJ might have been feeling for so long disoriented her and made her tense.

Alex had spent so much of the last few weeks vacillating between optimism and fear. Elaine Wheeler's words of warning kept returning. Knowing that she and CJ couldn't merely resume their relationship in the same place as they had been when CJ left worried her. What if their marriage had been damaged beyond repair by the havoc wreaked by Laurel Halliday? What if CJ had had a change of heart since leaving? Nine months was a long time, especially without a word of communication between them.

She left because she loved me, Alex repeated to herself. *She'll want to come home for the same reason. All I have to do is find her.*

A few minutes later, a fragment of conversation caught her attention.

"...the most amazing meatloaf I've ever had," a woman one aisle over was saying. "I mean, you expect enchiladas or something, but this was fantastic."

"Seems like an odd thing to order in Santa Fe," the other woman replied.

"Well, the wonderful thing about it was that it was listed as New Mexico meatloaf. It had this kind of spicy red sauce over it, and there were green chiles chopped up in the meatloaf—"

Alex almost sprang from her chair, startling the two women. They couldn't have looked more like tourists, from their massive colorful totes to their apparently brand-new turquoise jewelry.

To calm them, Alex said soothingly, "I'm so sorry to interrupt. That description of the meatloaf sounds wonderful. Where did you have it, may I ask?"

The first woman said, "At the Hotel San Pasquale, where we're staying. It's about two blocks down from the plaza."

Maybe it was a coincidence, but she had to know.

A few minutes later Alex entered the lobby of the Hotel San Pasquale with trepidation. The room was large and decorated in a way that made it look for all the world like she'd entered a monastery. There was what seemed to be a baptismal fountain in the middle of the space, filled with water. At one end was a massive stone fireplace with couches and chairs carefully arranged around it. There were plain plastered walls with crosses and crucifixes hung liberally, some plain wood or iron, others hand-carved and ornate. The registration desk was tucked into one corner of the room behind a wooden counter that looked at least a couple of hundred years old. In the other corner, dominating that half of the lobby, was a huge bar, also wooden, beaten and battered but full of character.

She went to the reception desk and asked to see the manager on duty. When he arrived, she showed him her badge and asked for someplace private to talk.

He led her to a tiny office wedged behind the reception desk, just about big enough for the two of them to sit down, almost knee to knee. He was wearing a white shirt and black vest, which apparently served as formal management attire for a New Mexico hotel. The armholes of the vest were too big for he was perhaps the slimmest man Alex had ever seen, his sleeves showing delicate wrists and long, bony fingers. His face was thin too, his cheekbones almost knife-sharp.

"What is this about?" he asked her, frowning.

"I'm looking for someone, someone I believe may be working at the hotel, probably in the kitchen. My information is she has been here some months."

He was already shaking his head. "We don't have anyone like that," he said firmly. "And you still haven't told me what this is about."

Alex had thought this through carefully on the drive into Santa Fe. "The woman I'm looking for is a witness in a case in Colfax," she explained. "She hasn't done anything wrong, and she's not in trouble of any kind. I just need to speak with her."

It was only a slight stretch of the truth, after all. CJ had certainly witnessed the shooting that had left David dead, and Alex did most urgently need to speak with her, even if the two facts weren't exactly related.

"You're not here to arrest her or anything?"

"Nothing like that."

"We still don't have anyone who's been here less than eighteen months," he said.

Alex tried to curb her anxiety. It had just been a hunch, after all. She persisted. "I still have every reason to think she's here, or has been here."

"What's her name?"

Another delicate point. It seemed unlikely to Alex that CJ would register under her own name, since she was being careful about being traced. Alex responded, "I'm not sure which of several names she might be using. Her full name is Christabelle Johnson St. Clair."

His frown changed into a more wary look. "Maybe you could describe her," he ventured.

Alex felt her pulse flutter. *He knows something.* "She's Caucasian, thirty-six years old, five ten, about one sixty-five, pale complexion, green eyes. She's a natural redhead, but she may have changed her hair color. She talks with a bit of a Southern dialect." Suddenly she remembered the photo she'd shown to Edgarton, and dug it out of her briefcase. "This photo is about three years old," she said, showing him the picture.

He took it with his slender fingers and stared at it a moment. Finally he said, "This is you, isn't it? In the picture with her."

"Yes," Alex admitted.

"This doesn't sound like you're looking for a witness," he said, with a touch of belligerence. "I think you should leave."

The change in attitude surprised Alex. Perhaps she shouldn't have shown him the photo, but she was certain that he'd recognized CJ and was now, for some reason, trying to protect her.

Alex said slowly, "Everything I've told you is true. It's also true that I have a personal relationship with her, and that I need to talk to her."

He stood up, and in the small room he seemed to tower over her. "I mean it," he said firmly. "Leave, or I'll call the police and we'll have you escorted from the premises."

Alex held up her hands in a mollifying gesture. "Please give me one more minute," she said, trying not to sound as desperate as she felt. If he threw her out, how long would it be before she could connect with CJ?

He sat down again, reluctantly, and continued to glare at her as she thought frantically. Why was he so defensive?

A thought occurred to her, and she took a deep breath, trying to figure out how much to gamble. At last she said, "I think I know what happened here. She came to you and explained that she was concerned about someone, someone who might be looking for her, and you shouldn't reveal that she was here just in case that person was dangerous for her. Is that about right?"

He sat back wordlessly, but she could see from his expression that she was close to the mark. Carefully, she continued, "She was telling you the truth. She was in some danger, but I'm here to bring her home. What can I tell you that will convince you that I'm the person she wants to see, not the one she was in hiding from?"

The manager continued to stare at her for a minute, then said, "How do I know you're really a police officer?"

Alex exhaled, back on firmer ground. She handed him her card. "You don't have to take my word for it. Go online and find the home page for the Colfax Colorado Police Department. There's a link to a page for the command staff. My photo is on the page. If you like, you can call someone in the department and have them confirm my identity to you."

He took her card and left without another word. In the five minutes before he returned, Alex felt as if she'd lived a lifetime or two.

When he returned, he said, "All right. You are who you say you are. But that doesn't necessarily mean it's safe for her to see you."

Alex said, "Call her. Tell her I'm here. I'll meet her in this office, in the lobby, in your bar, anywhere public you want to name. I just need to see her." She met his eyes and added softly, "Please. I need to see her."

He gave her one last, appraising look, and then said, "She's the Assistant Catering Manager."

Alex was nearly sick with relief. "Okay," she said.

He continued, "Christa Johnson is the name she gave us. She's in the kitchen now. I'll take you back there."

Alex felt as if her heart would beat out of her chest as he led her down a hall, past the small restaurant, empty in the midafternoon sunlight, and through a pair of swinging doors.

The kitchen was filled with stainless steel counters, the floor covered with slip-resistant mats. Everyone she could hear seemed to be speaking Spanish while they were cleaning up workstations or doing food prep, chopping or stirring. The man nearest her was stuffing green chiles into chicken breasts.

Beside her the manager was looking around for CJ, but Alex saw her right away, as if her eyes could see only the woman she sought. Her heart lurched against her breastbone.

CJ was standing with her back to them, talking to an Hispanic man who was gesturing over a large pot on the cooktop. She couldn't hear what they were saying over the other conversations and clatter in the kitchen, but as she watched, CJ took a spoon from the stainless metal canister next to the stove and dipped it into the pot. She tasted whatever it was, and the discussion resumed.

CJ had changed her hair, cutting it above her shoulders and coloring it darker, almost to auburn, but Alex knew her without seeing her face, without a moment's doubt. The shape of her was the same. Alex knew intimately the arch of waist into hip, the curve of her backside. She was wearing black trousers and a white, long-sleeved shirt with the sleeves rolled up. On her left hand, the hand holding the spoon, Alex saw the flash of the diamond on her ring finger.

Warmth surged into Alex's chest. CJ was wearing her wedding ring still, the ring Alex had given her. She still belongs to me, Alex thought in quiet exhilaration.

The manager had spotted her, and began to call out, but Alex stopped him with a hand on his arm. Instead she came up behind CJ and said, "I'm here."

CJ turned quickly, and the spoon fell with a clatter onto the metal countertop. Alex drank her in, thirsty for the sight of her face.

She looks tired, was Alex's first impression. The pale skin had dark smudges under her lower lashes, the lines around her eyes seemed more pronounced, as if she had aged too quickly. But her eyes were still the same vivid green, and as she met Alex's gaze, the light in them seemed to flare like fireworks.

"Alex," she breathed. "Oh, my God, Alex. Are you real?"

Whatever Alex had planned to say seemed far away as she took one more step toward her and said only, "I'm real."

CJ leaned toward her, then stopped herself, obviously aware of her surroundings. Behind Alex, the manager asked, nervously, "Christa, are you okay?"

"Yes, yes," CJ managed. "Ramón, I need five minutes. We'll be on the patio, all right?"

Still worried, he said, "Sure, of course. I just wanted to make sure it was okay for me to bring her back here. If you want me to make her leave…"

CJ tore her eyes away from Alex long enough to say to him reassuringly, "It's fine, Ramón. Thank you. I'll be back in a few minutes."

* * *

The patio was empty, the iron tables and chairs neatly aligned after the lunch crowd had disappeared. Blue- and white-striped umbrellas with the hotel name emblazoned on them shaded most of the tabletops. The patio was surrounded by a low adobe wall covered with some trailing plants with small yellow flowers brightening the spring afternoon.

As soon as they were alone, CJ turned to Alex and murmured, "I can't believe you're really here."

Alex moved into her arms. "Oh, God, sweetheart. I was afraid I'd never see you again."

CJ hugged her so tightly Alex could feel CJ's body trembling. Alex moved her hand to CJ's lower back and rubbed her lightly.

"I'm here," she said, over and over. "I'm here, baby."

Alex turned her head into CJ's neck and inhaled. She smelled faintly of wood smoke and chile peppers, but underneath was the scent that meant CJ to her, the sweet fragrance of flowers after a spring rain. Alex took in the perfume of CJ, drew it into her lungs, into her bones, let it settle into her skin.

After a couple of minutes, CJ finally released her, brushing back a single escaping tear. "I'm sorry I only have a couple of minutes," she said. "I have to get back to work."

"Do you?" Alex said with low intensity.

CJ seemed to withdraw from her, just a little. "I do," she said. "They're depending on me. I'm going to be late tonight, and unfortunately I have to be back pretty early in the morning. I'll be done after lunch tomorrow."

Alex frowned in distress. "Sweetheart, I understand you feel responsible, but…"

CJ stepped back farther and lifted a shaking hand. "Alex, please," she managed. "I do have to work."

"No, you don't," Alex said, more forcefully than she intended. *What was going on?*

"I can't just walk away from my responsibilities, you should understand that," CJ said, her eyes troubled. "And I…I need some time to deal with this."

Alex searched her face, trying to understand. "Deal with what?" she demanded. "It's over, and I've come to take you home. What is there to deal with?"

"Alex, please try to understand," CJ was pleading with her.

The pain felt like a hard punch to the stomach. She'd told herself over and over that Dr. Wheeler might be right, that the road back might be difficult, but seeing the reality of it in the anguish of CJ's eyes was more than she could bear.

"What do you want me to do?" Alex whispered. "Just go away and leave you?"

"No," CJ said softly. "Just…I just need time to talk to you, and we don't have it now." She reached into her pocket and pulled out a keycard. "I've been living here, in the hotel, room four eleven. Why don't you go upstairs? I'll come up as soon as I can tonight. Did you drive down from Colfax?"

Alex took the card and answered, "No, I rented a car in Albuquerque. I flew out from Savannah this morning."

"Oh. Of course." Her expression softened. "How is Roger?"

"Fine. He's fine. But he's worried about you. As is everyone we know. CJ, please—"

CJ lifted a hand to stop her. "Don't. We'll talk later, okay? I really have to go."

She walked away. Alex stood on the patio staring after her, clutching the keycard in her fingers so tightly her hand began to hurt.

* * *

After getting her overnight bag from the rental car, Alex went upstairs to CJ's room. It had two windows looking out on the street in front of the hotel. Alex went over to look out. The narrow sidewalks had people filling them, but they weren't nearly as busy as they would be when tourist season kicked off in a couple of months, she supposed.

The maid had been here already, and Alex smiled a little at the neatly made bed. Probably CJ's idea of heaven, she thought, somebody to come in to clean up her room and make her bed every day.

The next moment she flinched at the thought. CJ wasn't happy, Alex knew that. She looked exhausted and worn, and she wasn't acting naturally. Alex understood why CJ had been miserable—God knew Alex herself had been anguished for months.

It hadn't been just their separation, but the reasons for it that had caused Alex so much pain. All that time not knowing why, wondering what she had done wrong, only to discover that it was someone else who had caused it all.

Irrationally, Alex resented CJ for a moment. The months that Alex had had no idea what had happened, CJ had known, and hadn't called her, hadn't even sent her one lousy email.

She sat down heavily on the side of the bed and tried to relax. CJ was protecting her, Alex reminded herself. And for all the pain of uncertainty Alex had endured, at least Alex had still had her work, her family, her friends. CJ had had no one, nothing, except her fear for Alex's safety, to keep her company.

What was CJ feeling? It was driving her to distraction, not knowing. Before this, she'd almost always known exactly what CJ was thinking, and now not knowing frightened her. Restlessly, Alex got up and spent three minutes unpacking, putting her toiletry case in the bathroom, hanging her sweater up in the tiny closet.

The closet had another of CJ's uniforms, still in the bag from wherever she had it laundered, a pair of jeans, some shirts. There were only three pairs of shoes jumbled on the floor of the closet: a pair of plain black oxfords, spare work shoes she figured, tennis shoes and a pair of sandals. Alex looked down at them and mused that having only four pairs of shoes was undoubtedly a new adult record for CJ.

She finished unpacking and put her bag in the closet to get it out of the way. The room looked like a pretty standard hotel room, nothing personal or homey about it. CJ had the clock and telephone on the nightstand on her side of the bed, to Alex's right as she stood at the foot of the king-sized bed looking down at it. Alex wondered if CJ was paying for the room, or more likely staying here as part of her package as the Assistant Catering Manager.

Catering Manager. Alex shook her head. She should have figured that CJ would get a job where she could both talk to people and work with food all day. It surprised Alex that it hadn't occurred to her that CJ would be working, but it made sense. What else was she going to do with herself without a job? After all, CJ might not have known how long she'd have to be away. And it would have been impossible for her to pass a background check so that she could work as a police officer, especially using only part of her name.

She looked around again, and noticed something on the nightstand she hadn't seen before. Crossing to that side, she picked up a single framed photograph.

CJ must have had the picture on her phone or laptop, and had had it printed and framed. It had been taken at Christmas, the

Christmas before CJ left. David had taken it, Alex remembered suddenly. Charlie was proudly displaying the new bicycle he'd just received from his aunts, and Nicole was with him, smiling down at him. Alex was standing with CJ behind them, hugging for the camera. They all looked happy, giddy almost.

Will we ever be that happy again? She couldn't stop herself from asking the question.

But she tried to comfort herself with the thought that CJ had looked at this picture every morning before she got up, and every night before she turned out the lights. She had been trying to hold on to her family, trying to remember love and life and hope while she was in exile from them.

The photo blurred in Alex's vision.

CHAPTER TWENTY-THREE

It was almost midnight before Alex heard a knock on the door. She got up from the chair, where she'd been staring out the window at the city lights, her book unread in her lap.

She checked the peephole, then opened the door to CJ.

"Sorry." CJ smiled ruefully. "I gave you my card and forgot I'd need it to get back in. I'm sure I woke you up."

Alex, dressed in T-shirt and shorts, said, "Not hardly." How on earth could CJ think Alex would be able to sleep?

CJ lifted an eyebrow. Alex noticed that CJ had dyed her brows as well, to match her new, darker hair color. It was a good job, done no doubt in some expensive salon, but Alex preferred her natural shade of red.

Alex locked the door and said, "You look exhausted."

CJ went wearily into the room and sat down to take off her shoes. "I am. We had a rehearsal dinner in the meeting room tonight and the food was not spicy enough for the bride's family and much too spicy for the groom's family." She shook her head tiredly, and added lightly, "I give the marriage two years, tops."

Alex sat down on the bed across from her. "I bet you sorted it all out."

"As well as possible," CJ admitted. "We couldn't do anything about the tamales themselves, but we split the green chile to smother them in half, thinned one pot with some more stock and dumped a lot more Hatch chiles in the second. That seemed to satisfy everyone except the groom's grandmother, who probably would have found the food too hot if I'd just waved a single poblano over the pot."

Alex looked at her, faintly amused. "Look at you, talking about chiles like a native."

CJ smiled a little, and said, "It's impossible to be a chef in Santa Fe without being fluent in chile peppers, believe me."

Just sitting there, talking about the day with CJ, made Alex's chest ache with longing. She asked, "Has this made you want to open a restaurant?"

CJ slumped back in the chair and laughed a little. The laugh sounded forced to Alex. "Heavens, no," she admitted. "Just the opposite. I love to cook, but running a kitchen is hell on your body. My knees hurt, my feet hurt, my back hurts. And it plays havoc with your hands."

She turned them over for Alex's inspection, and Alex leaned across to take them into her own hands. She felt, rather than heard, a tiny intake of breath from CJ, and she felt the sensation from the touch run up her arms into her own body.

Alex looked down at CJ's palms. Her right hand had a couple of scars, healed knife cuts, which made sense since CJ would have had a knife in her left hand. Her left hand had a nasty burn scar on the fleshy pad below her thumb. It, too, was completely healed, but Alex winced at the sight of it. "Jesus," she exclaimed. "That must have hurt like hell."

CJ said ruefully, "It did. You should have heard me when it happened. I said curse words I don't think I've ever actually used out loud before."

"I'll bet." Alex was still holding her hands, and she ran her thumbs lightly across CJ's palms, caressing the small scars. The next minute, CJ withdrew her hands and stood up.

"I'm really beat," she said. "I'm going to take a quick shower to get the chile aroma off me, and go to bed. I have to be back downstairs by seven."

Alex, disturbed at CJ's matter-of-fact tone of voice, said, "Okay. Is there anything I can do for you?"

CJ hesitated, then said, "No. I'll just be a couple of minutes."

She left and went into the bathroom. A moment later Alex heard the water start in the shower. *Jesus Christ. She can't even get undressed in front of me.*

Alex turned down the bed, stood looking at it, then muttered aloud, "The hell with this."

She stripped off her T-shirt and shorts, then got into the clean sheets naked, on her side of the bed. She listened to CJ turn off the shower after a minute, then heard a brief whirr of a hair dryer. Less than ten minutes after she'd gone into the bathroom, CJ emerged, clean and pink-skinned, the ends of her auburn hair still lying damp against her neck. She was wearing her green silk robe, her favorite.

Alex turned on her side facing her, said, "I missed seeing your robe hanging on the back of the door every morning."

CJ seemed to freeze. "CJ," Alex said softly. "Talk to me."

CJ sat down on the side of the bed, turning to face Alex.

"Talk to me," Alex said again.

"I can't," CJ said quietly. "Not yet. I'm still sorting out things, and I'm just not up to it tonight, all right? I'm sorry I had to work, and that I have to go in tomorrow, but I just can't do this right now."

Alex felt her heart breaking with every word. "Okay," she said at last. "We'll sleep, and you'll go to work, and then we will spend some time together tomorrow, alone, and talk. Can you do that?"

She watched CJ's shoulders relax a little. "Yes," she said. "I can do that. I have a couple of days off after tomorrow, and so we'll have some time. I just need to sleep, all right?"

Alex knew what she was asking, and her heart broke again. *Don't touch me. Don't try to touch me tonight.*

"Yes," Alex said, trying to conceal her sadness. "I understand."

Something in CJ's eyes flashed, and Alex thought perhaps that CJ saw her pain anyway. CJ had always read her so well, better than anyone. But CJ said nothing, just leaned over and turned out the lamp.

In the pearly light from outside, edging the closed curtains with silver, Alex watched CJ take off her robe and toss it onto the chair. She could see just the pale outline of CJ's shape shining in the darkness for a moment before she slipped between the sheets. Alex lay motionless, feeling CJ turn on her side, away from Alex, then felt her shifting slightly toward the center of the bed.

Alex found that she was holding her breath. The heat from CJ's body, trapped with Alex under the sheets, surrounded her like a wave of warm water washing over her. The aching need rose again in Alex, her craving to touch, enfold, to claim CJ again, almost overwhelmed her.

She stayed where she was, wondering how on earth she was going to be able to sleep with this yearning running through her. Then CJ shifted a little closer and said, in a voice that was barely a whisper in the darkness, "Do you think you could hold me?"

Alex couldn't answer aloud, afraid she would cry or scream or just come completely apart. Instead she eased into CJ, pressing her front against CJ's back. Just feeling the soft warmth of CJ's skin against her breasts began to unravel the knot of anxiety inside of her.

Alex wrapped her arm securely around CJ's waist, and dropped a single soft kiss onto her shoulder. "I'm here," she said, one last time. "It's going to be okay. Sleep, sweetheart."

The moment she felt CJ relax into sleep, Alex followed her.

CHAPTER TWENTY-FOUR

Alex slept through CJ's alarm, her shower and CJ getting dressed. When she awoke, bright sunlight was peeking through the edges of the blackout curtains on the windows, and she looked at the clock in astonishment. She tried to remember the last time she'd slept until after nine.

There was a note on her nightstand.

I couldn't bear to wake you up. Eat something, please, room service or otherwise. There's a good breakfast place a block down from the Plaza called El Lugar, if you want to go. I'll be back by around 2 p.m. and we can spend the rest of the day.

Alex stared at the words a moment. No "Love, CJ" at the end. She sighed, and got up to shower and dress.

Sitting there, waiting for CJ, waiting to find out what was happening was going to drive her insane. She walked two blocks to the Plaza, the town square built in colonial Spanish style. In the middle of the square was a small park, with iron benches, the grass and sidewalks already populated with tourists and vendors. On the four sides of the Plaza were buildings built in traditional

Spanish colonial adobe, with wooden vigas visible as supports for the rooftops. Three sides had commercial enterprises, jewelry and clothing stores or restaurants. The north side of the Plaza was taken up completely with the Palace of the Governors, the seat of government for New Mexico which was, according to the plaque she read, the oldest public building in the country.

Beneath the shelter of the narrow overhang on the Palace, sellers of handmade jewelry lined the sidewalk, native woven blankets spread out to display their carefully wrought pieces. The sellers were all Native Americans from the various New Mexico pueblos, she supposed. Most were middle-aged or older women, but there were men and children, too. There was no raucous calling out to buyers. Instead, tourists strolled up and down, looking at the displays, and negotiations seemed to be conducted in quiet, respectful voices.

Something about the scene appealed to Alex, and she joined the slow line of onlookers despite her usual indifference to shopping of any kind. Her spirits were buoyed, not that she really understood why. She was suddenly and inexplicably in the mood to buy. In the space of less than an hour, she bought a necklace and matching earrings set with turquoise for Nicole, and a heavy silver-worked bracelet for Betty Duncan. She selected a handsome bolo tie for Rod Chavez, at least in part to thank him for his help in solving David's murder. She'd seen him wearing a bolo several times. On impulse, she bought one for Paul, too. He seemed unlikely to wear it, but Alex liked the deep red color and got it anyway.

She wanted to maintain her momentum, so she crossed the park to go into a store on the other side of the Plaza that sold Santa Fe items, and bought food supplies for Ana Chavez: a sweet spices blend, and dried adobada marinating spices. In the rear of the store was a children's section, and she debated over a gift for Charlie. The toy pearl-handled pistols tempted her, but she'd never discussed guns with Nicole, and after David's murder, it occurred to her that Nicole was unlikely to approve. Instead, she bought a set of child-sized cowboy duds—a hat, fringed gloves and chaps.

She walked back to her rental car and locked her packages in the trunk, feeling satisfied that she'd accomplished something. She found El Lugar a block south of the Plaza, and patiently waited in line for a seat in the tiny restaurant.

They were still serving breakfast, and she ordered fresh-squeezed orange juice, coffee and an omelet with green chiles. The omelet was enormous and she couldn't finish it, but the flavorful, mellow chiles were the best she'd ever had.

Santa Fe was only a few hours from the Denver area by car, pretty much a straight shot south down Interstate 25. Why hadn't she brought CJ down here before? Alex wondered. Museums, art, killer food. They would have to put it on their list for the next long weekend. That is, if CJ ever wanted to see Santa Fe again.

Alex walked slowly back to the hotel, the worry she'd been avoiding all morning catching up to her thoughts. It could not be that she had suffered all those months, longing for CJ every hour of the day and night, to find her again and then lose her to...what? Regret, or anger, or some other emotion she couldn't even name? It didn't look as if CJ had created any real life for herself here, to Alex's immense relief: no home, no real career, she hoped. No new woman, thank God.

So what was wrong? Why was CJ so cold? No, not cold, exactly, just...distant. What was it that was lying between them, what barrier was Alex failing to see?

Only CJ could tell her, Alex realized. Somehow, some way, Alex needed for CJ to tell her what she was feeling, so that they could talk it out, or go to therapy, or do anything else they needed to deal with whatever it was.

Because she couldn't live like this.

* * *

The Santa Fe River wound its way a few blocks south of the Plaza. There was a small parkway on either side of the trickle of water, the trunks of cottonwood trees just shading the benches and picnic tables as the limbs started to bud.

The April afternoon sun was bright and warm as Alex walked with CJ down to the park. "Not a lot of water," Alex remarked, as they found an empty bench and sat down.

"No," CJ agreed. "New Mexico dammed the river upstream somewhere, since it supplies a lot of the water for the city. This state has even less water than Colorado does."

Another conversation about water, Alex thought, the bane of living in the West. She hoped they weren't going to be reduced to talking about the weather next.

She studied CJ, her face so familiar and yet now changed. CJ had always looked young to her, fresh and unburdened by life. Now it seemed as if Alex could see every lonely moment marked in her face. CJ's skin was fair, but now she looked pale, almost ghostly.

CJ said softly, "If it's okay, I think I'd like to know how everybody at home is. I feel like I've been on some other planet all this time."

Her eyes were hidden behind sunglasses, but Alex heard the longing in her voice. Alex said, "I don't know where to start."

CJ wasn't looking at her but over the trees toward the Sangre de Cristo mountains west of town. The peaks still had traces of snow from the winter just past.

"How's Charlie?" she finally asked.

"Charlie," Alex answered, "is really okay. Kids recover faster sometimes. He still misses his dad, talks about him sometimes, but Nic says he's really managing just fine. He's doing well at school. No nightmares or anything. I think you saved him from a lot of that, the day it happened."

Something shifted in CJ's expression, but all she said was, "And how is your sister?"

Alex considered how to answer. "She's starting to mend, I think," she said at length. "It was really bad for a while, not just the shock, but the day-to-day living without David."

It was hard for me, too, living every day without you, Alex wanted to say. But CJ knew exactly how hard it had been.

"Nic actually went on a date a little while ago," Alex added, trying to sound upbeat. "She told me she's seeing the light at the end of the tunnel. She will be all right, eventually, I think."

"She's a strong person," CJ said, and Alex could see a slight easing in CJ's expression. The burden of feeling responsible for David's death must have been almost too heavy for her to bear.

"She is strong," Alex agreed. "I keep forgetting that. When we were growing up, I was always trying to protect her, be the big sister, you know? Sometimes it's hard for me to see her as the woman she is now."

CJ nodded. "It's always tough to see our families as they really are. We're always seeing them through the lens of growing up with them."

Alex said suddenly, "I didn't know you had a niece."

CJ turned to her in surprise, a slight smile on her face. "I do," she answered. "She'll be fifteen this year. It's sad to me that I've never met her. You and Roger must have had quite a conversation," she added.

"We did, actually," Alex said. "He sends his love. He seems very fond of you."

CJ smiled again, sadly this time. "He's been wonderful to me, especially after my father..."

She seemed to choke up, and Alex put her arm around her shoulders.

"It's okay," CJ said, after a moment. "I'm just...it's an emotional day, I guess."

"Yes," Alex agreed, giving her a squeeze before reluctantly dropping her arm away.

"And how's Vivien?" CJ seemed to need to change the subject.

Alex laughed. "When I tell you, you won't believe it."

She saw CJ lift her eyebrows. She slid her sunglasses down and her green eyes held some curiosity. "Try me."

"She's involved."

"That's not surprising. Viv falls in lust on a regular basis."

"Not just lust this time, she says. She insists it's the real deal. She actually took me to lunch to talk to me about how to deal with being in love."

"You are kidding me." Her eyes widened.

"Not a bit. They've been living together since last fall."

Alex was rewarded by CJ's blatant astonishment. "She's *living* with her? My goodness, Viv rarely even lets a woman spend the night! You cannot be serious!"

"I am. I've met her. She is the picture of stable maturity, despite being a few years younger than Viv, and Vivien acts like a lovesick kid around her."

CJ shook her head, still thunderstruck. "Poor Viv," she said, to Alex's surprise. "She must be terrified out of her mind."

"She is," Alex agreed, after a moment's thought. "But she's really happy, too. Love will do that to you, make you ecstatic and afraid at the same time. It's like giving someone else a loaded gun pointed right at your heart and hoping they'll never pull the trigger."

CJ's face twisted in pain.

"Sweetheart, I didn't mean..." Alex began.

CJ reached for her hand and gripped it hard while looking away again. They sat in the sunshine, CJ's grip squeezing Alex's fingers until Alex couldn't feel them anymore. Finally, CJ said quietly, "I went online every morning and read *The Denver Post*. I read every inch of the local news section. I didn't even know what I was looking for after awhile. 'Fatal Condominium Fire.' 'Police Officer Found Dead.' 'Runner in Fatal Hit-and-Run Accident.' I kept doing Internet searches for your name, making sure I hadn't missed anything." Her voice rose with anguish and anger. "I read the *fucking obituaries*, Alex, terrified every morning that I would find your name there. I died a little every day. It was killing me.

"And then...then last week I read the story on the front page, about the shooting, about...Oh, God, Laurel. I couldn't believe it, I didn't believe it. After all this time..."

Alex put her other hand over CJ's and gently released her numb fingers from CJ's grip. "Listen to me, sweetheart," Alex said. "I don't know what the shrinks are going to say, but I was there in Tony's office with her long enough to know that she is mentally ill, in a serious way. Tony had no idea, apparently, no one did."

CJ used one hand to claw her sunglasses from her face, and Alex saw the tears threatening. "Why?" she choked out. "How did this all happen?"

"Honey, I can't tell you why. Laurel apparently worked on her brother's book, and somehow thought she was entitled to the money or the credit, probably both. She told me his suicide was really a homicide. She said she killed him. Tony's got the Georgia Bureau of Investigation working with local law enforcement to reopen the case."

CJ's eyes, still teary, opened wider. "Jackson? She shot him? Alex, no."

"That's what she said. We got the ballistics tests back on the two guys she hired to run me off the road, the two who were in the car in the park that day. She shot both of them with Tony's gun. Between the evidence and her confession, she's never getting out of custody, whether they find her criminally insane or not."

CJ wiped the moisture away from her cheeks. "You had to shoot her, the paper said," she whispered.

Alex swallowed and then said softly, "She didn't give me a choice, sweetheart."

"I know. I know that. I'm glad she didn't die, I suppose."

"Are you?" Alex said, shaking her head. "I guess I am, too. Nicole feels differently, as you might imagine. God knows Laurel will never be the same."

CJ looked at her questioningly. "The paper just said she was seriously injured, but she would recover."

"They had to amputate her right arm above the elbow," Alex said gently. "I'm sorry."

CJ looked at her in horror, and Alex had a moment of dismay. Had CJ still, somehow, cared about Laurel? The next instant, CJ murmured, "Oh, darlin', I'm so sorry for you. It must have been so awful. You must have been terrified."

"You know how it is," Alex said, trying to recover her composure. "You're a lot more shaky after it's over. In the moment, all I could think about was how to get to my backup weapon and keep her from blowing Tony's head off."

CJ cried out suddenly, "I just don't understand why! I haven't seen her for twelve years, and then she murders all these people, and she tries to *kill* you, Alex. Twice."

"Obsession doesn't really make sense to anybody but the person who's suffering from it, I suppose," Alex said. "I'm guessing the trigger was her decision to murder her brother. Once she had the money she needed to find you, everything just snowballed, I imagine." She stroked the back of CJ's hand. "But it's over now, honey. As terrible as it was, it's over now."

They sat in silence a long time. The sun began to ease down toward the top of the mountains, and the shadows lengthened across the grass, creeping toward their feet.

Finally Alex said, very quietly, "You have to tell me how you're feeling. Sweetheart, please."

"I don't think I can," CJ answered.

"Try. You have to try. I can take your anger, CJ. I can deal with how much pain you had, I swear I can. What I can't take is your silence."

CJ looked down at the shadows. "Maybe silence is all I have left," she answered softly.

Alex felt her heart aching. "Please," she said, desperately. She took a breath to try to calm down, and then continued, "No. You have me. I'm your friend, your lover, your partner. I'm your wife, CJ, and you're mine. Whatever we've been through, we still have each other. I've been angry at you and hurt and sad. Being alone was awful. And it was terrible for you, too. You've felt all those things, anger at me and guilt for what happened. We have to find our way back to each other, my love. Please help me."

CJ sat silently, rubbing her thumb across the old burn scar on her left palm.

"Oh, baby, please." Alex was trying not to break apart inside.

"How can you be so sure?" CJ whispered. "How do you know we even can find our way back? I ran away from you, when you needed me."

"You didn't just run away from me," Alex was trying to gather her wildly strewn emotions together, "you were trying to protect me."

CJ met her eyes for a moment, and Alex could see the pain she was carrying, deep within her, marking her like the scars on her hands. "I should have told you. I can't imagine how much I hurt you, Alex."

"You did what you thought was best, honey, I know that. Whatever we wish we'd decided differently, it's over now."

CJ shook her head. "It doesn't work like that, I know it. You can't just say you understand and pretend it didn't happen. Every time you look at me, you'll remember that I left. You'll remember that David died because of me. Charlie is without a father because of me. You're going to wonder the rest of your life whether I'll leave you again if something else happens. I can't live with that, Alex. I can't see that moment of doubt in your eyes every time you see me. I can't."

She dropped her head into her hands in despair. Alex regretted that they'd chosen to come here, a place where she couldn't comfort CJ the way she wanted to, the way she'd always had, with her hands and her body.

Alex got off the bench, heedless of anyone who might see, and knelt in front of CJ. She gently pulled CJ's hands away from her face, then lifted her chin up until CJ had to meet her eyes.

"I promise you," Alex said, her voice throbbing with intensity, "I promise I will not let this destroy us. I promise we'll work on trying to leave the past behind us. I promise to let you look into me and see that I am not afraid. All you have to do is promise me you'll never leave me again. I don't care what happens, or what anyone says. Just stay with me, and it will be okay."

CJ searched her face. Was she looking for the doubts she feared to find? Alex didn't know. She knew only that she would risk anything, dare anything, give anything, to get CJ back again.

"CJ," she murmured, "you have everything I am, and everything I ever will be. If I'm afraid, I'll give you that, too, and you will make it go away. Just come back to me."

So softly she could barely hear it, she heard CJ whisper, "I'll try."

Without another sound, Alex stood up and took her hand.

* * *

There were no words between them on the way back. CJ unlocked her hotel room door, and as it shut behind them she stood on one side of the tiny foyer, looking across at Alex for a moment. Alex finally asked the question she'd been swallowing all day.

"Tell me," Alex began, "why you didn't tell me about the threats? Didn't you trust me? We could have faced whatever it was together."

"I was afraid for you," CJ whispered. "That's all I have to tell you. I've regretted it every minute since, but the longer it went on, the more afraid I became. Alex, I'm so sorry. So very sorry. I missed you so much…"

Just the gaze from the hot green of CJ's eyes, and Alex felt the long-dead fires of her desire rise up and begin to consume her flesh, the flames flashing through her, down her arms and legs, wrapping around her body, so hot that she wondered if CJ could feel the heat rising from her.

If she couldn't touch CJ, she knew she would be quickly consumed, burning to ashes in front of her. Only CJ could soothe the burning, satisfying the flames and pouring the cool relief over her.

Alex started to push off the wall, to go to CJ, but to her surprise CJ came across to her first and gripped her by the shoulders. CJ found her mouth, not a tender kiss of reunion, but a bruising demand against her lips.

Alex brought her arms up and pulled CJ closer as CJ continued to kiss her hard, then harder. When Alex had to pull away a moment, gasping for air, CJ moved to the side of her neck. Alex felt CJ's teeth against her skin and couldn't repress another small gasp, this one a sound of pure wanting.

The noise from Alex's throat seemed to ignite CJ further, and she moved to the tender muscle between Alex's neck and shoulder and bit down lightly. Alex lifted herself into CJ's arms more firmly, her body ebbing toward the contact, any point of contact with her lover.

She's never been quite like this, Alex thought, her head dizzy with overwhelming desire surging through her. But Alex wanted nothing more in this instant than to be taken, to give herself over completely.

She managed to get her hands in CJ's hair, pulling her head back to meet Alex's mouth once more. Alex was frantic to taste her lips again and CJ used her height and weight advantage to hold Alex firmly in place as she continued to press hard against her.

Alex groaned and groped for CJ's hands. She managed to find her wrists and dragged CJ's fingers to her breasts, pushing them against her. To Alex's frustration, CJ slipped away. CJ brought her hands up again, this time beneath Alex's T-shirt.

Alex broke the kiss again to throw her head back with pleasure as CJ caressed her through her bra. Alex made a noise she didn't recognize as coming from her own throat when CJ managed to unhook the bra and push it up and out of her way.

Now the heat in her body focused in her nipples as CJ touched her. How long had it been, how many lifetimes, how many dreams since CJ had touched her last?

She was so swollen the touches were almost painful. CJ took her hands away and pulled the T-shirt roughly over Alex's head, taking the unfastened bra with it. She actually lifted Alex a few inches up against the wall, so that she could bend and get her mouth on Alex's breasts, and Alex thought she might come apart with CJ's lips caressing her. Desire, gratitude, love swirled through her as CJ used her tongue to arouse her even more.

CJ's hands were on Alex's hips, holding her up. Then CJ stopped supporting her, let Alex slide helplessly down to legs that were close to refusing to hold her up. CJ, breathing almost as hard as Alex, unzipped Alex's jeans and pulled them down as far as she could reach. Then she straightened.

"Look at me," CJ demanded quietly.

Alex managed to lock her eyes on CJ's gaze as CJ slid her hand into Alex's body. Alex cried out, her grip on CJ's shoulders bruisingly tight.

She moved with CJ's movement inside her, the rhythm that was both universal and theirs alone, as familiar to her body as breathing. CJ began to caress Alex's center with her thumb and Alex felt herself falling.

Her eyes closed against the flood of the release beginning to rise up through her body, but CJ said, "No, look at me, Alex."

Somehow she forced her eyes open and CJ whispered urgently, "I love you."

Alex cried out and let her orgasm cascade through her, her head landing hard back against the wall with her climax.

Moments later she felt herself beginning to slip, but the next second she felt CJ's arm around her, heard her saying, "I've got you, darlin'."

CJ eased her down to the floor, Alex in a sodden heap. Alex couldn't stand, couldn't move, but CJ wrapped her up and held on, making soothing sounds that weren't quite words.

* * *

In a couple of minutes, Alex managed to stand, though she was still a little shaky. She kicked the rest of her clothes away. CJ stood with her, unfolding her long legs, and they went together into the room.

CJ pulled down the cover and Alex sat down on the side of the bed, still trying to reorient herself to their sudden physical reunion. Making love had always meant reaffirming their connection to each other, but especially so for CJ, who wanted their sexual bond whether she was feeling good or bad, when she was feeling lonely or sad. Alex had always treasured CJ's desire for her, like a gift of trust and comfort, but this felt different to her in some way she couldn't identify.

Her disorientation increased when CJ leaned down to kiss her mouth slowly and deeply, then knelt down in front of her and gently pushed Alex onto her back.

"CJ, sweetheart—" Alex murmured.

"Hush now," CJ responded, and she kissed her way up Alex's bare thighs, then down the soft crease between hip and leg.

Alex leaned back and shut her eyes when CJ's mouth touched her wetness. As CJ loved her with deliberate, caressing strokes, Alex felt herself surrendering, her heart as well as her body. She let CJ take her hurt away, erase the loneliness, destroy all the fears Alex had carried for so many months. She gave CJ all of her pain, and when her body surged triumphantly upward, tears welled up within her, joy and release.

CJ came up to the bed to lie with her, and Alex realized she was getting CJ very wet, from the leg of CJ's jeans resting between her legs to the shoulder of her blouse where Alex was weeping quietly.

Alex lifted her head at last, and CJ brushed her tears from her cheeks. Alex welcomed the slight roughness of CJ's scarred hands. She kissed each palm and said, "Come to bed, please."

CJ undressed quickly and slipped in beside her. But when Alex turned over to face her, circling CJ with her arms, CJ kissed her softly and said, "Sleep a little, darlin'. It's okay. I'm here."

CJ did what she often did, slipping down to rest her head on Alex's shoulder, compensating for the difference in their height. They fit together with perfect comfort. She curled around Alex's side and Alex relaxed into her embrace and fell asleep almost at once.

* * *

When Alex awoke with a start, the room was pitch-black. She sat up, trying to shake off the dark emotions from a dream she couldn't remember.

Reaching out, her hand found only vacant sheets and an empty pillow. *Oh God, oh God. It was just a dream.*

She was still alone. CJ was still gone. She cried out incoherently.

An instant later, CJ was there at her side, asking, "What? What's wrong?"

Alex collapsed a moment later into CJ's arms, grasping her hard. "Oh, darlin'," CJ said, soothingly, her hand stroking down Alex's back. "I'm here, Alex. I'm here."

"Sorry," Alex managed after a minute. "Just a bad dream. I'm fine."

CJ snapped on the bedside lamp, and Alex could see her eyes searching Alex's face, looking for the truth. Alex wasn't going to tell her that truth, not this time. CJ didn't need to know how many nightmares there had been or how many sleepless nights, the fact that she was seeing a therapist. Alex could see the feelings of guilt surrounding CJ like an aura.

"I'm fine," she repeated.

Looking doubtful, CJ handed her a water bottle. "I needed a drink, and I thought you might, too. It's a dry climate and we've been using up a lot of extra moisture."

Alex tried a half grin, and said, "We have, one way or another."

CJ returned the tentative smile and said, "Drink, Irish."

Alex took two long swallows of the cool water and handed the bottle back. "You're right," she said. "I needed that."

CJ finished off the water, then went around to get back into bed. "Are you hungry? I'm afraid we missed dinner, but I have kitchen access. We could go down and rustle something up."

"Rustle something up? Such a Westerner you're becoming."

CJ smiled and laid on her thickest southern drawl. "Ah reckon y'all has done converted li'l ole me," she batted her eyelashes.

Alex actually started laughing, and CJ joined her. "Oh, God," she said after a minute. "I really missed that."

"What's that?"

"Laughing with you. In bed."

CJ lifted her eyebrows. "Not laughing *at* me, darlin'?'

Alex slid over to her and wrapped her arms around her. She felt CJ withdraw, just a little, and Alex leaned back to meet her eyes. "Baby, what is it?" Alex asked.

CJ drew one finger down Alex's jaw. "You didn't answer my question. Are you hungry?"

"Not particularly. Not for food, anyway."

CJ tensed, just a little more, and Alex frowned. "You didn't answer my question, either," Alex persisted. "What's wrong?"

"Alex, I…" CJ stopped. Alex waited, but CJ only dropped her eyes and said, "I'm just not ready yet, I guess."

"Ready," Alex repeated, her frown deepening. "You don't want me to make love to you, is that it?"

"I just can't," CJ said unhappily.

Alex said in frustration, "I don't understand. You were so wonderful to me. I've missed you so much. What is it?"

"I can't," CJ repeated helplessly.

"I know you're feeling guilty, is that it?" Alex persisted. "You can't…what, you don't deserve to be loved, is that it?"

CJ looked away, unable to meet her gaze any longer, and bit her lip. "Yes. I don't know, exactly. I just can't right now. Please don't be angry."

Alex felt her heart breaking. "Jesus, CJ, I'm not angry. I *love* you. When you hurt, I hurt, don't you know that?"

"Oh, Alex." She blinked hard.

Alex sighed. Had she really thought it would be easy for them? Nothing in their relationship ever had been simple before, after all. "CJ," she began slowly. "I've been seeing someone."

She felt CJ go rigid in her arms, and a moment later she realized her mistake. "A therapist," she said quickly. "I've been seeing a psychotherapist, baby. Sweetheart, I didn't mean I've been *dating*, for God's sake."

CJ searched her face. "I didn't even think about—Alex, I want you to know that there hasn't been anyone, since I've been gone. No one. Just you," she added quietly. "In my dreams."

Alex leaned in to nuzzle her neck. "I know. I know. Me, either. I haven't even thought about it."

Against her ear, CJ asked, with soft hesitation, "Not even Chris Andersen?"

Alex sat back so that CJ could see her face. "Absolutely not," she answered firmly. "I don't want to be with Chris, or anybody else, as long as you're breathing. Okay?"

CJ gave her a small nod, and snuggled closer. "Okay. So tell me about your therapist."

Alex did, explaining why she had gone and what work they had done together. Then she said, "I want us to meet her together when we get back. We have things to talk about, and she said she'd help. Is that okay?"

CJ nodded against her shoulder. "Very much okay. I'm proud of you, Irish. I know how you always try to go it alone, and I'm glad you went to get help. I'm just so sorry I hurt you so much…"

"Stop," Alex kissed her, then said against her lips, "stop it. You did what you thought was right. We were both hurt, okay? We'll talk about it with Dr. Wheeler when we get back." After CJ nodded, Alex said, "We are going back, right? Together?"

CJ murmured into her shoulder, "I told Ramón I had to leave. He understood. I told him—I said the love of my life had come for me, and that I had to go home."

"Yes," Alex said. "That's exactly right."

CHAPTER TWENTY-FIVE

As CJ pulled her car into the parking lot of their condominium, she said, "Alex, what did you tell your sister when you called her this morning?"

"Not much. Just that we were driving home from Santa Fe. I wanted her to know she didn't have to pick me up at the airport. Why?"

CJ pulled into her assigned spot and said, "Your detective instincts may be slipping, darlin'. Check out the guest parking spaces."

They got out of the car, and as they pulled their suitcases from the trunk, Alex looked around. "Oh," she said, after a moment spent noticing cars. "Nicole, Vivien, Paul, and that looks like Rod Chavez's car, right?"

"Right. I do believe your sister used her key and that we have a welcome home party waiting upstairs."

Alex stopped her and took her hand. "If you're not ready for this, tell me. I can go upstairs alone and tell them all to go home. There's no rush."

CJ squeezed her hand. "Alex, I've wanted to come home since the day I left. And in case you didn't know it, you and our friends are my home. I'm just scared."

"Tell me why."

CJ stared out the window, not letting go of Alex's fingers. "Everything that happened to you, to David and Charlie and Nicole, was because of me. I didn't do it, but it was still because of me. How am I supposed to face everyone? How can I ever face your sister?"

"I don't know everything," Alex said quietly. "But I do know this. Whatever happened, whatever we both did wrong is in the past and we can't change it. We can only go forward. I want to try to do that together. Don't you?"

CJ continued to stare out the window.

"CJ?"

"Yes," she whispered. "I do want that."

"Nicole doesn't blame you for David's death. Come upstairs with me."

When they stepped into the foyer, Alex called out, "If you're hiding, it didn't work. Come on out!"

Vivien made it to them first, wordlessly throwing her arms around CJ. Alex stepped back and CJ circled her friend in a hug.

"It's okay, Viv," CJ said, fighting tears. "I'm back."

"God damn you," Vivien said. "Don't do that again, okay?"

CJ released her. "Don't worry," she said, mustering a reassuring tone. "Alex has already made me sign a notarized statement to that effect."

"You idiot," Vivien said. "You scared the shit out of us."

"Viv," CJ managed. "I'm sorry. I truly am."

"Well, as long as you're really, really sorry," Vivien said, wiping her eyes. "There's someone I want you to meet."

CJ lifted her eyes to the tall woman hovering protectively behind Vivien. "You must be Marja Erickson," she said, offering her hand.

Nicole was next and she hugged CJ fiercely. "Thank God you're home," she murmured into CJ's ear. "She was falling apart without you."

"Me too," CJ whispered. "I'm so sorry. About David, I mean, it…"

Nicole looked at her. "I told Alex this, and I'll tell you. None of this was your doing. I'm just so glad you're home."

"Is Charlie here?" she asked, looking around.

"No, he's at a friend's. I didn't want to impose him on you, in case…"

In case you're not staying, CJ mentally supplied. "When can we see him?" she asked.

Nicole smiled at her in happy relief. "Dinner, tomorrow? Okay?"

"You two come over here," CJ urged. "I'll cook. I have one or two or a hundred new recipes."

Rod and Ana Chavez got her in a group hug, and then Paul stepped up with Betty. He stuck out his hand and said, "Glad you made it back, St. Clair."

Betty, a short, round woman with a modest Afro said, "Oh, for heaven's sake, Paul," and reached around to give CJ a bear hug. "Welcome home, honey," she said. "Pay no attention to Mister Stiff-and-Formal here."

Paul looked a little uncomfortable as he turned to Alex and said, "I wasn't completely sure you wanted us here, but when Nicole called, Betty said it would be all right."

Alex said, "You and Betty are welcome in our home any time, you know that."

She emphasized the word "our," and CJ looked from Paul to Alex and back again. She realized that she was going to have to find out more about this conversation at another time.

Paul said to CJ, "Once you're settled back in, come and see me. I think we need to discuss your job."

CJ looked at him in stark surprise. "My job?" she echoed. "You know I resigned."

"Yes, well…" he rubbed his shaved head. "There was some paperwork mix-up, or something. Apparently you've been on unpaid administrative leave for the last nine months. There's been some delay in hiring your replacement and…well, we'll discuss it."

She continued to stare at him in frank amazement and he said, "Just call me, all right? We'll talk about it later." She looked at Alex, who shrugged in disbelief.

The crowd made it back into the living room. There were four more people waiting.

Nicole said, "Alex told me how much Chris and Frank helped solve David's…the case, so I thought you'd like to see them, too."

Frank, now well on the road to recovery, and Jennifer Morelli welcomed her back warmly. Then Chris Andersen's girlfriend, Beth Rivera gave her a gentle embrace. "Oh, Inspector," she said. "We're so glad to see you again. You must have missed being home so much."

CJ blinked hard but managed another smile for her. She'd befriended Rivera when Beth had worked as an evidence clerk at Colfax PD. "Beth, thank you for being here. Yes, I'm very glad to be home."

Behind her, Chris Andersen was standing awkwardly. CJ felt Alex begin to move beside her, but CJ went first, going to Chris and initiating the hug.

"Chris," CJ said warmly. "Alex told me how much you helped get me home. I want you to know how thankful I am for you."

And she was grateful, she realized. It wasn't easy to let go of her resentment of Chris, but she knew she could trust her, and that she could trust Alex with her.

Someone had found the extra leaf for the dining room table, and the table spilled out into the living room, every chair in the condo pressed into service to get them all seated. Alex could identify Ana Chavez's enchiladas, a roast chicken from someone else, and Betty Duncan's green bean salad as they sat down.

"It's just like Thanksgiving," CJ said happily to Alex.

"Your favorite holiday," Alex replied, smiling.

"Of course," CJ agreed. "Because it's all about the food!"

Suddenly, Alex stood up again, facing them all. "This really is Thanksgiving Day, for me, for all of us. I have a toast."

Everyone took up their glass, and CJ had to fight her tears once more, happy tears this time.

Alex lifted her wine and locked her gaze on CJ. The blue gaze seemed to go on forever. CJ could see eternity in Alex's eyes and wondered again how she had managed to live even a single day without seeing her.

"To the three things in the universe that last forever," Alex said, with as much passion in her voice as CJ had ever heard. "To faith, and to hope, and to love."

"To love," everyone said in unison.

* * *

When Alex walked in the front door to the condo on Friday, the first thing she noticed was CJ's shoes. A pair of beige pumps lay strewn on the floor of the foyer. The sight of them almost brought tears to her eyes.

Alex hung up her jacket, and tossed her keys on the table. "Where are you?" she exclaimed.

"In here," CJ called out.

Alex walked down the hall and into their bedroom. CJ was sitting on the side of the bed.

Alex said, "I almost tripped over your shoes again. What is it with you and neatness?"

CJ looked up at her wonderingly. "You noticed?"

Alex admitted, "I missed them when they weren't there."

"Did you? I guess that shows you how important it is to be flexible."

"No, it shows me what a slob you are."

"This is a surprise?" CJ smiled tentatively.

Alex returned the smile. "Oh, honey, I already knew about that minor character flaw."

"And you wanted me back anyway?" CJ ventured.

Were they still talking about her untidiness? Alex thought not. "I wanted you back every day, every hour, every minute," Alex said quietly.

CJ looked up at Alex. "Do you still want me?" CJ whispered.

Alex felt her heart speeding up wildly. "Yes," she answered softly. "Do you want me, too?"

"Yes, please," CJ said softly.

Alex went to her. She gathered CJ's face in both hands and leaned down to kiss her, a lingering kiss. Alex felt CJ's lips part under hers, and she teased CJ with her tongue, waiting for CJ's invitation.

CJ kissed her harder, and sought out the warmth of Alex's mouth. Alex responded, dropping her hands to CJ's shoulders, then moved them lower, cupping CJ's breasts in her palms.

"Oh, Alex," CJ pulled away to whisper brokenly.

Joy rained down on Alex, submerging her in desire. She gently pushed CJ back onto the bed beneath her.

* * *

CJ was lying on her stomach, sprawling limp and untidy on the sheets. Alex had her head resting comfortably in the small of CJ's back, idly stroking her hand up and down the back of CJ's bare legs.

"Why is your back always warm?" Alex asked.

"I come from a warm climate," CJ muttered.

"Hot-blooded, are you?" Alex teased.

"Apparently so. Oh my goodness, I cannot move a muscle."

Alex dropped her fingers down into the valley between CJ's legs, and CJ pulled her away with a weak hand. Alex laughed and said, "See, I knew you could move if given proper motivation."

"Oh, stop being a tease."

Alex shifted upward and CJ rolled over to face her on the same pillow. "I wasn't teasing you a few minutes ago." Alex smiled.

"That's true," CJ agreed happily.

She gave Alex a couple of soft kisses. Then Alex said, "Are you all right? I mean, why now?"

CJ blinked at her. "Do I need a reason for you to make love to me?"

"You do when you haven't wanted me to touch you since you came home to me, sweetheart. Tell me what changed for you."

CJ saw more than a trace of worry in the gray-blue eyes. She ran one hand up Alex's arm and said, "I'm sorry."

"Don't ever apologize for that again, CJ. Just talk to me."

"What happened to you?" CJ tried a little teasing. "You were the one who always wanted less talk and more action."

"Stop it," Alex said seriously. "I never want to wonder what you're thinking again. Answer the question."

CJ lay back and Alex propped up on one elbow to watch her face. With her other hand she trailed gently down CJ's torso to rest low on her belly. CJ covered the hand with her own and said softly, "You feel good. Your hands on me feel so good."

Alex stroked her gently and said, "Please quit ducking the question."

"I forgot the question."

"Why now, sweetheart? What changed?"

CJ closed her eyes to concentrate on the feel of Alex's fingers on her belly and said, "I was thinking about what Dr. Wheeler said to me when we met with her."

"Which of many things that she said might that have been?"

"Do you remember when she told me the only way we really know how other people feel is by what they say and what they do?"

Alex nodded.

"You kept telling me you didn't blame me, that you forgave me. And I thought if I couldn't find a way to stop feeling guilty about leaving you, and about everything Laurel did—well, we weren't going to make it. And I need to be with you, Alex. We belong together." She met Alex's eyes. "You told Dr. Wheeler you were getting better every minute. And I thought, 'She's getting better because I'm here.' That's right, isn't it, darlin'? It's because we're together again that you're healing?"

Alex leaned over to kiss her. "You know it is."

"When I came home this afternoon, I just, well, I realized being with you again could heal me, too. If I let it. If I let you." Her tone lightened, and she added, "So I just thought I'd give you a chance to show me how you feel about me."

Alex said wryly, "Oh, this was all for my benefit, was it?"

CJ laughed. "Exactly. It only looked as if I were the one having all the fun. It was really all about you."

Alex laughed with her a moment, then grew serious. "Are we okay, CJ?"

"We will be, darlin'," CJ answered her, with confidence. "We will be."

Alex moved to take CJ in her arms again. The night was endless.

Bella Books, Inc.

Women. Books. Even Better Together.

P.O. Box 10543
Tallahassee, FL 32302

Phone: 800-729-4992
www.bellabooks.com